TWISTED

FIC Harri

Harrington, L.
Twisted.

PRICE: $10.02 (ya/m)

LISA HARRINGTON
AUTHOR OF *LIVE TO TELL*

Copyright © 2014 Lisa Harrington
This edition copyright © 2014 Cormorant Books Inc.

No part of this publication may be reproduced, stored in a retrieval system or transmitted, in any form or by any means, without the prior written consent of the publisher or a licence from The Canadian Copyright Licensing Agency (Access Copyright). For an Access Copyright licence, visit www.accesscopyright.ca or call toll free 1.800.893.5777.

 Canada Council for the Arts / Conseil des Arts du Canada

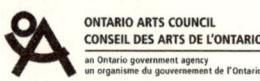 ONTARIO ARTS COUNCIL
CONSEIL DES ARTS DE L'ONTARIO
an Ontario government agency
un organisme du gouvernement de l'Ontario

 Canadian Heritage / Patrimoine canadien — Canadä

The publisher gratefully acknowledges the support of the Canada Council for the Arts and the Ontario Arts Council for its publishing program. We acknowledge the financial support of the Government of Canada through the Canada Book Fund (CBF) for our publishing activities, and the Government of Ontario through the Ontario Media Development Corporation, an agency of the Ontario Ministry of Culture, and the Ontario Book Publishing Tax Credit Program.

LIBRARY AND ARCHIVES CANADA CATALOGUING IN PUBLICATION

Harrington, Lisa, author
Twisted / Lisa Harrington.

Issued in print and electronic formats.
ISBN 978-1-77086-413-9 (pbk.).— ISBN 978-1-77086-414-6 (html)

I. Title.

PS8615.A7473T85 2014   JC813'.6   C2014-905118-2
                                    C2014-905119-0

Cover art and design: Angel Guerra/Archetype
Interior text design: Tannice Goddard, Soul Oasis Networking
Printer: Trigraphik LBF

Printed and bound in Canada.

FSC MIX Paper from responsible sources FSC® C107623
www.fsc.org

The interior of this book is printed on 30% post-consumer waste recycled paper.

DANCING CAT BOOKS
AN IMPRINT OF CORMORANT BOOKS INC.
10 ST. MARY STREET, SUITE 615, TORONTO, ONTARIO, M4Y 1P9
www.cormorantbooks.com

Chapter 1

She mills around the kitchen with an air of familiarity. I don't like it. I don't like her. I have my suspicions, but that's all they are, suspicions. She pops up the cap on the dish soap and fills the sink with water.

"I can do that, Mary," I say.

Giving me a dismissive wave, she slides in a stack of dirty plates.

Frustrated, I sit there at the table, trying to think of a way to get rid of her.

Once she has everything in soaking, she comes over and sits beside me. "The minister did a wonderful job. It was a fairly good turnout, don't you think?"

I lift the corners of my mouth. Not a real smile.

She sniffs, pulls out a crumpled tissue from under the sleeve of her black dress, and wipes her nose. "I'm going to miss her terribly."

Liar. I stare back, taking in her blonde hair streaked with grey, red lipstick, ivory powder packed like clay into the wrinkles on her face. So different from my mom, but yet here she is, my mother's oldest and dearest friend. Mom must have been blind. She was blind about a lot of things.

I keep quiet, and Mary pinches her lips together at my silence. I think she knows I suspect. After a moment she says, "Your father isn't too happy about you leaving."

"Vince isn't my father," I correct. "And he doesn't care what I do."

"Of course he does. Don't say things like that." She scolds me as if she now has the right or something.

"Well, I'm eighteen. He can't stop me," I say.

She gives me a disapproving look. "And what about your mother's café? Who's going to run that?"

"Vince will probably sell it."

"She loved that place. He'd never do that to her memory."

I raise my eyebrows. Who is she kidding? "*You* could always run it." I throw it out there just to see her reaction.

Immediately she becomes flustered and claps her hand to her chest. "I know nothing about that kind of thing. I sell *real estate*."

"Right." I nod. "Of course."

She gets up from the table and returns to the sink. I want to laugh at her attempt to get me to stay here. I know it's an act. She can't wait to see the back of me.

Then she starts to hum. It grates on my nerves, like something digging at the inside of my skull. She keeps rinsing out the same coffee mug, wiping the same spot on the counter. It's so obvious she's killing time, waiting for Vince. Probably wants him to walk in and see her acting all domestic. She's going to have a long wait. He's been MIA ever since the funeral. My guess, he's at the cabin. He could be gone for days.

Finally I can't take it anymore. I stand and noisily slide out my chair. "I have to pack, Mary."

"Well," she huffs. "I can see you're not going to listen to a word *I* say." She dries her hand on a dish towel and reaches for her purse. "Tell your father if he needs anything, anything at all, he can just call."

"He's not my father," I say again.

She sighs. "I wish you would show him a little sympathy. This has been extremely hard on him. He loved your mother very much."

I fold my arms.

"She wasn't herself for a long time, you know," she reminds me, like I need reminding. "Long before we knew what was wrong."

"Yes, I'm sure it was terrible for him. I'm just happy he had a shoulder to cry on." I cross the kitchen and hold open the screen door.

She shoots me a nasty look as she brushes past me.

I SMELL HIM BEFORE I see him. My heart sinks. I was hoping to be long gone by the time he resurfaced.

He leans against my bedroom door, an almost empty bottle of some kind of amber liquor in his hand. He looks sweatier and puffier than usual. His white shirt is unbuttoned at the top and stained under the arms. There are other stains. A splotch that's brownish red, another that's translucent, probably grease. His green tie hangs limply from his front pants pocket like a wilted plant.

I start packing faster, scooping stuff off my bed and stuffing it in the duffle bag. My hair falls forward — a curtain so I don't have to look at him. I hear him slowly circle the perimeter of my room like an animal stalking its prey. I feel his eyes on me. My mouth goes dry. He's going to try to stop me. I strain my ears, listening for the sound of Caroline's car on the gravel. Nothing.

"It would kill your mother, you leaving," he says. His words are sloppy, all running together, but I'm used to "Vince speak" and can easily translate.

"She's already dead," I say flatly.

"This is your home. Your place is here."

The idea of staying, having to share the house with him ... I swallow down whatever's inching its way up my throat.

The bottle sloshes as he takes a drink. "You think that college dipshit is going to welcome you with open arms? That he's going to be happy to see you? He's moved on by now."

At that moment I hear the *beep-beep* of Caroline's horn. My body floods with relief. But Vince hears it too. Our eyes lock, and we both stand perfectly still. The horn sounds again, breaking the spell. He lunges toward me and grabs my arm. His breath almost blinds me. With my free hand I push hard against his chest and wrench myself free.

I catch the handle of the duffle bag as I run for the door. He comes after me, but I'm faster — his movements are slow and clumsy, like he's wading through deep water. Once in the hall, I yank my door closed behind me and hold on tightly to the knob. My hand shaking, I slide the deadbolt across. It snaps into place with a click, trapping him inside — just as he did to me all those nights.

Bet he regrets the day he installed that lock.

WHEN CAROLINE SEES ME running toward the car, she reaches across and flings open the passenger door. I toss my bag in the back and collapse into the seat.

"Drive," I say.

She puts the car into gear and backs out of the driveway. "Are you okay?"

"I am now."

Like a good best friend, she knows better than to ask any more questions.

As we pull off the lane onto pavement, I feel my heart rate slowly return to normal. The last traces of a late autumn sunset beats in the side window, and I roll it down a crack to let in some cool air. The car is instantly filled with the smell of low tide. Will I miss it? Being close to the water? *There's water in Halifax*, I tell myself.

We pass by the Jenkins farm. All the cows are clustered along the fence. It's like they know I'm leaving and they've come to say goodbye … or maybe it's just going to rain tonight.

Caroline and I drive in silence the whole way up the Cape John road.

In the village I see Alex and Jessica coming out of the KwikWay. I wave. They wave back. They don't know this is the last time they'll ever see me, that I'm never setting foot in River John again.

After a while the quiet feels too heavy. "Thanks, Caroline," I say. "I don't know what I would have done … you know … how I'd make the bus."

"No worries. I'm always looking for an excuse to go into Truro." She smiles and looks at me sideways. "Frenchy's has 'fill a bag for five bucks' this weekend."

We both fall silent again. I can't bring myself to make small talk.

This time she speaks first. "The funeral was nice."

I nod and pick at something crusty on the armrest.

"The lilies," she says. "This time of year. How did you get them?"

Mom's favourite flower. "Mary got them somewhere."

Caroline winces. "Sorry." Then after a moment: "You still think she and Vince are messin' around?"

"Yup."

"My mom told me Mary always had a thing for Vince in high school, even though he was your mom's boyfriend."

My head snaps up. "Yeah? So?"

"I'm just saying, maybe she never got over him."

"Are you making excuses?"

Caroline gives me a horrified look. "Shit no! Like there'd ever be an excuse."

I watch her shift uncomfortably in her seat.

"Why wasn't Kyle at the funeral?" she asks — her attempt to change the subject.

"He had a term paper due. Plus it's a two-hour drive, if he could even find a ride. I told him not to come."

She scrunches up her nose. "Still … your girlfriend's mother dies … you think he'd show." She never hid the fact she wasn't his biggest fan.

"His parents were there," I say. "That was enough."

"Does he know you're coming?"

"No."

"So you're just going to show up?"

"Surprise!" I exclaim, but my voice sounds deadpan.

She raises her eyebrows.

"What?" I twist to lean my back against the door. "You don't think he'll be happy to see me?"

Shrugging, she says, "You should have given him a heads-up, that's all. What if he's not there?"

"He's working on his paper. He'll either be at his residence or the library," I answer.

"I just don't want to see you get stuck." She gives me a worried look. "You know ... you could always call Aidan, like if you can't find Kyle."

The mention of Aidan's name causes a million different emotions to churn together in my stomach. I turn away from her and stare blindly out the window.

"I saw him at the church," she says. "I forgot how cute he was."

I keep staring out the window so she can't see my face. I can't believe he was here.

"But then he disappeared," she continues. "Did you see him, talk to him?"

"No," I whisper.

"Oh." She coughs. "Well, it was really crowded. I don't think he stayed long. He didn't go to the reception."

"If he had wanted to talk to me, he would have found me." I sigh. "I don't know what we would have said to each other anyway." I turn from the window. "Wait. Why did you say I could call him, like if I got stuck?"

"I heard him talking to Stevie. He's in Halifax."

I digest this bit of information.

"At least there'll be another person in town that you'll know," she says. "You should get in touch with him. He is your brother after all."

"Step," I say.

"Fine. Stepbrother. Whatever." She looks at me sideways. "Lyssa. You can't still be mad at him for leaving, for getting a life."

She doesn't know the half of it. No way would she understand the rest. And I can't explain it to her. Aidan made it bearable. He promised he'd always be there for me. Then one day he left without a word, leaving me alone.

He never got in touch. Never told me why.

We haven't spoken in over two years.

I missed him every day. And I'd get so mad at myself because I missed him.

I still miss him.

Caroline has her lips pressed firmly together, chin all puckered and dimply. I know she's annoyed with me. I should say something, make up an answer. But I'm too tired, so I let the moment pass.

I close my eyes and pretend to sleep. About an hour later we pull into the bus station parking lot. Caroline turns off the ignition and reaches for her purse. "You've got a long wait. I'll come in and stay with you, keep you company."

Without thinking, I say, "No." She looks hurt. "It will be easier to say goodbye here, now," I add quickly. "Instead of saying it later."

After a second she nods, and we both slowly crawl out of the car. She opens the back door and passes me my bag.

"Thanks again for the drive," I say, but my words are drowned out by the roar of a bus leaving the parking lot.

Caroline stretches out her arms and wraps me in a hug. She squeezes me tight. I pull away first. Though it's dark, I can see a film of water in her eyes.

"I can't believe this is it. That this is goodbye," she says in a gravelly voice.

"I know."

"Email me or something. Keep me in the loop. Let me know how you're doing."

"I will."

We hug one last time. "Bye, Lyssa. Good luck," she whispers into my hair. "And break down and get a friggin' phone, would ya?"

I smile. "Goodbye, Caroline." I thought it would be harder to say. I sling my bag over my shoulder and walk across the lot to the entrance of the station.

I don't look back.

chapter 2

The hum and vibration of the bus lulls me to sleep. I sleep deeply. For the first time in a long time I don't dream.

A tap on my shoulder drags me out of the darkness. "We're here," someone whispers.

It takes me a moment to remember where I am, and I blink a few times to bring the face into focus. It's the older woman who was sitting across the aisle. "Thank you," I say. When I stand to stretch, I see that there are hardly any people left on the bus.

Still groggy, I lean my elbows on the seat in front of me and wait for the rest of the bus to clear out. The driver turns. "Need some help?" His tone says, *Time to leave.*

"No." I pull my duffle bag down from the overhead and slowly make my way to the front. Before I step off, I dig a piece of paper out of my pocket and ask him, "How do I get to Glengary Apartments? They're on Edward Street."

"Cab or Metro Transit." He checks his watch. "I think it runs on the half-hour ... so another fifteen minutes."

I can't afford to waste money on a cab, and I don't feel like waiting around the bus station. "Is it a long walk?"

He scratches his bald spot. "No, probably about twenty minutes. Go right up South Street."

"Thanks." I hop off the bus.

"Hey, missy!" he calls after me. "You shouldn't be walking alone at night!"

"Don't worry," I call back over my shoulder. "I'll be fine!" *I'll be just fine.*

THE HALLWAY IS DIMLY lit and smells stale and damp, like our cellar with the dirt floor. I turn a corner and catch a whiff of beer and takeout food. Not great on an empty stomach.

Music blares from behind a door, combined with loud, out-of-tune, drunken singing, but once I pass by, the rest of the floor seems quiet. It's Saturday night. Enough happening on campus and downtown to lure students from their caves.

I stop and pull an elastic out of a side pouch on my duffle bag. After trying to comb my hair with my fingers, I sweep it back into a loose ponytail. My eye catches a white sock tied to a nearby doorknob, and it makes me smile. I thought they only did that on sitcoms. Continuing down the hall, I scan each door, searching for the right number. 205, 206 ... the next one is Kyle's, 207.

I plaster on my best and brightest smile, hoping the hell of the day won't show. I've missed having someone to talk to. It feels like I've been alone forever. But that's all behind me now. It's finally my turn. This is my new beginning.

Taking a deep breath, I knock lightly on the door. After a second I hear footsteps on the other side. "I told you not to come back before mid— !" The door flings open.

"Surprise!" I manage to work up some enthusiasm.

Kyle's eyes bulge out of his head. "Jesus, Lyssa?" He grabs on to the edge of the door, looking like he's about to pass out. "What are you doing here?"

The look on his face isn't the one I imagined. He should be happy, sweeping me into his arms, kissing me. It throws me off balance. "I — I left," I tell him. "I came to be with you, just like we planned."

He rubs the back of his neck. "You should have called me first."

A weird sensation works its way up my spine. "Aren't you happy to see me?"

"Of course I am." He clears his throat and swallows. "Just let me change and we'll go grab some coffee."

"Grab some coffee?" I echo. "Can't we have coffee here?"

"Uh ..."

Something's not right. I take a step back and survey the scene. He's wearing pyjama bottoms and no shirt. His hair is all tousled like he just crawled out of bed, but it's only — I check my watch — just after ten o'clock. Behind him I see a table covered with empty beer bottles and dirty glasses. "I ... thought you had a term paper."

His cheeks flush, and he takes a quick look back at the mess. "I, uh, I do. My, uh, roommates don't, though." Then, as if becoming aware that he's only half dressed, he grabs a hoodie from a hook by the door and slips it over his head. "I was just trying to get some shut-eye while they were out," he continues. "I've been working non-stop."

Of course. The roommates. I blast out a breath of relief. That explains it. "Let me in, loser," I say, playfully pushing him out of the way and tossing my bag on the floor.

"Lyssa, wait —"

"Kyle!" I hear a voice call. "You're out of sham—"

We see each other at the same time. She's coming out of another room, a plastic bottle in her hand. A jolt of electricity shoots through my body. She's wearing his pyjama top. Her long blonde hair has the same messed-up look. They match. They're a pair.

There's ringing in my ears, an airy feeling in my head.

Kyle swears under his breath, and his chin drops to his chest. "Rosalyn, could you leave us for a bit?"

Her cheeks flush like his. "Yeah, uh, sure, sorry." And she scurries away out of sight.

My mouth starts moving, but no sound comes out.

"Lyssa." He reaches out and touches my arm. I jump back. Stung.

He takes a step toward me and tries again.

I find my voice. "Don't touch me," I say. "Don't come near me."

"She's nobody, Lyssa," he says desperately. "She means nothing to me."

I roll my eyes. "You couldn't come up with anything better than that? Isn't that every cheater's slogan? When they get caught?"

"But it's true!"

"You sleep with her and then tell me she means nothing, that she's nobody?" I shake my head in disbelief. "I don't know who to feel more sorry for — her or me."

"Lyssa. It was just a stupid mistake, that's all. I love you. You know you're the only one."

Wow. He doesn't even deny it. A high-pitched, hysterical kind of laugh bursts out of me. It's all so ridiculous. "You have a half-naked girl in your bed!"

His eyes fly to the bedroom door, now closed. He has no response. There isn't one.

As I watch him struggle, a coldness settles over me and smothers all my other emotions. It scares me a bit, how little I feel. Making two fists, I dig my fingernails into my palms. It barely registers. I'm numb. I bend over and gather up my duffle bag. "Goodbye, Kyle," I say.

"Goodbye ...?" He says it slowly, like he doesn't know what the word means. "But —"

"Yeah. I'm telling you goodbye," I say. "It's more than you deserve."

He seems stunned as I shoulder my way past him and start down the hall. I'm almost to the front door when I hear his feet thumping on the stairs behind me. He follows me out to the sidewalk.

"You can't just leave," he says. "Where are you going to go?"

I don't answer. I just keep walking. I know he's in bare feet and won't get very far.

"Lyssa!" he shouts. "I'm sorry!"

His voice sounds far away.

I don't look back.

chapteR 3

A horn blares as I step off the curb. "It's a crosswalk, asshole!" I yell. The car honks again and speeds away. I give him the finger, reaching my arm in the air as high as it can go.

Once I'm across the street, I sit on a low stone wall at the edge of someone's front yard. I wait for the tears to start, but they don't come.

It begins to rain. I tilt my face upwards and let the water wash away the horrible day. It feels good. I like it here on this wall. I picture myself staying in this spot forever, turning to stone, becoming a giant garden statue.

As the rain soaks through my jacket to my clothes, so does reality. Where *am* I going to go? Stranded in the city, no friends, no place to stay. I should be a little more freaked out. I had no plan B. Or did I?

Never go back. Not to home. And now not to Kyle either.

That's ... sort of a plan.

A clap of thunder brings on a heavy downpour. I have to move. I try to keep under the trees, but after I walk for a few minutes, there's no point — I'm completely drenched.

Through the sheets of rain, I'm able to make out an "open" sign. When I get closer I see it's an old house converted into a coffee shop. I run up to the door and pull it open. Warm air hits me, sending shivers through my whole body. I didn't realize how cold I was.

The wood floor creaks as I step inside. The place appears empty. I wipe my face with the cuff of my jacket and take a look around. There are a dozen or so round tables scattered along both sides of the room, leaving a clear path to the counter. Funky red pendant lights hang low over each table, throwing off a soft glow. Benches with piles of cushions line the front windows. There's a brick fireplace — the bricks cover the entire wall. A massive, antique-looking mirror leans on the mantle.

I hear something and glance down. Water drips off my jacket onto the floor. When I look back up, there's the reflection of someone standing behind me in the mirror. I spin around.

He puts up both hands. "Sorry," he says. "Didn't mean to scare you."

My heart is jammed in my throat. I swallow, hoping it slides back to where it's supposed to be.

"Really sorry," he repeats. "Are you okay?"

I nod, feeling stupid. The *ping* of the water falling from my clothes to the floor sounds extra loud. A puddle the size of a small lake surrounds me and my duffle bag. He probably thinks I'm a homeless person.

"Can I get you something?" he asks. Then before I can say anything: "Bet you could use something hot."

"Tea," I whisper.

"Green? Chai?"

"Plain tea, please."

He grins. "Sure."

He goes to the counter, drops a tea bag into a mug, fills it with steaming water, and grabs a few sugar packets and creamers. "Listen," he says. "Sit over here. There's still a bit of a fire left." He puts the mug down on a table across the room and angles the chair closer to fireplace. "Might help you dry out."

Peeling off my jacket, I follow him and take a seat. Goosebumps explode over my skin as the heat from the fire starts to seep through my wet clothing. I wrap my ice-cold fingers around the hot mug and lift it to my mouth. It burns my throat going down, but I don't care.

He watches me.

"Thank you," I say.

"I think we have some soup left. Not enough to bother saving. I'll get it for you." He doesn't wait for me to answer.

I take another sip of tea. *Yup, he thinks I'm homeless.* In a way, he's right.

My eyes follow him as he returns to the counter. At school we would have called him a lank. He has a nice face, a nice smile. His hair is wavy, almost black, long enough that the ends curl at the bottom and touch his shirt collar. His bangs are so long, he keeps tossing his head to flick them out of his eyes.

He's back in a couple of minutes with another steaming mug. A spoon handle sticks out of the top. "Hope you like beef vegetable."

It smells delicious. "I do. Thanks." I start shovelling in the soup. I've had nothing to eat since this morning.

"May I?" He points to the other chair.

"Sure."

He sits down across from me. He's holding his own mug of something, coffee or tea because he dumps in multiple packets of sugar.

The soup makes me feel human again. "This is the best thing I've ever tasted."

"Hmm. You might want to re-evaluate your standards."

"Oh?"

"I do a lot of things well, but making soup isn't one of them."

I feel myself smile. I notice his brown eyes, how they're fringed with long lashes most girls would kill for.

He smiles back, takes a drink from his mug, and makes a face. "So ... rough day at the office?" he asks, adding another sugar.

"Sort of," I say. "Do you ever sometimes just really hate your life?"

"Oh yeah." He tilts his chair back and locks his hands behind his head. "Every morning when my alarm goes off at 6:05."

"I went to my mom's funeral this morning." The legs of his chair slam to the floor. "Cancer." I take another spoonful of soup.

"I — I'm so sorry."

I wipe my face with a napkin. "No, I'm sorry. I don't know why I just said that." And I really don't.

"Maybe you needed to," he says, sweeping hair out of his eyes. "Like, maybe you needed to say it, hear it, or something."

I roll that around in my head for a second. "Yeah, maybe."

"I feel like an idiot, though, whining about my alarm."

"It's okay. I don't like it when my alarm goes off either."

It's quiet except for the rain on the windows and the hissing from the dying fire.

He glances down at my duffle bag. "Are you just passing through?"

There are a few drops of spilled soup on the table. I drag my spoon through them until they're all joined together. "I came to ... surprise my boyfriend. It turned out to be" — I make a popping sound with my lips — "not a good time."

"Oh," he says knowingly. It's all quiet again. Then he makes a fist and flexes his arm muscles. "Do you want me to rip his lungs out?"

"Um ..." I stare up at the ceiling like I'm seriously thinking it over. "Thanks for the offer. But you might get caught, sent to prison. I'd feel responsible."

"Okay." He shrugs. "Just trying to help."

"Yes, well, thanks for the offer."

"So what are you going to do now?"

That's the million-dollar question. I think of the 238 bucks sitting in my bank account. With no job or place to stay, it's not going to last me long. "I'm not sure yet."

"Is there anyone you can call? Someone else you know? I have a car. I can drop you wherever."

I don't answer. There's a long thread hanging from the corner of the tablecloth, and I weave it through my fingers, over, under, over, under.

The faint pattering of rain on the roof is comforting. It would be so easy to drift off... A snap from the fire jerks me back.

"Look," he says. "I've still got to do the cash and stuff. Take your time, stay and think about what you want to do." He gets up and goes to the door, flips over the "closed" sign, and slides across the deadbolt.

Click.

Instinctively my chest tightens and I sit up a little straighter in my chair. I've just let myself be locked up with a stranger.

As if reading my mind, he says, "Don't worry, I'm not a psycho or a serial killer. Though the 'rip his lungs out' thing might have made you wonder."

I stare at him, really hard, like I'm looking for something, a sign.

He tilts his head and stares back, like he's trying to figure me out too. His hair flops over one eye, and he brushes it away. Then, as if something dawns on him, he reaches for the deadbolt. "I can leave this unlocked, but you'll have to be in charge of chasing people away."

I feel myself relax a little and shake my head. "No, it's okay."

As he starts to make his way back to the kitchen, he stops and holds out his hand. "I'm Liam, by the way. Liam Stewart."

His hand hangs there, waiting. I take a deep breath, slip my hand into his, and shake. "Lyssa," I say. "Lyssa Thomson."

"Okay, Lyssa Thomson. I'll be done here in about ten minutes. Then, like I said, I can drop you anywhere you want."

"Thanks."

I take my tea over to the window and watch the water rush along the street gutters. I have only one option. "Do you have a phone book?" I holler out to Liam.

"Yeah," he answers. "Over by the cash register. The phone's there too."

The number is easy to find. There are a million Mackenzies, but the one I want is at the very beginning. I lift up the phone and punch in the number.

He picks up after the second ring. "Hello?"

For a second I freeze.

"Hello?" he repeats.

"Hi, Aidan," I finally say. "It's me."

CHapteR 4

The rain drums loudly on the hood of the car. A film of condensation covers my side window. With my finger I draw a happy face on the glass. Liam must think I'm crazy. We've been parked here in front of this house for more than a few minutes and I haven't made the slightest move to get out of the car. Out of the corner of my eye, I look at him. He's listening to Arcade Fire on the radio and tapping his fingers on the steering wheel, like he finds nothing at all weird about this situation. Maybe he's the crazy one.

I know I can't stay here forever. I erase my artwork with the palm of my hand. "Thanks again for the drive," I say.

"No big whoop." He sweeps his hair out of his eyes. "It's on my way home."

I still make no move to get out of the car.

Liam turns in his seat. "I'm not trying to be nosy or anything, but you kind of remind me of myself when I had to go for a root canal last month."

I let out a laugh, more of a grunt really, but I don't say anything.

He rolls down his window and looks at the house. "This guy's your brother, huh?"

"Step."

"My Spidey senses are telling me you're kind of ... I dunno ... anxious about seeing him?"

"It's a long story."

"It usually is," he says.

I reach behind me, pull my duffle bag from the back seat, then fling the car door open. My stomach cramps up. I know it's nerves. I sit with my body half-in, half-out and breathe deeply. I don't care that the rain is soaking my legs all over again.

"Hey." He touches my shoulder. "No matter what, he's family, right?"

My head turns. He makes it sound so simple. "Right."

But he must see something in my face, and his eyes turn serious. "Do you want me to come to the door with you?"

"No," I say quickly. "Not necessary." I feel guilty about all the time he's wasted on me, a complete stranger. It's time to let him off the hook.

He stares back at the house for a second. "Are you sure?"

"Yeah." I try to sound convincing. "You've gone above and beyond."

"Well ... I *did* spend a few years in the Boy Scouts."

"And it's obviously paid off." I force myself to smile, to reassure him.

The car door is now dripping wet. I finish getting out, hook my bag over my shoulder, and walk around to the driver's side window.

"Thanks for everything, Liam," I say.

"Like I said, no big whoop. And drop by the coffee shop sometime. I'm there most nights."

"Okay. Maybe." I step back from the curb and wave.

He sticks his head out. "I'm going to wait here until you're in."

I nod and make my way up the walk. When I get to the front step I turn and look back. I realize the upset feeling in my stomach isn't completely about seeing Aidan again; a bit of it is about saying goodbye to Liam. Liam, who only knows me as Lyssa — anonymous Lyssa. In spite of all the crap that came earlier, this past hour has been my first taste of normal in a long time. And it was ... nice. Then again, I guess it depends on your definition of normal.

The lights are on inside the house, but the porch is in complete darkness. I go to ring the bell, but the door swings open before my finger makes contact.

There he stands, the brightness from inside the house making him look like he's glowing around the edges, like he's not real, like he's an angel. Or a ghost. My breath catches, blocking my words. I didn't expect to feel this way.

I hear Liam toot his horn and drive off.

Aidan looks past me over my shoulder and frowns. "I could have picked you up, you know."

My words are still blocked.

He glances up at the porch ceiling. "Sorry, the bulb's burnt out. Come in. Here, let me take that." He holds a hand out for my bag.

Wordlessly, I pass it to him and step into the hall.

For a long moment we study each other. I take in every tiny detail. The changes are subtle. His dark eyes are the same, but set in a face that looks older. His brown hair is slightly shorter, not so long and "Shaggy from *Scooby-Doo*" anymore. He's still tall, but he looks even taller because he's lost weight. I wonder what he thinks about me. Do I look the same as I did two years ago? Then I remember ... he was at the funeral. He would have seen me this morning.

Aidan moves first. He sets my duffle bag down, circles his arms around me, and envelops my body with his. All I want to do is hug him back, but I'm hurt. Hurt about this morning, hurt about the last two years. My body remains completely rigid. I'm a cardboard cut-out.

He gets the message and lets go. I back away from him. I don't know what to do with myself, where to look, what to say. Using my front tooth, I scrape at a dry flake of skin on my lip until I taste blood.

He nosily clears his throat. "I'm sorry about your mom, Lyssa."

Finally I speak. "People said you were there this morning."

"Yeah." He nods.

"Why didn't you come and talk to me?"

He drops his eyes. "I didn't know if you'd want me to."

A few seconds go by. "What about Vince? Did you talk to him?"

His head jerks up. He looks insulted. "No."

"Then why did you come?"

He drops his eyes again. "She was always good to me, your mom. I know I didn't make it easy."

That's an understatement. Aidan was the poster boy for "troubled teen." I knew he smoked drugs; I could always smell it on his clothes. I'm sure Mom could smell it too, but she ignored it, probably to keep the peace. I figure Vince was more an expert in "eau de alcohol." Calls from the principal came on an almost daily basis — Aidan was always getting into fights, which I could never understand, because he was a complete loner. He barely passed high school. I think they pushed him through just to be rid of him.

"She loved you, Aidan."

"I don't know how many times she stopped Vince from beating the shit out of me. She ran good defence."

More seconds go by.

"I've missed you, Lyss," he says. "I think about you, worry about you, all the time."

I'm not sure I believe him. Everything he says is only making me more confused. "You're the one who left, remember?"

"I know. And I'm sorry."

I stare back at him. Does he really not get it? What his leaving did to me? "I'm sorry? That's it?"

"You don't want to get into this whole thing right now, do you?" he sighs.

"I kind of do."

"I promise. When the time is right, I'll explain it all," he says.

"When the time is right, you'll explain it all?" I repeat. "What does that mean?"

"Trust me about this."

"Aidan. You have to give me something, *anything*."

Frustrated, he runs his hands through his hair. "Think about the day you've just had, Lyssa." He checks his watch. "I can't imagine how exhausted you must be. I don't know how you're still standing."

It's like Aidan saying it out loud suddenly makes it true. I hit a wall. I feel a little off balance, my vision blurs. I reach for the arm of the sofa and ease myself down onto the seat.

He starts to tug off my wet jacket. I let him. Then he unfolds a fleece blanket and drapes it over me. "Just lie down and shut your eyes."

I try to keep them open. Just before I fall asleep, I hear him whisper, "Everything's going to be okay now."

CHAPTER 5

My eyes are closed, but I can still tell it's morning. I burrow down deeper into the sofa, pull the blankets around me tighter. I feel a puff of warmth on my face, smell a bad smell. Still half-asleep, I drag my eyes open. A mass of ginger fur is all I can see. My heart stops. Before I can think, I swat at it with my arm. I hear a high-pitched meow, the sound of nails scraping along the floor.

Aidan comes rushing in. "Beat it, Bingley!" He takes a menacing step toward the cat, stomping his foot loudly. "Sorry," he says to me.

The cat arches its back, hisses, and runs out of the room.

"Hate that damn thing," Aidan mutters.

I'm now fully awake and sitting up. I toss back the blankets and instantly feel cold. My clothes are still damp.

"Last night, I left for two seconds to put your stuff in the spare room," Aidan says. "When I got back, you were dead to the world. Instead of moving you, I just piled on the blankets and hoped for the best. Were you warm enough?"

I nod.

The cat reappears, stretches lazily, and weaves itself, nose held high, in and around Aidan's feet like he owns the place and everything in it.

Aidan curls his lip and pushes it away with his foot.

"I never thought of you as a cat person," I say.

"I'm not. It's Marla's. She can't have pets in her apartment."

"Marla?"

"My girlfriend."

"Your girlfriend?"

He smiles. "You seem surprised."

"I, uh, am."

"Why?"

"In all the time I've known you, you never once had a girlfriend, never really showed any interest in ... any girl." I get up, attempt to fold one of the blankets. "After a while ... I just ..."

"What?" he demands. "Thought I was *gay*?"

I pause. "It crossed my mind."

"What about Tammy Johnson? I really liked her, wanted to ask her out. *You* told me to stay away, told me that she was trailer trash."

"Well, she was. *Is*. You know she's got two kids now, by two different guys."

He shakes his head. "I can't believe it. I *can't* believe you thought I was gay."

"I actually thought that might have been why you left."

"Because Vince wouldn't take too kindly to having a gay son?" he says sarcastically.

I shrug.

"Yeah, well, I'm not. And that's not why I left."

There's anger in his voice. I wait, but he doesn't offer any more of an explanation. He motions with his head toward the hall. "Your room's the second door. The bathroom's right next to it. I'll make you some breakfast."

After I'm showered and dressed, I take a moment to check out the house. It's old. The furniture's worn and faded but looks comfortable. It doesn't feel like a guy lives here.

Aidan comes out into the hall to find me snooping around the dining room. "Do you still take milk and sugar in your tea?"

I quickly set down the porcelain figurine I'm holding. "Just black."

"What do you think of the place?" he asks.

"Uh ... nice?"

He laughs. "This all belongs to Mrs. Collins. She lives upstairs, owns the house. In return for cheap rent, I do all the odd jobs. You know, shovelling, mowing the lawn, any repairs. She's eighty-five."

"Oh."

"I sort of inherited all this stuff from her," he continues. "I used to live upstairs, but then last year someone tried to break in. It scared her. She didn't want to be at street level anymore, so we switched. Even after she moved up everything she wanted, it was still full of furniture down here. It was easier to just live with it than put it in storage."

I nod.

"Come on. Breakfast is ready."

I follow him into the kitchen. He puts two plates of scrambled eggs on the table, two cups of tea. I can't help but smile when I see the processed cheese slice melting over the mound of eggs, taking on their lumpy shape. He nudges the bottle of ketchup toward me. We used to take turns making this exact breakfast every Saturday morning. Only this time we eat in silence.

He sighs and shoves back his plate. "I don't remember you being this quiet."

I look at him over the rim of my cup. "Just tired."

"You grew your hair," he comments.

More silence.

"Okay. Is this how it's —"

"Can I walk to King's College from here?" It's like he expects me to act like nothing happened, like we can pick up where we left off two years ago. Part of me wishes I could. It would be so easy. But I'm all a jumble. I'm not sure how I should feel. Or act.

"Um, yeah. But I can drive you."

"No thanks."

"Is this where you're heading?" He holds up a crumpled piece of paper. "It fell out of your jacket last night."

Kyle's address. It suddenly occurs to me that Aidan doesn't know about Kyle or what happened. In fact, now that I think about it, he never even asked me what I was doing here, why I needed a place to stay. Guess I should be grateful, grateful he feels so guilty.

"No. I just told you, I'm going to King's." I reach for the paper, but he snatches it back.

"Who's Kyle?" he asks.

Damn. I wrote "Kyle new cell #" above his address.

Aidan glances back at the paper. "The Glengary ... it's a Dalhousie residence ... so, someone from home?"

I don't answer.

Then Aidan makes a face like he just ate something rotten. "Not Kyle Matthews. Please tell me you weren't going to see Kyle Matthews."

I debate lying, but it would only create more questions. "Not anymore."

"Good." Aidan dumps sugar straight from a two-kilogram bag into his tea.

I'm kind of taken aback when he doesn't ask me anything else about Kyle. Maybe he figures I won't tell him.

"He was an arrogant little prick," he adds.

Much to my surprise, I become a bit defensive. "You didn't even *know* him."

He shrugs. "I knew *of* him."

"Any right you had to offer an opinion, you gave up two years ago," I add.

"Maybe. But it doesn't stop me from having one. A *right* one," he says, all smug.

"Could you be any more of an asshole?" I try kicking him under the table, but he's too quick and shifts his legs.

He balls up his napkin and throws it at me. "Probably," he jokes.

I narrow my eyes. Did he really think I'd find that funny?

"Okay, okay, time out," he says. "I'll take you over to King's. Why do you want to go?"

"To do *stuff*."

"Lyssa. It's just a question. I'm only trying to help."

"Fine," I say. "I want to go to the registrar's office, see about my student loan, see if I can start taking some classes in January, see if there's any student housing available."

"Wow." Aidan sits back in his chair. "That's quite a list. I kind of thought, with your mom and everything, you gave up on university."

"Well, I didn't."

"That's great. Good for you," he says, but he doesn't sound like he means it.

"Thank God I have your approval."

He smirks. "Nice to see you still have that sarcastic edge I so admire."

"Practice makes perfect."

Shaking his head, he says, "Hey, listen. Don't waste your loan money on a place to stay. Stay here."

I push my eggs around on my plate.

"Come on, Lyss. The residences are all full by now. Classes started a couple of months ago."

"I'll check at the student union building. Someone might be looking for a roommate."

"Oh, right, and risk ending up with some crazy?"

"Well, when I meet them, I'll make sure to ask for their mental health records."

"But I have an extra bedroom. You're fifteen minutes from the university. You'd be nuts not to stay here."

"No … I dunno …"

He doesn't say anything for a minute, then: "I know it hurt you when I left like I did. So let me at least start to try and make it up to you — I owe you. Stay here. Come and go as you please. You don't even have to talk to me if you don't want. Please, Lyss."

I close my eyes, pinch the bridge of my nose. I feel like a checker piece blocked in on all sides. I'm out of moves — no money, no job, no place to stay, a student loan that might not even exist anymore.

"Come on, Lyss. It'll be fun. We used to have fun, didn't we?"

We did. We did used to have fun. My shoulders slump. "All right, I'll stay. For now."

"Why just for now?"

"Because I need a change. I want to try living on campus, meet new people, do all the things you're supposed to do when you go to university."

"You can do that all from here."

It's like he really thinks living here would be the same as living on campus. "I said I'd stay. For now. Take it or leave it."

"Guess I have to take it," he says. "For now."

Chapter 6

Aidan has an exasperated look on his face. I've refused to let him drive me to the university. He's offered three times.

"I want to walk," I say, pulling on my jacket. "I have to start finding my way around."

"Well, do you at least want directions?"

"No. I think I got it."

He's still jangling the car keys in his hand and muttering under his breath as I walk out the door.

It's sunny, and the fresh air feels good — cold and crisp. I pause and take a second to think about which direction Liam brought me from last night, and then head that way.

The rain has left scattered patches of ice. There are chunky bits of salt sprinkled on the sidewalk, and they crunch loudly beneath my feet.

Back home they use sand. It's dirty. Gets everywhere.

After a few blocks I come to a busy street. Two lanes each way, divided by a boulevard. I glance up at the sign. Robie Street. I store it in my memory.

I keep going. The next corner brings me to University Avenue. This has to be it.

The fact that almost everyone is carrying knapsacks or messenger bags tells me I'm in the right place. Rather than wasting a ton of time wandering around like a moron, I approach a bunch of kids waiting at a bus stop. "Could you tell me where the King's registrar's office is?"

"Sure," one guy says. He's dressed all in black — black hair, black eyeliner, multiple facial piercings. He drops his cigarette on the ground and grinds it to a pulp with the heel of his pointy black boot. "Keep going, first right, then next left. You'll see a sign, and a courtyard. It's in there."

"Thanks."

I find the office no problem. The lady I speak to, Ms. Watson, is really nice. I explain my situation, how I was all registered, supposed to start in September, but had to withdraw. Because of my mom. Because she got sick and died.

Giving me a sad look, she says, "I'm so sorry."

"Oh. Um. Thank you."

"Did you want to go ahead and see what we can find out?"

I nod.

She wiggles her computer mouse to wake it up. "What's your full name?"

"Alyssa Kathleen Thomson."

"Okay ..." She punches my name into the computer and leans in close to the screen. "What do we have here ..."

She tells me that the circumstances surrounding my withdrawal are all in my file and that my student loan has been put on hold but the funds are still available.

The relief is so overwhelming, my knees feel weak.

"You'll have to fill out some forms," she says, handing me some papers. "You'll find all the instructions online."

I slide the papers into my bag.

"Once they get proof of enrolment, you'll get notification and you can submit your pre-study report."

"Pre-study report?"

"It might end up getting you some more money." She smiles. "It's all on the website."

"Okay."

"Just remember, the funds won't be deposited into your account until a week or so before the next term starts."

My face falls. "Oh." I'd kind of hoped to dip into a bit — if only to get a phone, maybe a laptop ...

She hands me a course calendar. "You probably already had all your courses picked out."

I nod.

"But take this. It's likely you'll have to make some changes. You can do this online too — see which January classes still have space."

"Okay."

"If you were interested in living in residence, I can put your name on a waiting list. We're full right now, but it's not unusual to have the odd student drop out or not return for semester two."

"Yeah, that would be great. Thanks."

Outside the office I notice a giant bulletin board on the wall with pamphlets, homemade flyers, students selling books, looking for books. There are a bunch that say, "looking for roommate," "looking for apartment," but I can tell they're old, mostly covered by new stuff. I take down a piece of paper advertising a party in the Ward room on September 8 and flip it over. I write that I'm looking for accommodations to share for January. I add my name, have to stop and go back to the office to borrow a phone book, write in Aidan's phone number, and re-pin it right in the centre of the board.

As I leave the building, something new begins to stir inside me. Something unfamiliar. Hope.

Suddenly the idea of wandering around isn't so bad. I zigzag up and down the tree-lined streets, looking at the beautiful old homes. Every so often I go by one that has obviously been rented out to students. The signs are all there — bed sheets as curtains, beer cases piled on the porch, even the occasional sofa. The next thing I know, I'm standing on the exact same corner as I did last night, directly across from Liam's coffee shop. I stop, *smack*, as if there's an invisible wall blocking my path. If I'm here, that also means I can't be far from Kyle's — a couple of blocks at the most. That new feeling, the hope, it's gone before I even get a chance to enjoy it.

I clench my jaw. Kyle ... Rosalyn ... I see the whole scene in my head all over again. I *hate* myself for being so stupid. I thought I was so smart, smarter than everyone else. Kyle said it was a vibe I gave off. It used to drive him crazy. Guess he showed me.

Minutes pass while my feet stay glued to the sidewalk. I want to go into the coffee shop, get warm, and read through my calendar. But I hesitate, rolling my calendar into a tighter and tighter tube. It's because of Liam. I don't want to see him. Only because he'd think it was weird, me showing up the next day like some kind of stalker. Yeah, he said come by, but everyone says stuff like that.

Wait. He said he worked most evenings. It isn't even noon. I'm safe.

When I pull open the door, it's just like last night — heat wraps around me like a thick blanket. I breathe in the aroma of fresh coffee and cinnamon, and let my eyes adjust to the low lighting.

A table of older ladies glance up as I walk to the front counter.

"What can I get you?" a girl about my age asks. She has fluorescent pink highlights in her pigtails. Her eyeshadow and lipstick are the same fluorescent pink.

"Umm ..." The menu board with a zillion beverage combinations looms on the wall behind her. "Uh ..."

She gives me that look — that "sometime today would be nice" look.

I decide to take a risk, think outside the box. "Small vanilla latte, please. No, wait ... make it a medium."

After paying, I survey the room while the cup begins to burn my hand. Two girls, student types, are getting up from the table by the fireplace where I sat with Liam. I hurry over to lay claim before they've even finished putting their coats on.

I sit, sip my latte, and stare into the flames, zoning out for a while.

The pink girl behind the counter shouts out an order and snaps me back. I open my calendar and start reading, folding down the corners of the pages that interest me. As I drain my latte, I feel a rush of cold air. Someone's come through the front door.

"Yo, Erin!"

Shit. Liam. Whipping the calendar up in front of my face, I slink down real low in my seat. Maybe he won't see me. He walks right past my table and starts talking to the pink girl. I hear him laughing, hear him say, "You bet, see you at six."

He's leaving. I hold my breath and try not to move. That's when a finger appears on the top edge of my calendar. Liam slowly pushes it down, revealing my face. "Personally, I've never found course calendars to be that captivating."

"Really?" I fight to keep my tone casual, but my voice cracks anyway. "The part *I'm* reading is absolutely spine-tingling."

Smiling, he flicks his hair out of his eyes and sits down in the other chair. "I see you're at your usual table," he points out.

"I hovered until I drove the other people away."

He nods. "Impressive."

"Thanks."

"So you must be staying for a while." He reaches for my calendar and fans through it.

"Yeah. I just came from the registrar's office … I didn't know it was so close by … thought I'd pop in and grab a coffee …" I feel the need to explain my presence.

"What are you thinking about taking?"

"I'm planning on —"

"Don't say a bachelor of arts."

"A bachelor of arts." That isn't what I'm planning to take at all, but I can't help myself.

He sighs dramatically, shaking his head. "That'll get you a fine career in waitressing."

"Oh?" I raise my eyebrows and glance around the coffee shop. "Is that what you took?"

"Pre-med, missy." He pokes at his chest. "Pre-med."

"So you're a degree snob."

He laughs. "I've been called worse. Just offering some friendly advice, that's all."

"Thanks," I say dryly. "I'm taking journalism. But only if that's okay with you, of course."

Leaning back, he squints at me. "Aren't *you* a funny one?"

I shrug. "I have my moments."

He laughs again, then stands and slides his chair back in. "Well. Got my paycheque. Time to head out."

"K. See you around."

"Yeah. Nice to run into you."

"Yeah. You too."

He's halfway to the door when without thinking, I call out, "And thanks again for last night." A handful of people turn to look at me. I smile back weakly, feel my cheeks turn hot.

Liam's shoulders shake. "The pleasure was all mine," he calls back.

After he leaves, I wait a few more minutes and then leave myself.

It's not as cold as it was this morning, but it's clouded over and looks like it's about to rain. A second later it does. *Damn it.* I stuff my calendar inside my jacket and pick up my pace.

A car honks its horn, slows, and pulls up to the curb a little ahead of where I'm walking. The rain is coming down so heavily, the car just looks like a giant dark blur.

It can only be one of three people. Aidan, Kyle, or Liam — I don't know anyone else here. Cautiously, I lean over sideways to see.

The window slides down. "Get in!" Liam hollers.

I yank the door open and jump inside.

He puts the blinker on and pulls back into traffic.

"Thanks for the lift. *Again*," I say, tucking my wet, stringy hair behind my ears.

"Don't worry about it. Are you on your way back to your brother's? Stepbrother's?" He corrects himself before I can.

"Yeah," I say.

"Then it's like I said last night, you're on my way."

"I know. But it's starting to feel like all I ever do is thank you."

"Didn't I tell you I was half superhero? I'm used to being constantly thanked."

"You told me you were a Boy Scout. There was no mention of your being half superhero."

"Well, I am. On my mom's side. You're just lucky I had to go to the bank machine or we might have missed each other." He turns down Aidan's street. "It's all about the timing, you know."

AIDAN IS STANDING IN the living room window with his arms crossed, frowning, when I come through the front door. "That the same guy from last night?"

"Uh-huh."

"You'll take a drive from him, but not from me?"

"I just ran into him at a coffee shop. It's *pouring*, in case you haven't noticed."

His frown stays put. "Well, do you even know this guy? Anything about him?"

"*Hello*. What happened to, 'You can come and go as you please. You don't even have to speak to me'? You said that, remember?"

"I'm your brother. I'm only trying to look out for you. It's sort of my job."

I hold back the response that's formulating in my brain, the one about how he quit that job a long time ago. He really seems genuinely concerned. "Thanks, but you don't have to get all protective. He's a nice guy. I think you'd really like him."

chapter 7

When I wake up, the first thing I notice is that the door is partly open. I'm sure I closed it before I finally crawled into bed last night. I slip on a pair of socks and thread my arms into my furry housecoat. Maybe it didn't catch.

Sticking my head out into the hall, I listen. It's all quiet. I wait a minute, then two. Nothing.

Yesterday after supper, I flaked out on my bed to read more about courses. I promptly fell asleep, but not before I heard Aidan leave and the car pull out of the driveway. Around 1:30 a.m., I got up for a glass of water. The car was still gone, and there was no sign of him. It could be he never came home.

Stretching and yawning my way to the kitchen, I put on some water to boil for tea and shuffle out to the living room. My footsteps slow down. An unknown head of hair is visible just over the back of the sofa. It's a girl. She's holding Bingley up to her face and talking ... cat talk.

She must sense I'm there and twists around in her seat. "Lyssa. Yay! I've been waiting for you to wake up."

"Uh ..." My brain's not working yet.

"Aidan told me to stay away, give you a few days to settle in, but I totally couldn't wait to meet you."

"Uh ..."

"Sorry." She stands and brushes cat hair off her skirt. "I'm Marla."

At last it clicks. "Right. Owner of Bingley."

"And Aidan's girlfriend," she adds.

"Right, and Aidan's girlfriend," I repeat, looking behind me down the hall. "Where *is* Aidan?"

"I popped by to throw in a wash." She reaches out, grabs my hand, and gives it a squeeze. "I was hoping you'd be here. I just know we're going to be best friends."

I glance at the clock on the mantle. Quarter to nine. "And Aidan is …?"

"Oh, he's probably off doing the cash."

"The cash?"

She nods. "It usually doesn't take him more than a couple of hours."

It dawns on me that I don't have a clue what Aidan does, where he works. "So he does the cash for …?"

"The bar, silly." She scrunches up her eyebrows. "He's the manager now, you know."

I stare back at her blankly.

"Good grief. Didn't he tell you about his promotion?" She shakes her head. "That's just like Aidan, never wants to talk himself up."

While I continue my staring, something else dawns on me. Marla's under the impression we're normal. She doesn't seem to know about us, our family, our dysfunction, our … estrangements. What in the world has Aidan told her? More importantly, what hasn't he told her?

"You guys haven't had a chance to talk much yet, huh," she says, coming up with her own theory.

"No, not really." I leave it at that.

Marla curls back up on the couch, and Bingley immediately leaps into her lap. It's obvious she has no plans to leave anytime soon.

She looks at me, big green eyes, all full of smiles, waiting for me to speak.

I rock back and forth on my heels, run my tongue along my teeth trying to think of something to say. At the same time I give her a good once-over. I guess I never really pictured Aidan's type, but she's pretty in a natural sort of way — tall, model thin. Her hair is dark blonde with highlights, good ones, and cut into a sleek shoulder-length bob. I actually attempted that same style a while back but gave up after Caroline pointed out I spent half my life with a hair straightener in my hand.

Those big eyes are still on me, still waiting.

"So, uh, how did you guys meet?" I finally say. "At the bar?"

She frowns and tilts her head. "You mean he didn't tell you how we met *either*?"

I can tell she's hurt Aidan hasn't shared their story. "No ... wait, he might've. It's like you said, we haven't had much time to talk. I think he mentioned ..."

"The hospital?" she finishes.

"The hospital?"

"Okay, the psych ward to be more precise."

"Um. *What*?"

Confusion flickers across her face, then her big eyes get even bigger and her hand flies to her chest. "You didn't know ..."

I slowly shake my head.

"Uh ..." She stands, puts the cat down, and begins tugging hard on the ends of her hair, over and over. "I kind of wondered why no one ever came to visit. Don't tell him I told you. I mean, how could I know you didn't know?" She whispers like she's afraid someone's listening. "I mean, I just assumed ... God, I'm not supposed to even be here."

All I hear are the words *psych ward* playing on repeat in my brain. I bury my shock deep inside, save it for later, mainly because Marla looks like she's about to cry. "It's okay, just sit down," I soothe and guide her back to the couch. "I won't say a word. He's probably waiting for the right time to tell me, that's all."

Her head is shaking back and forth in tiny, jerky movements.

I sit beside her, put my hand on her arm. "I promise. Really, I won't say a word. Everything will be fine."

She looks down to where my hand is resting and rolls her arm over.

I follow her gaze and see that the tips of my fingers are touching a pinkish, slightly raised line stretching across the inside of her wrist. My breath catches in my throat when I realize what it is, and I pull my hand away. Extending her other arm, she holds them both out and presses them together. "Twins," she says, attempting to smile.

"Uh ..."

"I read somewhere that when you slit your wrists, if you're really serious, you're supposed to cut up and down, not across."

My mouth falls open.

"Guess I'll have to remember that for next time." She laughs and gives my shoulder a shove. "That was a joke."

I try to laugh with her. It comes out more like a squeak. But she doesn't seem to notice and scoops up Bingley, who's crouching at her feet.

My thoughts run in circles inside my head. Aidan? Was in the psych ward? With Marla ... and her wrists? I don't even know where to start. "Marla, when was Aidan in the psych ward?"

Her eyes get all dreamy looking. "I met him two years, one month, eighteen days ago."

That's around when he left home ... "But why? Why was he there?"

She chews on her bottom lip. "I've spilled too much already. I — I don't think I should talk about it anymore. It's up to Aidan to tell you."

I comb my fingers through my hair, let out a frustrated sigh. She's right. It's not fair of me to try and pump her.

"It was all over a stupid boy, by the way," she says.

My mind is working overtime, trying to process everything, trying to keep everything straight. "Sorry, what?"

"Why I was in there. It was because my boyfriend dumped me."

I resist the urge to say "I know how you feel" and instead say, "That can be rough." My eyes automatically go back to Marla's wrists.

"I don't know what I'd do without Aidan," Marla gushes. "He makes my life worth living."

"Oh." That's all I can think of to say.

Marla checks her watch. "Whoops. I'm going to be late." She jumps up and grabs her coat off the bench in the hall. "I work at a bookstore, just off Spring Garden. Come visit me."

"Sure," I say, following her to the door.

She turns and puts both hands on my shoulders. "It was so great to meet you." Then she hugs me. "And you won't say anything to Aidan?"

I nod.

"Talk soon?"

I nod again.

After she leaves I sink onto the bench where her coat used to lie. My head falls back against the wall. The day has only just started and already I'm completely exhausted. I shut my eyes and think about Aidan. What happened? What happened to him? Then I think of Marla and her whole suicide thing. What is it like to love someone so much that you'd want to end your own life at the thought of losing him? I lost Kyle, but not for one second did I ever consider killing myself. Him, maybe ...

I get up, go to the window, and watch her walk down the street.

chapter 8

I'm sprawled across the bed, feet dangling over one side, arms over the other. I can just reach the edge of the rug, and I unravel a piece of the fringe.

Bingley's nose pokes through the door. I pick up my sneaker and throw it. "Get out!"

He yowls and scampers away.

My head is pounding, but I'm too lazy to get up and hunt for some Advil. I roll over and stare at the ceiling. Is that why Aidan left home? To go to the hospital? Or did that happen *after* he left? Why didn't he tell me? I would have come to see him. I hate that he was there all alone.

There's no one to ask.

Except Aidan. And I can't do that. Because I promised Marla.

I hear keys being tossed on the hall table. Aidan's home.

His footsteps pause briefly outside my door then continue on.

I get up and follow him into the kitchen.

He's hanging off the fridge door. "You must be hungry," he says without turning. "Can I make you something to eat?"

"That'd be great!"

His head twists around, eyebrows raised in surprise at my oddly enthusiastic response. "Okay. I think there are some bagels down in the freezer. Be right back."

A carton of eggs sits on the counter. As I pull down a bowl from the cupboard and start breaking shells against the edge, I worry about how hard it's going to be to act like I don't know anything.

Aidan returns holding a plastic bag full of bagels. He looks pale.

"There's a pile of wet clothes on top of the dryer," he says. "Were you doing a wash?"

"No."

"Well, who …" He puts it together. "Marla was here?"

Uh-oh. "Um, yeah … She was just leaving when I woke up. Said she was late for work."

"So …" He licks his lips. "You guys didn't —"

"It was strictly a hi-bye thing," I say.

"Good, good." He nods. "I mean … I want you to meet her and everything, I just hoped maybe we'd all go for dinner or something."

"Sure. I'd like that," I say. "But not anytime soon. Not till I can help and chip in."

"I'm talking one meal, here," he sighs.

"Yeah. One meal," — I sweep my arm around the room — "a place to live," — I point to the eggs — "groceries. I want to pay my own way. As soon as I can. Retroactive."

"Christ. You're so stubborn," he says, pouring the eggs into a frying pan. "Fine. Your share so far comes to about a buck-fifty." He reaches over and drops a bagel into the toaster. "I'll figure out the interest later."

When the eggs are ready he divides them onto two plates. "I'm out of cheese slices. Want ketchup?"

"Yup."

He takes the bottle from the fridge. I hear the ketchup burp as he squeezes. When he sets the dish in front of me there's the outline of a red happy face on top of my eggs. It catches me off guard, and I laugh out loud.

"Throwback Thursday, huh?" He grins. "There's no charge for the ketchup, by the way." He unfolds a copy of *The Coast*, places it on the table beside his breakfast, and begins to read.

I smile and let my mind wander — all the way back to that first happy face.

I storm out of the house, slamming the screen door behind me. My eyes sweep the yard. There's no sign of anyone around. I walk to the edge of our property, where the land drops away, down to the beach below. I grab on to the stair rail and lean out so I get a good view of the shoreline. There's Aidan, a few metres from the bottom of the steps, ankle deep in the water, skipping rocks.

"Did you do this?!" I holler, waving the piece of yellow paper.

He looks up at me.

I scramble down the rickety steps. When I get to him I hold the Post-it note right up to his face so it's touching his nose. "Care to explain?"

He laughs and pushes my arm away.

"Well?" I demand.

"Calm down. It was only a joke. You're always in such a bad mood."

"Stay out of my room."

"It was like half a foot, just to put it on your light switch."

"O.U.T."

"You can't hate me forever, you know. We're kind of stuck with each other."

"I don't hate you. I don't know you yet."

"Okay. Let's do something then ... " He looks up the beach. "Let's walk around the Cape. See if we can get to the other side before the tide comes up."

"Um." I chew on my lip. "I ..."

"Come on. It'll be fun."

"Uh ..." I can't think of an excuse. "Okay ..."

From then on, we became brother and sister, best friends. What helped strengthen our bond was our mutual dislike for Vince. We could handle anything as long as we had each other.

I look over at him. Aidan, who always knew when something was wrong and would leave happy faces in my sneakers, my binders, my lunch bag, on my frosty window, in the sand on the beach, all for me, to cheer me up ... sometimes to say he was sorry. But now he's Aidan from the psych ward. What did I miss? Why couldn't I tell when something was wrong with *him*?

I have a hundred questions I'm dying to ask, fire at him like a machine gun. But I can't, so I keep my lips mashed together tight, in case the words try to fly out on their own.

The food turns cold on my plate. How long will I have to pretend? Should I really care so much about betraying Marla's confidence? Someone I've known for five minutes? I flash back to those wrists covered in scars. I don't dare break my promise.

The black and white kitty-cat clock hanging on the wall ticks loudly, its tail swinging one way, its eyes rolling the other.

"Well, they trashed every movie I planned to see," Aidan says, his fork clattering onto the plate. As he turns the paper to a new page he notices my untouched eggs. "You okay?"

"Not as hungry as I thought I was, I guess." I pick up my bagel and wrap it in a napkin. "I'll take this with me. I'm going to head out. Got stuff to do."

I start walking up the street, retracing my steps from yesterday. I take a couple of bites of my now hard bagel then toss it in a garbage can. There's a newspaper vending machine right next to it, and I dig out some change. Paper in hand, my inner homing device leads me directly to the coffee shop. I'm not surprised — it's one of the only places I know how to get to. Where else would I go?

The same girl is behind the counter when I go up to order. "Medium vanilla latte, please."

At least she doesn't roll her eyes this time. Progress.

I turn to find a seat. The place is pretty full. Then I see Liam across the room, sitting at my table by the fireplace. He's staring into a laptop screen and holding a mug against his chin.

No point pretending I don't see him. I like it here. I know I'm going to keep coming back. If he thinks I'm some kind of stalker, then so be it. Taking a deep breath, I make my way over.

"Hey," I say.

He looks up. "Hey." He pushes out one of the other chairs with his foot. "Fancy meeting you here. Take a load off."

"Thanks." I unzip my jacket and drape it over my seat.

"So how's it going with the bro?"

"Oh, you know, it's going." I peel back the tab on my coffee lid and take a sip to test the temperature.

Noticing my newspaper, he slides his laptop to one side of the tiny table. "Here. You want some room to read that?"

"I'm good. I'm only interested in the classifieds — easily foldable."

"Ah. The big job hunt."

I hold up my cup. "These lattes ain't gonna buy themselves."

"I'll give you a hint. If you can downgrade to just plain ol' coffee, order it in a mug and you get free refills."

"I dunno. The latte's in my blood now."

He laughs, closes his laptop, and sets it on an empty chair. "Let's get out the want ads, have a look then. Anything particular in mind?"

After pulling out the classified section, I lay the rest of the paper on the floor. "The CEO of a major conglomerate would be kind of cool, but I guess I can't afford to be too picky."

"Plus, rarely are those CEO jobs part-time. It'd be hard to juggle with school," he says all serious, but I see the corners of his mouth twitching.

"Good point." I nod.

"So what *are* you looking for?"

"My mom owned a bakery café type place," I say. "I worked there after school. That's my only real experience. The odd babysitting, of course."

His eyes widen. "Erin!" he shouts to the girl behind the counter.

She pretends not to hear.

"Erin! Come here!"

Sighing loudly, she does something to the cash register, comes toward our table, stops halfway, and crosses her arms. "What?"

"Did Janet find someone to cover Lauren's shifts yet?"

"How should *I* know?" she asks sarcastically. "Anything else?"

"No. Thanks, Erin. You can go back to spreading your rays of sunshine."

"Gee, can I?" She returns to the counter, shaking her head.

"She's secretly in love with me," Liam whispers.

"Yeah," I laugh, "obviously. So ... what's with Lauren?"

"She works here. Another student. She's out with a concussion. Hockey. We need someone to fill in. You'd be perfect."

I would *be perfect*.

"It could turn into something longer," he continues, "what with exams coming. Then there's Christmas break. Most of the staff is students, so they go home and stuff."

"I would *love* to work here," I say eagerly.

"I'll see Janet tonight — she's the owner. Then I'll let you know, probably by tomorrow. Give me your cell number."

"Uh. Don't have one."

"Email?"

I do have email, but I don't remember seeing a computer at Aidan's. "I'll just come by."

"Okay."

I finish my coffee and try to keep my excitement in check. Could it really be this easy? I fold up the classifieds, add them to the rest of the paper on the floor. My eyes land on Liam's laptop sitting on the chair. I should try to get a message to Caroline. I'm a shitty friend. It's been a couple of days, and I know she's probably wondering if I'm still alive. "Speaking of email ... would you mind if I checked mine?"

He's texting on his phone. "Sure, help yourself."

His laptop takes a second to wake up. "It's asking for a password." I turn it toward him so he can key it in.

"L.Y.N.N.I.E," he says, still focused on his phone.

I shrug and type the letters. "Lynnie?" I ask. "Let me guess, your first pet."

He chuckles to himself and finally looks up. "No. My girlfriend."

chapter 9

"Oh. Right. Girlfriend." I laugh and wave my hand in the air. "Pet. What was I thinking? Lynnie's not a pet name." I want to stop talking, but words keep tumbling out. "Like, who's going to name a dog Lynnie, right?"

Liam gives me a funny look. "Well, not a dog. A cat maybe."

I rub the back of my neck, like I'm seriously debating the dog/cat thing. "Yeah," I nod. "Maybe a cat."

He gives me another funny look. "I'm getting a refill. You want anything?"

"Nope. Nope, I'm good."

While he's up at the counter, I take a moment to congratulate myself. *Well done, Lyssa. You* are *the queen of smooth. Did you actually think he didn't have a girlfriend? A guy like that?* Not that it even makes a difference. I wasn't thinking about him like that anyway ... That's the *last* thing I need.

"So yeah. Done deal," I say out loud.

A woman at the next table looks up from her book.

I flash her a smile before ducking behind Liam's laptop screen.

He comes back to the table. "Success?"

"Sorry?"

"Did you check your email?"

Caroline! "Um. Yes ... just finishing up." I quickly log on to my email. There are four messages from Caroline. All with the same subject line: "???????!!!!!!" I don't bother reading them and type in, *I'm here. I'm fine. Don't worry. Hoping to get a cellphone soon. Will fill you in then. Xo, L.*

As soon as I press the "send" button, I feel guilty about my lack of information. This is the kind of thing that will make Caroline's head explode.

"All done. Thanks," I say and slide the laptop back. "Guess I should get going." I feed my arms into the sleeves of my jacket while it's still hanging off the chair.

"I'll see you tomorrow though, right? I usually pop in for some breakfast if you want to come by then."

"You really think you'll have an answer for me that soon?"

"Oh yeah. Janet will be in tonight to do office work. Don't sweat it. She loves me. It's in the bag."

I raise my eyebrows. "You think *everybody* loves you."

He grins. "What can I say? Have you met me?"

tHat niGHt i Dream about Liam. We're having dinner with Vince and my mom — she's still alive. She reaches across the table and hands Liam a set of keys. "The café. For you and Lynnie. A gift from us."

"But I'm not Lynnie," I tell her.

"I know," she says. "Lynnie's right there."

I look over my shoulder to where she's pointing. There's no one there. Only darkness.

My eyes fly open. It takes a moment for me to remember where I am. The clock says 8:07 a.m. I flick back the covers. Then I see my door.

It's open. Just an inch or so. Again.

I step out into the hall. "Hello?" No answer. I sit on the edge of the bed and stare at the door. Aidan probably checked on me when he got home last night, or maybe he peeked in to see if I was awake before he left this morning.

After a hot shower, I throw on some clothes and grab my jacket off the hall bench. I'm coffee shop bound. I'm dying to find out if I have a job.

The car's not in the driveway. The past couple of days, Aidan's schedule has been pretty much the same. Gone early in the morning. Home for a while. Then gone again until late at night. I wonder if he ever takes a day off.

The wind chill is brutal, and I zip my jacket up as far as it will go. As I walk my mind drifts back to Marla, and how I'm sworn to secrecy. I wish Aidan would just sit me down and tell me everything so that it's all out in the open. Why doesn't he?

Liam must have seen me coming because when I step inside the shop, he's dangling an apron from his finger. "Welcome, coffee wench."

A huge smile spreads across my face. "Really?"

He nods and tosses me the apron. "Suit up."

"Now?"

"Unless you have something better to do."

"No, no. I'm good to go." I take off my jacket and slip the apron over my head. As I wrap the ties around my waist, I can't stop smiling.

"I offered to train you," Liam says. "I don't think you're emotionally prepared to work with Erin yet."

"Gotcha."

"Plus, I figured it would be an easy gig," he says as he holds up a binder, "as I've got to write a paper on genetics. Quieter here than at the apartment with three roommates."

My smile fades. "Yeah, but, you're going to be behind the counter with me, till I know what I'm doing ..."

"You know how to use a cash register?"

I look over at the machine. It looks like Mom's. "Yeah."

"Debit machine?"

"Yeah, but —"

"Congratulations. You've just completed your training." He pulls out a chair and dumps his books on the table.

"You're kidding me, right?"

"Relax. I'll be right here."

"But what about all the fancy coffees? I don't know how to make any of those."

"I believe in learning as you go. We'll worry about it when someone orders one."

"But —"

"Shhhh." He puts a finger to his lips and holds up his binder again. "I'm trying to do research."

I don't know whether to laugh or cry. Thank God the place is spattered with only a few people, and everyone seems to be already drinking something. I go and stand behind the counter and pray that the next person who walks in doesn't order anything difficult.

There's a laminated menu with all the prices lying beside the register. I pick it up and start memorizing.

"It says the muffins and scones are baked fresh daily," I call over to Liam. "Do we do that here, or does someone bring them in?"

"I make up the batter at the end of the night and put it in the fridge. Whoever has the early shift does the baking."

"Okay." That sounds easy enough. I did that kind of thing at Mom's place.

After going over everything on the menu a couple of times, I feel a bit better. The only things that scare me are the lattes, cappuccinos, and espressos.

I'm checking out the muffins and stuff in the display case when I hear the bell over the door tinkle. Someone's come in. I've got my first customer. Smoothing the front of my apron, I turn to face the counter.

You've got to be kidding me.

It's friggin' Kyle.

Instantly my legs go all rubbery. For a second I worry they're not going to hold me up.

He doesn't see me. He's still back by the door, looking for something in his knapsack. I watch him. His hair is all windblown, and his cheeks are rosy from the cold. It reminds me of all the times we went tobogganing, had snowball fights, drank hot chocolate from a Thermos. It reminds me of how much we were in love — at least, I thought we were.

He hasn't seen me yet because he's holding his phone, texting, as he walks up to the counter. Suddenly it occurs to me whom he might be texting, abruptly ending my warm, fuzzy memories. What was that slutbag's name? Oh yeah. Rosalyn.

My nails dig into the edge of the counter. I better get ready.

He keeps texting away and doesn't even look at me. "Yeah, uh, I'll have a medium ... Colombian, black, to go."

I spin around and start pouring his coffee. Setting it on the counter, I keep my head bent down. What are the odds he'll leave without ever realizing it's me?

"Two seventy-five," I mumble.

He slaps down a toonie and a loonie.

As fast as I can, I scoop up the coins and replace them with a quarter. *Please, please, turn and walk away. Turn and walk. Turn. Walk.*

"Could you put a lid ..." There's a long pause. "Lyssa?" he whispers in disbelief. "Holy shit! What are you doing here?"

I look up. "Working," I say.

He rakes his hand through his hair. "Where have you been? I've been going crazy."

"Yeah, sure you have," I say.

"I *have*! Where are you —?"

"Excuse me, miss? Could I get a large mocha latte, double decaf, half-caf, extra foam?" Liam is standing behind Kyle, arms folded across his chest.

Kyle moves closer to the counter, trying to block Liam. "Please, Lyssa, we need to talk. Pick a —"

"I'm kind of in a hurry, miss," Liam says loudly.

Kyle turns to Liam. "Cool your jets, buddy." Then he turns back to me. "Tell me when you're off," he pleads.

"You're holding up the line," I sigh.

"I'll come back later," he says.

I shake my head and slide the quarter to the far edge of the counter. "Take your change, Kyle."

"A second chance, Lyssa. I deserve it. You know I do."

Liam taps Kyle's shoulder. "Dude."

I raise my hand, signal Liam to stop. "How do you figure that, Kyle?"

"When you wanted to stay back and look after your mom, did I make a big deal about it? No. Even though you kind of hung me out to dry. We were supposed get an apartment together, remember?"

Open-mouthed, I stare back at him.

Liam moves around the counter and stands beside me. "I think you should probably move along," he says to Kyle.

"Who the hell are you?" Kyle demands.

Liam ignores the question, snaps on a lid, and holds out the cup. "Here's your coffee, *buddy*."

Kyle grabs the coffee and makes for the door.

His quarter is left sitting on the counter. I pick it up and whip it at his back. "Take your goddamn change!"

I don't care that everyone's looking.

chapter 10

My shift ends, and I plunk myself on a stool. My back aches. I'm not used to being on my feet for so long.

"Do you want a coffee or something?" Molly asks. "You're allowed. It's free." She came in for her shift early to finish supervising me. Liam had to leave to meet a prof. "You deserve it. You did awesome," she continues.

She wasn't here for my little outburst, so for now she thinks I'm just regular folk. "No," I sigh. "I'm good, thanks." I pull on my coat and get ready for the walk home.

As soon as I push open the front door, my breath catches in my throat like a hiccup. Kyle. He's on the other side of the street, leaning against a telephone pole, waiting for me. For a second I think about backing up through the door — it hasn't even closed yet, I can still smell the coffee. But we've already made eye contact. And he'd probably just follow me in. I sigh and drop my chin to my chest. Might as well get this over with.

He waits for a car to pass then runs across the crosswalk.

Folding my arms, I stand with my feet slightly apart. Bring it on.

"Hey," he says. "Thanks for not taking off."

I don't say anything.

"I'm completely frozen, you know." He rubs his hands together. "But I knew you'd have to come out sooner or later. Can we go inside, grab a coffee?"

I raise my eyebrows. "What do you want, Kyle?"

"Lyssa, please," he says. "Give me a chance to explain."

"No."

"Look. I'm sorry about what I said, you know, about you owing me, about you hanging me out to dry. That was out of line. I wasn't thinking."

"Really? *That's* what you want to apologize for?"

"Well, no, I mean, yes, but there's more." He stumbles over his words. "Of course there's more."

"Kyle," I say calmly. "Just turn around and go."

"So you need more time to cool down. I get it."

"I don't think you do. I don't need time. We're done." I pull my gloves on and start walking.

Behind me I hear his footsteps crunching in the frozen slush. "Are you staying with Aidan?" he suddenly asks.

I keep my back to him and say nothing.

"He's here in town," he says, still following me. "I've seen him."

I pick up my pace.

He picks up his pace too. "You are, aren't you?"

"None of your damn business!" I say over my shoulder.

"The guy's insane!" he shouts.

Stopping, I spin around. "Why would you say that?"

"Trust me. He is. You don't know how lucky you are that he left town."

"And how do you figure that? Because I had to take care of my mom by myself while her brain got eaten away by cancer and Vince was busy drinking the town dry?"

He doesn't say anything.

I shoot him a final glare of disgust and start off, back on my way.

"I know it was Aidan who did that to Mark and Todd!" he calls out to me.

I feel my feet slow, feel the *thump, thump* in my chest. He doesn't know anything. He's bluffing.

"I know you know!"

I just keep going.

Kyle catches up and grabs my sleeve. "Why do you protect him?"

"Go to hell!" I snatch my arm away, turn, and break into a run.

"Lyssa!"

I don't look back.

my lungs feel like they're on fire. When I finally stop, I have to bend over to hack up a gob of phlegm. Then I see I'm only a half block away from the stone wall, the one I sat on in the rain that night — right after I found Rosalyn in Kyle's apartment.

I trudge toward the wall, my legs full of tingles. As soon as I sit, the cold from the stone turns my butt numb, but I don't mind. I feel oddly comfortable here.

It's been over three years, but just hearing their names, *Mark and Todd* ... it's as if it happened yesterday.

We were so cool, the chosen ones. Caroline and I had been invited to this giant party thrown by the captain of the high school hockey team. We were only in grade nine, so yeah, it was a big deal. The place was swarming with hockey players. And about four times as many girls, all vying to be the special make-out partner of some random Sidney Crosby wannabe.

My mistake was leaving the security of the cluster of people I knew. But I'd had two coolers and needed to pee. I made my way through the crowds and headed down the hall to the bathroom. And there they were, Mark and Todd, two star hockey players, lying in wait. For me? Or for anyone?

I gave them a nervous smile and stayed focused on getting to the bathroom.

When I came out, they were still there.

There was something about the way they looked at me. I swallowed and started walking, but they blocked my way.

"I've had my eye on you ever since you got here," Mark said.

Todd pinned me against the wall with his arms. "You don't look like you're in junior high."

They were drunk. I could hear it in their voices, the way they slurred their words.

I shoved Todd's arm away and tried to walk past. Whichever side of the hall I went to, they went too. I laughed so they wouldn't guess I was scared. I gave them both another shove, but then they shoved me back and into an empty room.

Next thing I knew I was on a bed, flat on my back. I screamed, but the music was so loud, no one could have heard. I thrashed, twisted, and kicked, but Todd was twice my weight and size and easily held me down, while Mark pushed up my top, hauled up my skirt, and clawed at my panties. All I smelled was his breath — beer. Then I felt the burn of Mark's stubble scraping along my face, neck, and chest. I must have tried screaming again because Todd slapped his hand over my mouth. I opened wider, found his thumb, and bit. He swore and smacked me back, above the ear, hard enough I could hear ringing. Then he held me down using even more strength.

Play dead. It'll end quicker. I closed my eyes and made my body limp, made my body numb.

And then it was over.

Mark rolled off me.

I heard him zip up his jeans.

Guess Todd wimped out.

Mark gave me a wink as he left, like he just did me a favour.

I edged off the bed and straightened my clothes. Every move I made hurt.

After I threw up in the garbage can, I checked my face in the mirror. Dry. No tears. There was a brush on the dresser, and I used it to fix my hair.

Like a ghost, invisible, I floated down the hall and slipped out the back door. I don't remember the walk home except for the part where I stopped behind the Co-op, tugged off my torn underwear, and stuffed them into a dumpster.

For two days I stayed in bed. "Flat out with the flu," Mom told the school. I was an amazing actress when I had to be.

And that was what I was, for a while anyway. I didn't tell anyone, not Caroline, not Mom, not Aidan. Kyle and I weren't going out yet. I just went on like nothing had ever happened.

It must have built up or something, because one day I just sort of snapped. Aidan found me bawling my eyes out down on the beach. He wouldn't let up until I told him what was wrong.

I didn't want to. It was still all so raw, and embarrassing, and ... disgusting. But I did.

He listened without saying a word. Then he hugged me tight and left.

It wasn't until almost midnight that I saw the light from his bike coming down the lane. I waited for him to come inside. When he didn't, I went to look for him. Once outside, I circled around the house. He was sitting on the back porch step, staring off into space holding a rag, the nozzle of the hose resting by his foot.

The light coming from the porch lamp was enough for me to see the blood on his hands, under his fingernails and in the creases of his knuckles.

Not saying a word, I picked up the hose, gently squeezed the trigger, and ran some water over his hands as he scrubbed them with the rag.

All he said was, "I only did what needed to be done."

I nodded.

The next day at school, it was all everyone was talking about. Mark and Todd had been beaten to a pulp and were both in the hospital. No more hockey for them, not for a long time, maybe forever. No one had a clue who did it. Not even Mark or Todd. "It was dark," they said. "We were jumped from behind. We didn't see."

There were rumours, of course. Some thought it was drunken townies, or guys from the Northumberland High hockey team. There were the wild theories as well. Everyone under the sun *could* have done it. It was actually Kyle's brother who said he'd seen Aidan in the village that night, talking to Mark and Todd, and told the police. Aidan was questioned, said Mark and Todd stopped him to ask if he knew where to get some weed, and that was the extent of their conversation.

This all happened almost two weeks after the fateful party. There was no connection to me.

At the end of that summer, Mark and Todd went away to university. Mark had a permanent limp and never played hockey again. I never heard what happened to Todd.

Why did Kyle throw that at me now? In all the time I went out with him, he never once brought it up. I know Kyle's brother, and I guess Kyle, too, had suspicions about the beating, but that's all they would ever be. No charges were ever laid.

I hug my arms around my middle and rock back and forth on the wall until the rolling in my stomach settles.

Lock it back up. Put it all away.

There's a horrible taste in my mouth. I wonder if bad memories produce some kind of chemical reaction in your body.

chapter 11

A single strand of spaghetti hangs from Aidan's fork. He watches the sauce drip back onto his plate. "Is this from a can?"

"Yeah," I say, shaking some parmesan onto my pile of pasta. "But it's the good kind — thick and rich, that's what the label said."

Looking doubtful, he puts down his fork. "So why the fancy dinner?"

It's impossible to ignore the sarcasm in his voice. I sigh and lean back in my chair. He's all bent out of shape because I took the job at the coffee shop. He's barely said a word to me in two days.

"I thought it'd be nice to cook for *you* for a change." I shrug. "I made good tips today. Stopped at the grocery store on the way home."

"I could have gotten you a job at the bar, you know," he says for the hundredth time.

"Thanks, but I think the coffee shop's more my style."

He pushes the plate away. "You'd make more tips in one night at the bar than you would in a *week* at that coffee shop."

"How? I'm only eighteen. I can't serve liquor."

"You can bus, or hostess."

"I don't want to have to work late nights, especially once I start school."

"I'm the manager. I could have fixed your schedule," he argues.

There's no point continuing the conversation, so I don't. I can't figure out why he's so against the coffee shop. What difference does it make to him where I work?

I study him while he glares at the spaghetti. I've been doing that every chance I get — studying, searching for some kind of sign. What do people who've been in a psych ward look like? Act like?

He catches me staring, and I scramble to say something. "Remember when Mom used to cut up salami and put it in our spaghetti?"

"Yeah," he says, finally smiling. "She was an awful cook. No amount of salami could save her sauce."

"I'll never forget that time she made it in the pressure cooker."

He sucks in a breath. "Yes! Holy shit. She forgot about it and it exploded all over the kitchen. The cast iron lid was embedded in the ceiling."

I nod. "Yup. Then she had us on chairs with paint scrapers, scraping it off the walls."

"I couldn't move my arms for a week."

We both burst out laughing. It feels good.

I pick up a napkin and wipe my eyes. "Baking was more her thing, I guess."

He's quiet for a second. "You must miss her."

"I feel like she was gone way before she died. She wasn't herself ... wasn't all there ... for a long time."

"And I bet Vince wasn't much help."

"No." I stab my fork into a clump of noodles and twist. "No, he wasn't."

"I'm sorry," he says. "About Vince. And for not being there for you. I mean, I remember what it was like when my mom died. I could have helped maybe. Like with what you were going through."

My eyebrows shoot up. Aidan never talks about his mom. All I know is that she died in a house fire, in Vancouver, when Aidan was thirteen. I keep twisting my spaghetti, hoping he'll say something more about her.

But he doesn't. "Your mom was a nice lady. She deserved better than Vince."

I twist and twist, staring at the growing ball of pasta. "I can't understand how she ended up with him. How she couldn't see what he was."

"You mean a nasty drunk?"

I don't answer.

"It's okay," he says. "You don't have to watch what you say around me."

"He's still your father."

"And because of that, I know better than anyone."

The ticking of the kitty-cat clock echoes through the kitchen.

"I'm not sure if I'll ever understand. Or if I can ever forgive her ..." I whisper.

"For dying?"

"No, for marrying Vince."

Aidan gets up and carries his dish to the sink. On the way he stops and puts a hand on my shoulder. "Love. It can make people do some pretty fucked-up stuff."

"If Janet doesn't get this oven fixed soon, I swear I'm going to punch a hole in the kitchen wall!" Erin exclaims, loudly slamming down a tray of muffins.

The noise makes me jump. The fact is, she terrifies me, but I force myself to go over and see. "They don't look so bad," I offer weakly.

"Are you freakin' kidding me?" She picks up the tray and slams it down again, louder. "They're hard as rock!" One bounces out and lands on the floor. She kicks it across the kitchen, where it ricochets off the side of the fridge and hits the broom handle, causing it to topple across the recycling bin.

I've got to get her out of here before she trashes the place. "Erin. Your shift is over. I can totally do this. Go home."

Ignoring me, she whips open cupboards and drawers, assembling what she needs to mix up a new batch of batter.

"Erin!"

She looks up. "What?" She's gripping the spatula so tight, her knuckles are white.

"It's okay. I really do know what I'm doing." I say it in a low, soothing voice, like I'm trying to talk a jumper in off the ledge. "My mom owned a bakery." I carefully tug the spatula from her grasp. "I know how to make muffins."

Her shoulders sag, and she leans back against the counter. "Yeah, okay, maybe ... I've been here since seven a.m., you know. I was up till two working on a paper."

I nod. She doesn't fight me when I lift the apron off over her head.

"I think I'm having some kind of breakdown," she whispers.

I smile and pass her her jacket. "It's dead in here. Go home and get some sleep. I've got this."

Like a zombie, she slowly drags herself out the door.

The rest of my shift passes uneventfully. It's my third time working by myself, and I actually know what I'm doing now. My attempt at blueberry muffins is a success. I even tweak the recipe a bit — sour cream, a dash of cinnamon and nutmeg, just like Mom used to do.

And thank God there's been no sign of Kyle. That entire next shift, every time the door opened, I held my breath, thinking he was back to stir things up. Hopefully he got the message and is staying away on purpose.

But no sign of Liam either. He's been off for a couple of days. Not that he has to check in with me or anything. It's just, I've gotten used to seeing him. I think I ... sort of miss him. Not *him*, him, more like *talking* to him. He makes me laugh — something I haven't done a lot of lately.

The door opens. My eyes scan the group coming in, hoping Liam's in there somewhere. I know he works later tonight. No, it's Anna, here early to relieve me, and a couple of random students.

"I just wanna grab a bite before my shift starts, okay?" Anna says.

"Sure."

She takes one of my muffins from the display case, hesitates for a second, then reaches in and takes another. "I gotta bulk up. I'm working a double. Liam so owes me."

"Liam's not coming in?"

Anna shakes her head. "It's the girlfriend's birthday. He's taking her out for dinner or something."

"Oh, right ..." There's a burning feeling in my stomach. "The girlfriend."

AIDAN'S CAR IS IN the driveway when I get home. I hope he didn't eat all the leftover spaghetti.

Once inside, any thoughts of spaghetti leave my head.

Aidan is standing in front of my bedroom door, a screwdriver in one hand, a hammer hanging from his belt loop. He turns and says, "Hey." Then goes back to whatever it is he's working on.

"What are you doing?" I ask slowly.

"Putting" — he cranks the screwdriver a couple of times into the door frame — "a lock on your door." He stops and flexes his fingers. "The way it's mounted, it's not flush. I had to drill a hole in the casing. Got a blister."

I feel my eyes stretch wide. I rush over and smack the screwdriver out of his hand, sending it flying down the hall.

"What the hell?!" Aidan shouts.

"Why would you put a lock on my door!? Are you out of your mind?!"

"What is your problem? Jesus!" He stomps off to get the screwdriver that's still spinning on the floor.

"It's on the outside!" I cry. "Why would you put a lock on the outside?"

"*Because* ..." — he looks at me like I'm crazy, then disappears into my room — "... of this." When he returns he's holding up my course calendar. The cover's all shredded. "It's that goddamn cat. He was having a field day in there."

"Cat?" I blink a couple of times, trying to make sense of his words.

"Yeah, look." He closes my bedroom door, then, using one finger, pushes it open again. "I'm trying to do you a favour. The lock thing doesn't click. Didn't you notice?"

"No. Um. Maybe." The door. It's always open in the mornings.

Aidan pulls the door tight and shoves the deadbolt over. "Now you can lock the door when you go out and the cat can't get in. See?"

I slide down the wall until I'm sitting on the floor, my knees tucked up under my chin.

"Lyssa, what's going on?"

I look up at him. Does he really not remember? "Um, *Vince?*"

"Huh ...?" Then his jaw drops. "Shit." He drops the screwdriver and kneels beside me. "I'm so sorry. I totally forgot." He shakes his head, then looks up at the lock. "I can't believe I did that."

"I can't believe it either." I glance at the top of the door. "It's even the same kind."

"You know I never actually saw it — the lock. Once I moved to the shed, he never let me back in the house." He closes his eyes. "Not that it mattered. I swore I'd never darken his door again."

I stare down the hall at nothing. "That feeling of being trapped in my room ... I hated it."

After a moment, he says, "Vince was one twisted motherfucker. Damned if I know what he was thinking."

"He caught me sneaking home in the middle of the night." I lean my head against the wall. "I'm pretty sure he thought I was off drinking or screwing around with some guy."

"But you were really hanging out with me."

I nod. "It was the only chance I ever got to see you. Then he put that lock up the next day. And every night from then on, on his way to bed, I'd hear it slide into place."

"No more visits for me."

I spin sideways to face him and narrow my eyes. "You should have remembered," I snap. "I told you all this. Told you why I couldn't come anymore."

"I know you did," he says, scratching his forehead. "There was so much going on back then." He looks me right in the eye. "I find there's some stuff I don't remember."

"Oh." What if he was already suffering from ... whatever it was that landed him in the psych ward?

His hand reaches for mine and gives it a squeeze.

"It was awful in that house," I say. "I really missed you."

"I could spend the rest of my life apologizing for Vince and it would never be enough, but for what it's worth, I'm sorry. And I'm sorry about the lock. I'll take it down." He starts to get up. "I'll do my best to keep Bingley out."

"No, it's fine. I overreacted."

"Are you sure?"

"Yeah, I'm sure."

Chapter 12

"So when do I get to meet Marla?" I ask. "Like, for real."

"Oh, uh ..." Aidan doesn't look up from his newspaper. "Soon, I guess."

I push down the handle on the toaster. "Maybe she could come over for dinner tonight," I suggest casually. "Didn't you say you were off?"

"Yeah. But I think she works."

I'm not giving up. "Well, could you ask her?"

He ignores me, pretending to be deep into his reading.

I think for a second. "Actually, never mind. I'm going out later to see about getting a phone. I'll drop by her store. It's off Spring Garden Road, right?"

His head whips up. "How would you know that?"

"She told me. She asked me to come visit her sometime."

"You said you guys didn't get a chance to talk."

"Um ..." Thankfully my toast pops up. The bread's not done enough, and I slam the handle back down. "We didn't. It was literally two sentences. She just mentioned it on her way out the door."

He gives me a long look then says, "I have to go to the bank. I'll drop in, see what her schedule is."

"Great." I smile. "What should we have? Or I guess the real question is, what brand of pasta sauce does she like?"

My little joke goes unnoticed. He's distracted. I can tell by the way his eyes are flitting over the page. Does he feel tricked? Well ... he kind of was. But I want some answers. I'm hoping he'll spill the beans knowing I'm going to be around Marla. Can he risk not telling me himself?

"She's pretty," I say, spreading peanut butter on my toast.

"Huh?"

"Marla. She's pretty."

"Yeah."

"Where'd you meet her?"

"At the bar," he answers.

"Oh." I play dumb. *So much for that plan.* "Was it love at first sight? Did your eyes meet across a crowded room?"

Again he ignores me. Probably too busy planning how he's going to get to Marla and coach her so they have their stories straight.

"Do you ever think about going home?" he asks suddenly.

It throws me off. Apparently he wasn't thinking about plotting with Marla at all. "To River John?"

"Yeah."

"No."

"You haven't thought about it once?" He says it like he doesn't believe me.

"No," I repeat. "I haven't."

"But the bakery. You loved that place. I always pictured you taking it over and running it someday."

"What? You honestly thought that?" Offended, I throw my knife into the sink. "I would have hoped you'd have greater aspirations for me."

"You make it sound like it would be the worst thing in the world."

"It would."

"So you don't *ever* want to go back?"

Is he serious? My mind is blown. "No, not while Vince is still around."

"Right." He nods. "Of course ... but if Vince wasn't there?"

"Where is this coming from? Why are you even asking?"

"I dunno," he sighs. "I was just thinking."

"About *what*?" I ask incredulously. "You're actually telling me *you'd* consider going back."

He shrugs. "We moved a lot when I was a kid. I know I was only there for four years, but it was the only place that ever felt like home. I don't like the city." He goes back to reading his paper.

I'm stunned. Aidan thinks of River John as his home? After all the shit that went down? And he thought I'd want to spend my life slaving away in that bakery? That I'd be happy doing it?

Chewing angrily on my toast, I give him the evil eye.

He sits there, all oblivious, turning pages.

Who *is* this person?

I find myself thinking back to the first time I met Aidan. It was the summer I turned twelve. Mom sat me down at the kitchen table. Told me how she'd run into an old friend at the Co-op, someone she'd known from high school. He'd moved away years ago, and now he was back. Widowed. With a fourteen-year-old son. They came that night for supper. Aidan sat across from me at the table. I spent the entire meal glaring at my plate. We mumbled a few words to each other, but that was about it.

Mom and Vince got married three months later, that Thanksgiving Day weekend. We became a family. Sort of.

"Here. Do you still like to do the Word Jumble?" Aidan holds out a section of the paper.

I'm lost in thought. "What?"

"The Word Jumble. Don't tell me you've forgotten how we used to fight over the puzzle page. My thumb's never been the same since that time you sprained it."

"Right. That." I grin and take the paper.

I fold it and fold it again so only the part with the Jumble shows, and slide it under the edge of my plate. Vince didn't like anyone touching his paper, let alone writing in it, especially if he hadn't read it yet. It only took us one time, one screaming match, one grounding, to figure *that* out. So Aidan and I would wait till we were sure he was done and then we'd race from wherever to see who could get to it first. That turned into more of a game than the actual Jumble.

I feel Aidan's eyes on me.

"I lied," he says. "About how I met Marla."

"Oh. So how did you meet her?" Under the table I cross my fingers, hoping he tells me the truth.

He takes his time answering. "I, um ... I met her in the hospital." He pauses again. "In the psychiatric ward."

I decide not to react, in case it scares him off or something, and makes him stop talking.

"Vince," he continues. "He told Dr. Fraser a bunch of lies. Got him to sign some paper. Then he drove me straight to Halifax, dumped me in the hospital, and left me there. For *observation*," he adds.

Another puzzle piece slides into place. "That's why you were gone when I got back from camp. Why you never said goodbye."

"Didn't really get a chance," he says bitterly.

"They told me you just ... left. That things got so bad between you and Vince, you thought it would be best for everyone to leave."

"Well. Some of that's true."

"And then there was the shed ... all your stuff ... burned. Gone."

He shuts his eyes like the memory hurts.

"I kept waiting for you to email, or write, tell me what happened," I say. "But I never heard a word."

"I thought about it. But I knew Vince would intercept anything. I almost called Caroline, to go through her. Then I figured maybe I should just leave it alone. If I tried to make contact and he found out, you'd be the one he'd take his anger out on. Better to have you be pissed at me than have him pissed at you."

I feel guilty. I've been so mad, confused, and hurt for so long, and here he was looking out for me. It's what we used to do for each other. "I should have known it was something ..."

Pushing himself back from the table, he clears his throat. "It's all over with now."

"The shed," I say. "They told me *you* burned it down."

"Do you think I burned it down?"

I tell him the truth. "I don't know. I wasn't there."

Aidan opens his mouth as if to say something but then leaves the kitchen without a word.

chapter 13

I can't focus. I've screwed up two lattes already and that was in the first twenty minutes.

Why won't Aidan tell me what happened? Not just about the shed, but about all of it. We used to share everything. No secrets.

The mid-morning rush is over. I grab a cloth and start wiping down the counter. The answer has to be somewhere in those last couple of months before he took off. That whole summer was a mess — things went from bad to worse. It started on Aidan's high school graduation day. I'd just finished grade ten. He and Vince had some huge blow-out. No matter how much I begged, Aidan wouldn't tell me what it was about. But instead of leaving, he packed up his stuff and moved into the shed, to *live*. Vince made it perfectly clear, Mom and I were to have nothing to do with him. It made me crazy that she went along with it — now I blame it on her illness. I'd sneak out in the dead of night to visit him. Stay for a couple of hours. Sneak back.

That was until Vince caught me. "Where the hell were you?" he demanded, his breath stinking of booze.

"I — I heard something. I thought the cat wanted in."

His eyes swept the hall. "So where is it?"

"The cat?"

"Yeah."

"It wasn't him. I, uh … don't know what it was …"

I could tell he didn't believe a word I said.

The next day, I came back from the beach to find a lock on my door.

At the end of that summer, Caroline and I attended a weekend leadership camp in Truro. When I got home, the shed was nothing more than a pile of ashes and Aidan was gone.

"I think it's clean now," a voice says.

Startled, I look up. "Oh. Liam. Hey."

He leans both elbows on the counter. "You're scrubbing like you're trying to take the paint off."

He's so close I can smell his shampoo — coconutty. "There's like ink, or maybe it's marker ... someone must have signed a receipt ..." I peer down at the non-existent stain. "Yeah, I think I got it." I rub some more. "Yup, it's gone." Why am I talking like I've just downed a dozen shots of espresso?

"Sorry I haven't been in for a while," he says. "I should have given you a heads-up. Are you making out okay?"

"It's totally fine. Don't feel you have to —"

"I guess I still think of you as my trainee, that's all."

"I pretty much know the ropes now."

"No, I know. I didn't mean to make it sound like you *needed* to be checked up on or anything."

"Oh no, I didn't think that."

"It's just that I *do* normally come by every —"

"Yeah, but you *work* here, you shouldn't spend all your time —"

"I had a paper due, and then it was Lynnie's birthday dinner, and —"

"Really. It's all good. Everything's running smoothly ..."

At this point, the conversation peters out.

I fold up my cloth and hang it over the edge of the sink. "So, the dinner. Where'd you go?"

He rolls his eyes. "Some hipster place down on the waterfront. She's been wanting to go forever."

"And how was it?"

"Let me put it like this. I blew almost two hundred bucks and still had to stop for a donair on the way home because I was *starving*."

"Yikes. Can I buy you a coffee? You're probably tapped out."

He smiles and brushes his hair out of his eyes. "Yeah. That'd be great." He looks back over his shoulder. "So any sign of your friend? Has he been back?"

"Kyle?" I reach for a mug. "He's *not* my friend, and no." I don't feel like telling him about round two of his last visit.

The front door swings open.

I hold my breath. Part of me thinks it might actually be Kyle, because ... that's how my luck is going lately. But it's not. Surprisingly, it's Aidan.

He spots me and crosses the room.

Liam slides his body down the counter a bit, out of Aidan's way.

"Sorry." Aidan stops short. "Were you waiting to ...?"

"No, no. Go ahead. I'm just hanging out."

Aidan frowns.

"Aidan," I jump in. "This is Liam. Liam, Aidan." I don't tell him that Liam's the guy who drove me home or got me the job.

"Hey," Liam says.

"Hey," Aidan says back.

"Liam works here," I add.

Aidan looks at him for a second, like he's sizing him up, then turns to me. "Listen, Marla can come for dinner after all. She's going to grab some Thai on her way home from work."

"That's great," I say.

"I'm off to the liquor store. You want anything?"

"Oh, uh ..."

"Yeah, yeah." He smirks. "I know, you're underage ..."

I twist up my mouth. "Maybe a case of Bud Light Lime?"

Liam whistles. "Wow, a *case*."

"Well, it's not like I plan on drinking it all at *once*," I say.

Aidan slaps both hands on the counter. "Okay, then, I'll see ya at home." He turns and heads for the door.

"I'll pay you tonight," I call after him.

"Don't worry about it."

Liam watches Aidan leave. "So that's the bro, huh."

"Yup, that's the bro." I don't insert the word "*step*" this time.

If Liam notices, he doesn't say so.

AIDAN SLAMS HIS BEER bottle down on the kitchen table, knocking over the peanut sauce. "For shit's sake, Marla. Could you please stop talking about it?"

"What? So you're on medication," she says, blotting the spilled sauce with a napkin. "We both are. You, me, and a bazillion other people in Halifax."

Aidan has his lips pressed together. I can tell he's about to blow. The fact that he's on medication is something I didn't even consider. I'm dying to ask about it. But I can tell it will only end badly, so I keep my mouth shut.

"We should be able to talk about it," Marla insists.

"Yeah, but does it have to be the topic of conversation for the whole fucking evening!?" He looks at me from across the table. "It's for my mood swings, that's all."

If I blinked, I would have missed it — the look Marla gave Aidan.

"Can we all just drop it now?" he asks through clenched teeth.

Marla sighs. "Yes, of course. Sorry, Aidan."

He shoves his chair out from the table. "I'm going to get another beer."

All the beer is out on the back porch, nature's fridge, so Marla and I are left alone in the kitchen. There's a long, uncomfortable silence.

"I think he's still kind of embarrassed," she whispers. "He's worried you're going to think differently about him or something."

What she says makes sense. I probably do feel a bit differently about him. But not in a *bad* way. "So, Marla, Aidan's medication —"

"He's right. I shouldn't have brought it up."

I know she's not going to tell me anything. "It'll be okay, I'm sure he'll get over it." I gather my hair over one shoulder and start twisting it into a rope.

She watches me. "You have beautiful hair."

"Thanks, but I need a trim." I flip up the bottom of my hair rope so she can see. "Split ends."

"Oh. You can go to my girl, Ivy. She used to work at Fred's, but now she does it out of her house. She's really cheap."

"Sure." I smile. "Thanks."

She goes back to staring at my hair. "Sometimes I think about trying to grow mine long."

"I really like your cut. It looks great on you."

"I guess ..." She reaches up and touches her bangs. "It was Aidan's idea. He came with me to Ivy's, basically told her how to style it."

"Um." For a minute I'm at a loss for words. "And ... you were okay with that?"

"Yeah." She shrugs. "I mean, it's only hair, right? He said he saw it on some actress. Thought it would really suit my face."

"Well, it does," I admit. "He obviously has an eye for that kind of thing."

"You don't think it's weird? My roommate does, thinks he's being a total control freak."

I start collecting the takeout lids and placing them on the containers. There's something about Marla, something that has me believe I should choose my words carefully. Like she's made of glass, and if I say the wrong thing she'll break. "Different things work for different people," I tell her. "Every relationship has its own dynamic. She probably doesn't consider it to be typical boyfriend behaviour, that's all."

"Yeah, I guess." She passes me the unused packets of soy sauce. "Do *you* consider it to be typical boyfriend behaviour?"

I don't make eye contact. "I'm the *last* person you should —"

"You do. You *do* think it's weird, don't you?"

"No, no," I say quickly, trying to sound reassuring. "I don't think it's weird at all."

chapter 14

"That's *totally* weird," Erin says, one hand on her hip. "It'd be a cold day in hell before I'd ever let Josh tell me how to cut my hair."

I tie the strings of my apron into a bow and don't answer.

"He's not even allowed to *touch* my hair," she adds.

Liam shakes his head. "That Josh. He's one lucky guy."

"Oh, go fuck yourself, Liam." She makes a face and stomps out back to the freezer.

"See?" Liam says. "See how she tries to fight her love for me?"

Rolling my eyes, I start measuring out the coffee to make a fresh pot.

I don't know how or why I ended up telling them about the whole haircut thing. I think it was because it kept playing over and over in my head, like it was on a loop. Plus, Erin was right here, and besides Marla, she's the only other girl's opinion I have access to. Liam just happened to overhear while he was eating his breakfast.

"Marla's roommate thinks Aidan's a control freak," I say to Liam as I refill the napkin dispenser.

"Oh, I dunno. This one thing doesn't necessarily mean he's a control freak. I mean, he's *your* brother. *Is* he a control freak?"

I come around the counter and sit on the stool next to him. "We only lived together for four years, but I never noticed anything ... control-*ish*." I don't tell him about Aidan ending up in a psych ward.

"You know ..." he says, ripping open a sugar packet and pouring it in his mug, then another, and another. "It's possible you guys are blowing this out of proportion. Like, maybe the guy *did* see the haircut on some super hot actress, and he's just living out a fantasy." He stirs his coffee thoughtfully and smiles. "I should ask him his secret, actually."

WHEN MY SHIFT ENDS, I go out back to check the schedule. I picked up a shift for Anna, but I can't remember what time it starts. It turns out to be not until evening. I hold a little debate in my head. The lazy part of me wants to stay here and hang around the coffee shop for the rest of the day eating muffins and reading magazines, but I know there are more productive things I could be, should be, doing.

I head home.

Kicking off my shoes, I can't help but notice all the pebbles of salt in the vestibule, and the many families of dust bunnies living along the baseboards of the hallway.

Aidan arrives just as I'm unwinding the vacuum cleaner cord. "Hey," I say.

"Hey." He holds out a small brown paper bag.

I take it from him. "What's this?"

"Just wanted to say sorry I kind of acted like an idiot last night." He grimaces. "I think I had too much beer and not enough pad Thai."

"Oh." I shrug. "That's okay. Shit happens." I'm relieved he brought it up. Nice to know it's not his usual behaviour. I open the bag and pull out a doughnut. A Boston cream — my favourite.

"Look before you bite it," he says.

I laugh. There's a happy face drawn in the icing.

"I got inventive and used a straw."

"Clever." I sit on the hall bench, eat the whole thing in six bites, and sigh, "I needed that." I give my fingers one last lick then turn my attention back to the vacuum.

He takes my spot on the bench and fiddles with his car keys. "So I was wondering if you've given any thought to Christmas?" he asks out of nowhere.

I glance up from plugging in the vacuum cord. "Christmas? No."

"Well, how would you feel about going home?"

I squint at him. "What do you mean?"

"I just thought, I mean, maybe it's time."

"Time for *what*?"

He shrugs. "To bury the hatchet, mend some fences."

"Why are you bringing this up again?" I jam the hose attachments together. "I've told you before, Aidan. I'm not going back there. Not while Vince is *living* in my mom's house, *sleeping* in my mom's bed, *eating* off my mom's dishes."

"It's your house too."

"No, it's not. Not anymore. You just gotta let this go."

"But I don't think it's good, cutting yourself off."

"From what? And you're one to talk! You left your family and never looked back."

He gets up, slowly takes his coat off, and hangs it on a hanger. "I'm hoping Vince has had a change of heart. That if we go back together, present a united front, maybe he'll start to see things my way."

"Your way? What's *your* way? What does that even mean?"

I stand there, waiting, staring him down.

"Never mind," he says and turns to leave. "You're right. It's too soon."

"What's too soon? Aidan, please talk to me." As I go to follow him I stub my toe on the sofa leg. I wince and limp the rest of the way to the kitchen. He's opening a can of cat food.

"It's supposed to be freezing rain later," he says. "Do you want me to pick you up from work?"

This is what he does. I remember this from before. He shuts down after any sort of confrontation, pretends it never happened. Even if he's mad, he won't talk about it, so of course, there's never any resolution.

I play along. "No. Thanks. Anna has a doctor's appointment. I'm covering her shift till she shows ... so yeah, I don't know how long I'll be."

"Okay. Call me if you change your mind." He plops the food into Bingley's dish.

"Oh, and Bingley's back at it. My door was open again this morning when I woke up. The lock is only good for when I'm not home. I guess I need another one for the inside, for like when I'm *in* my room."

"He's nocturnal — does his best prowling at night."

"Yeah, well, I don't like the idea of him creeping around my room when I'm sleeping. He can just as easily trash my stuff at night as in the day."

He adds the cat food can to the bag of recyclables. "Sure. I'll stop at Canadian Tire later today."

WHEN I SHOW UP for my evening shift, Liam's behind the counter doing his cash.

"And how was your afternoon?" he asks, glancing up.

"Oh, you know." I hang my stuff on the row of hooks out back.

"Give me something. It must have been more exciting than mine."

"Aidan wants me to go home to River John for Christmas," I say. "Just sprung it on me, out of the blue."

"I'm guessing you're not too crazy about the idea," he says, sliding a stack of bills into a Ziploc bag.

"That's an understatement."

He reaches for a paper tube to roll loonies. "Would it be so terrible? Going home?"

"Leave the coin," I say. "I'll do it later."

"You didn't answer my question."

I nudge him out of the way. "Without getting into all the gory details — I swore I'd never go back. Not while Vince is there."

"And Vince is …?"

"Sorry. My stepfather. Aidan's dad."

A man comes up to the counter and orders a decaf, to go. I pour his coffee, take his money.

"Keep the change," he says.

"Thanks." I take out the difference and drop it into a cup beside the register. "But the thing is," I continue, "I wouldn't go back even if Vince *wasn't* there."

"Didn't you grow up there?"

"Yeah. But my dad died in a car accident when I was eight." I realize that probably doesn't explain much. "I don't really remember feeling very happy after that." It surprises me how it all just flows out of my mouth.

"Not a lot of great memories back there, then."

"No ... well, some ... not many, and certainly not lately." Then it hits me. No happy memories, no mom, no dad, no Kyle, no home. Suddenly I'm filled with self-pity. I have nothing. Nothing except Aidan. And then I think of Caroline. "I have a best friend there," I say.

He's quiet for a second. "Life is full of steaming piles of crap. But maybe there's only so much crap to go around. Maybe you've reached your quota and it'll be smooth sailing from now on."

I try to smile. I want to say, "Nice thought," but the words catch and don't make it out.

He slips on his jacket and slings his messenger bag over his shoulder. "I'm off to meet my study group. You're working for Anna?"

"Yeah."

"I might see you later then. A bunch of us are meeting here before a movie."

"Okay." A movie. What's it like to do something normal and fun like go to a movie?

After Liam leaves, it starts to get busy, which helps make the time fly. I'm down to only five muffins, so as soon as there's a break in the action I throw together another batch of batter. I just finish sliding a tray into the oven when I hear a voice.

"Excuse me. This mug seems to be dirty."

There's something in her tone. I can tell she's going to be a pain in the ass. I plaster on a happy face before turning around.

It doesn't happen right away. It takes me a few seconds to place her. She's rubbing the rim of the cup with her thumb and hasn't looked up. There's no doubt, though. I'm sure it's her. I'll never forget. Rosalyn. The slut in Kyle's apartment.

She finally lifts her head. Something flickers across her face, but I can tell she hasn't figured it out yet.

"Here," I say, pulling myself together. "Let me take it. I'll get you a fresh one."

Her eyes narrow slightly. "Thanks," she says.

I'm just handing her a new coffee when I see Liam come in. He strides up to the counter, a huge smile on his face.

"Hey," I say, smiling back. "How was your …?" I don't get to finish. My mouth falls open in horror as I watch him drape his arm around the slut's shoulders.

"I see you've met Lynnie," he says.

Chapter 15

There's an acidic taste in the back of my throat. I swallow, hoping to wash it away.

"Lynnie," Liam says, "this is Lyssa, the rookie." He looks at me and winks. "Well, you've been here over a week now, so I guess you can probably lose that title, right?"

"Um ..." I can't think. I'm not even sure what he just said.

But he doesn't seem to notice how stunned I'm acting. "Wow. Get a load of us. Lyssa, Lynnie, Liam. We should start a band." He gives the slut a squeeze.

"Yeah, you're so musical," she says out of the corner of her mouth. Then she turns to me. "Nice to meet you, Ly—" she pauses, tilts her head, "—ssa."

And just like that, she's figured it out. I hear her suck in a breath. She holds it forever. We both stand there, eyes locked. The very same way we did in Kyle's apartment.

She exhales and blinks a few times, touches her fingers to her temple. "I'll — I'll just wait for you back at the table," she says slowly to Liam.

"Okay. Did you want anything?"

"No, I, uh, Suzanne already bought me one." She holds up her mug. "But it had ... spots." And she walks away in a daze.

Liam frowns and shakes his head. "Don't mind her. She gets like this when she has a big assignment due."

I nod, make his latte, hand it to him, collect his money, all without uttering a single word. Again, he doesn't seem to notice as he gives me a loonie tip on a three-dollar coffee and joins Rosalyn at her table of friends.

I go out back to the kitchen and slump against the coolness of the stainless steel fridge. This can't be happening. What are the odds of Rosalyn being Lynnie? It's like something you'd see on *Gossip Girl*. And what am I supposed to do now? Say now?

"Hey, are you okay?"

Anna's voice startles me. "Uh, yeah, I'm fine."

She slips on her apron, moves closer, and peers at my face. "Are you sure? You don't look so hot."

"Just a headache," I whisper.

"Well, go home and lay down or something."

"I will."

"And thanks for covering for me," she says handing me my coat and hustling me over to the service entrance. "Take some Advil," she adds.

"Will do." I smile weakly, mock salute her, and march out the back door.

Thankfully, the forecasted freezing rain ends up being light flurries. I flip up my hood and stuff my hands in my pockets. Before I even step onto the sidewalk I hear, "Lyssa!"

Through the glow of the street lamps, I make out a figure, a girl, standing on the corner. I know it's Rosalyn. I stay where I am and watch her walk toward me.

"Aren't you supposed to be going to a movie?" I say.

"I told Liam I had to run across to the drugstore first," she says, her eyes darting back to the front door of the coffee shop, "because I had a headache."

"There's a lot of that going around."

She twists up her mouth, gives me a good glare. "Listen, I don't know what you're planning …"

"Planning?" I ask innocently. She's squirming, and I can't deny that I'm enjoying it a bit.

Then she turns on a dime. Her face falls, her eyes get all huge and glassy. "Please don't tell," she pleads. "I'll do whatever you want, just don't tell him."

I keep silent. I don't want to have this conversation with her. I don't want to have *any* conversation with her. And her ... emotionalness is making me uncomfortable.

"That's what you're going to do, isn't it? You're going to tell him." Her words come out fast and full of panic.

Part of me wants to say yes, push her aside, run screaming into the shop, and broadcast the news, but the other part of me ... the other part of me knows I'd never be able to pull it off.

"Haven't you ever made a mistake?" There's an edge to her voice now. I think she interprets my silence as a sort of power play. Maybe it is. "Haven't you ever met someone and totally hit it off, discovered you have everything in common? There's a spark. You don't want there to be, but there just is."

I find my voice, but I can't quite make eye contact. "Yeah, it happens. I don't sleep with them, though."

She sighs and pulls her jacket tighter around her body. "Kyle and I are in the same class, he's my biology lab partner. We spend a ton of time together. It was one mistake, one night. It didn't, and it won't, happen again. I love Liam."

I just look at her. Do I believe she loves Liam? Sure. Do I believe she and Kyle were a one-time-only thing ...?

"Everyone deserves a second chance," she says urgently, her eyes flying to the front door again.

Shaking my head, I turn away, start off in the opposite direction, and leave her standing there. Kyle said those exact same words to me. They didn't apply to him. I'm not sure they apply to her either.

By the time I get home, my headache is a reality. The throbbing is making a thumping noise I can actually hear. The house appears to be empty. I shuffle to my room and throw myself across the bed. My eyes land on the course calendar on the floor. It reminds me I have to go register for classes. I hang over the side, reach out, and slide it closer. The cover picture is unrecognizable, full of slashes running in straight lines from top to bottom. I trace my fingers along the torn ridges. *Stupid cat.*

As if on cue, Bingley sticks his nose in the door, struts across the room, and curls up on the rug under the window. I forgot to lock my door when I went to work, and my eyes do a quick sweep. No, no damage today. I watch him for a while, purring away, not a care in the world. I wish I were a cat right about now.

My mind makes its way back to the run-in with Rosalyn. She's got some fucking nerve, I'll give her that. Like I owe her *anything*. Who does she think she is? On the other hand, did I really want to be the one to tell Liam his girlfriend's sleeping around? The phrase "don't shoot the messenger" exists for a reason — there's zero glory in that job. The problem is I like Liam; he deserves so much better. I flip over onto my back. Or does he? I've only known him for a while. And apparently I'm not the greatest judge of character. Maybe he's a total asshole and I just haven't seen it yet. It would be so much easier if he were ...

The more I think about it, the more I don't believe Rosalyn about it being a one-time thing. I can still remember her there in Kyle's apartment, whining about the shampoo. She was too ... familiar. Then again, she may spend a lot of time there if they study together. Also, I can't ignore the fact that Kyle now knows where I work. If they *were* in a relationship, wouldn't he have warned her that I was working with her boyfriend? But then maybe Kyle doesn't know Liam or where he works. Kyle was standing right next to Liam ... there was no hint of recognition ... *shit*. That would point more toward the "one time thing" theory.

I rub my eyes, pressing my fingers into the sockets. God. I've got so much of my own crap right now. Do I really want to get involved in theirs?

I head to the bathroom to get the Advil I should have taken the moment I got home, but at the time I couldn't seem to make it those few extra steps. There's a dispenser of disposable Dixie cups mounted on the bathroom wall — it must be an old lady thing. As I pull one out, something catches my eye. On the floor, just behind the toilet, a tiny white pill. Puzzled, I kneel for a closer look. That's when I see another one, right beside the hinge of the toilet seat. Then another, nestled against the baseboard. It's white on white, almost impossible to see if I weren't down so low.

My eyes shift back and forth between the pills. Floor, toilet seat, baseboard, floor, toilet seat, baseboard, like watching a triangular tennis match.

I move to the medicine cabinet, open the door, and scan through all the stuff on the shelf. Tums, shaving cream, mouthwash, deodorant, bandages, nose spray, razor blades, nail clippers ... no pill bottles except Advil. I pop two in my mouth, take a sip of water, but I keep glancing back down at the pills.

I know Aidan's on medication — that cat was let out of the bag at our little dinner party. These pills are probably his. I check the shelf again. *Shouldn't there be a prescription bottle?*

Bending down, I scoop up the pills and hold them over the toilet. Something gnaws at me. I press down on the handle, release one, two pills into the water, watch them swirl around the bowl and disappear. The remaining one I set on the counter next to the sink. Crouching in front of the vanity, I lean forward until my nose is only inches away and study the pill at eye level. *Why were you and your friends on the floor?*

Then I tear off a square of toilet paper, fold the pill up inside until it's the size of a stamp, and tuck it into my pocket.

chapter 16

I'm off to the registrar's office again. After checking on the library computer, I discovered that I can't get into the program I want until the fall, so I figure I'll just take some electives in the new year. That will give me more time to work and make money, plus decrease my study load in September.

The same lady is working in the office as last time. She recognizes me, which is a relief, because I don't want to have to go over my whole sob story again. I explain to her what I want to do. She offers to register me online right now if I have my course numbers. Her fingers fly over the keyboard. She has everything finished in a matter of minutes.

I walk over to the King's bookstore. The guy working there looks up my courses and tells me what books I need. They're expensive, so I only spring for two. I tuck them safely into my bag. *Now I'm getting somewhere.*

Without even thinking about it, I head for the coffee shop. The outing to the registrar's office was a distraction, but now my mind is on one thing and one thing only — not Rosalyn and that whole mess, but the pills. I guess it's the TV detective in me. I mean, one pill on the floor, okay. But three? The only scenario I can come up with that would have that result is if someone were dumping, or *flushing*, a substantial amount of them.

And that can't be good.

I see Liam as soon as I walk in. I knew he'd be here. He has the afternoon shift. I only know that because his name is next to mine on the schedule. It's not like I have his shifts memorized or anything.

He's plowing through a before-shift sub from Subway, and I plunk myself down in the chair across from him. "You're in pre-med, right?"

He looks up and raises his eyebrows. "And hello to you too."

"Sorry. Hello. So you know about medication and pills and stuff, right?"

"Yeah," he says, all suspicious, leaning back and crossing his arms. "I can't write prescriptions, though, if that's what you're looking for."

It takes me a moment to clue in. "What? No, that's not what — wait. Here." I root around in my bag, pull out the tissue-wrapped pill, and place it on the table.

"Oh," he smirks. "Now it all makes sense."

"Just give me a sec ..." I peel back the tissue, exposing the pill. "I wanted you to tell me what *this* is, what it's for."

He gives the pill a quick inspection. "Sure. I'll bag it and send it to the lab."

"Really?"

"Noooo." He laughs. "This isn't *CSI*, you know."

I want to punch him for making fun of me, but instead I grab back the tissue, scowl, and slouch down further in my chair.

"Oh, come on now." Under the table he nudges my leg with his foot. "Don't be like that. Let me have another look at it, then."

I slide it toward him.

"Where'd you find it?" he asks, examining it closely.

"At ... home." I decide to leave out the proximity to the toilet.

"So it's your brother's?"

"Maybe ...?" It comes out more like a question.

"And that's all the background information you're gonna give me?"

I nod.

Flicking his hair off his face, he says, "Ian, one of my roommates, his girlfriend's in pharmacy. I'll take it with me, see what I can find out."

"Thanks."

"You owe me." He rewraps the pill, tucks it into his shirt pocket, and returns his attention to the last few bites of his sub.

I sit back and drum my fingernails on the table, wiggle my toes inside my boots. I'm full of nervous energy.

"Uh ..." Liam is staring at my noisy fingers.

"Sorry." I immediately ball my hand into a fist.

He crumples up his sub wrapper, scrunching it into a tight wad. "Anger issues?"

"What?" I ask, confused. Then I realize he sees my partially curled and shredded course calendar. I hauled it out when I was getting the pill. "Oh, that. No. Cat issues."

"A cat did that?" He picks up the calendar, gives the cover a good look. "How friggin' big is your cat?"

"*Normal* size." I snatch it from his hand. *Am I really defending Bingley?*

As I'm fitting the calendar back into my bag, my eye lands on Liam's laptop partially sticking out from under a stack of textbooks. I am so getting one as soon as I get my hands on that loan money. And a phone. God, I need a phone.

Again I feel a twinge of guilt about Caroline. I've made almost no effort to keep in touch even though she made me promise I would. I suck as a friend.

"Can I borrow your computer again to check my email?"

"No prob," he says, wiping mayo off his chin. "Remember the password?"

He doesn't see the face I make. "Oh yeah, no worries there."

"Lynnie," he tells me anyway.

I clench my jaw. "I know."

The laptop boots up in a few seconds, and I pound in the password using a bit more force than needed. I see Liam frown and glance at me out of the corner of his eye.

There's a bunch of junk mail and four messages from Caroline, all with her usual "????!!!!!!" in the subject lines. Two are dated yesterday, the other two, the day before. I click on the most recent one.

Yo Lyssa! What the hell? For the bazillionth time! Please email me or phone me or something. Saw Vince at the Co-op.

My stomach drops. I check my watch — two-thirty. Caroline is working for the Andersons, taking care of their kids, just for a year to raise money to go to Europe. She's probably chasing them around right now, but I know she has her phone on her.

I type in, *I'm here. What happened with Vince?* Then I wait. Caroline has it set up so her emails go right to her phone. About a minute later a message pops up on the screen: *What happened with Kyle? I know you're not with him. Details. Now.*

How does she know that?

Me: *On someone else's computer. No time. Short version, Kyle's a fucking asshole. More important, what happened with Vince?*

Caroline: *He cornered me, asked me if I'd heard from you. Said, no, BECAUSE I HAVEN'T! He said he saw Kyle down at the wharf — he's home for his mom's bday. Kyle told him you weren't staying with him and he didn't know where you were.*

Of course. Kyle. He never was very good at knowing when to keep his mouth shut. Before I have a chance to reply another email comes in: *Vince might be coming to Halifax to track you down. Think he's worried you are in homeless shelter or something.*

My jaw falls open. Shit. Why would he even care? But I feel Liam watching me, so I snap my mouth shut and concentrate on keeping my face expressionless as I type, *If you see him again say you heard from me and that I'm in student housing.*

Caroline: *K. But are you? Did you find Aidan?*

I think for a moment before I answer. *No. I am actually in student housing. Sharing with a Caper. Never drank so much tea in my life.* This time I choose to lie, knowing Caroline would only have a ton of questions about Aidan that I don't feel like answering. I press "send."

Caroline: *Phew. Sure I'll run into Vince again soon :(PS, Tell me what happened with Kyle. I'm dying.*

Me: *Thanks. Be in touch. Xo L.* She's probably having a meltdown at this very moment.

Liam is still watching me. "Bad news from the home front?"

"No, no." I fake a smile, and try to ignore the anxious tingle working its way up my spine. "Everything's fine, just fine."

CHAPTER 17

It's getting really crowded in my head — Rosalyn and the stuff she said the other night, Liam not having a clue, Aidan and the pills. Adding to the mess is Caroline and her run-in with Vince. Though it was an email, I hear the high pitch of Caroline's voice, the way she says things, as if we had the conversation face to face ... But I have to cram everything to the back corner of my brain and ignore it.

Today I'm making it all about Aidan.

I dig a handful of Cheerios out of the box and watch him. He's across the kitchen by the back door, arranging empty beer bottles in their cardboard cases. There are a lot.

"Wow, did we have a party I wasn't invited to?" I ask, making it sound like a joke.

"These have been here for a long time," he says without turning around. "I've just been too lazy to do anything about them."

"Oh." I suck on a single Cheerio until it turns to mush on my tongue.

The tick of the kitty-cat clock emphasizes the quiet.

"So, uh, Aidan," I start. "How are you feeling?"

Still crouching on the floor, he turns. "What do you mean?"

"Well, like, you *were* in the hospital, right?"

"That was a long time ago."

"How long?"

He presses his lips together so hard they turn white. "What is it that you want to know, Lyss?"

"I dunno," I say. "I guess I just want to know how you're doing. I care. Sue me."

"Look. I told you. It was all made up by Vince. There's nothing wrong with me. Never was."

"But Marla said you were on medication — that you *both* were. They don't just give you medication for no reason."

He sighs a long, deep sigh. I can tell he's fighting to keep control of his temper.

"It's for my supposed mood swings. Which, just so you know, is what they diagnose everybody with when they can't find anything wrong with them. So nothing for you to worry about." And he goes back to packing his beer bottles.

His tone plainly says, *it's none of your business*, but the more he withholds the information, the more determined I am to drag it out of him.

I picture those pills scattered on the bathroom tile, the way one was leaning against the base of the toilet. "And you're still taking stuff now?"

"Yup."

I almost tell him that I found a bunch on the floor, but for reasons I'm not even sure of, I chicken out. Instead I say, "Does it help?"

There's the harsh scraping sound of glass against glass as Aidan squeezes another beer bottle into the box. "There's nothing to *help*," he says.

"Then why —"

He slams two full cases of bottles onto the kitchen table. "I thought I made it clear the other night at dinner. I don't want to talk about it."

"Yeah, I know, but —"

"So I'm not mistaken. I *did* make it clear."

I can see the vein throbbing in his forehead, see the rise and fall of his chest. It used to take a lot to get him angry. "Like I said, Aidan, I care."

He goes to the sink and runs his hands under the water. "So how are you liking your new job? They certainly give you enough shifts."

I stare at his back. There he goes again, acting as if the last few minutes never happened. This time it must be his idea of a white flag, because I know he doesn't give a rat's ass about my job at the coffee shop.

When I don't answer, he turns, sees my expression, and comes toward me. His face softens. "I'm sorry, Lyss. I don't mean to bite your head off. I know Marla thinks it's all wonderful to be open and talk about everything ..." He pauses. "Only, that's not ... my way. Talking about it *doesn't* make me feel better. There's not really anything to talk about, anyway."

"If you say so ..."

"Look. The doctor says I suffer from mood swings. Does she know what she's talking about? No. But if it means keeping me out of that hospital ... some pills and a few therapy sessions are a small price to pay."

"You're in therapy?"

He shrugs. "It's a sham. You don't have to be a psych major to figure out how to work the system. I go in, tell her what she wants to hear, and she leaves me alone."

I think about that for a minute. I might do the same thing in the same situation.

He reaches for both my hands, gives them a squeeze. "You gotta trust me, Lyss. There's nothing wrong with me."

Looking in his eyes, I see a flicker of the old Aidan. "Okay," I say quietly.

"So we're good?"

"Yeah. We're fine, just fine."

I sit alone at the kitchen table, my hands warm around a mug of hot tea. Aidan has gone off to the bottle recycling place, then to work. Blowing on my tea, I let the hamster in my head do its thing. Around and around on the wheel it goes.

Marla. I should talk to Marla. She'll have the answers. She'll be able to tell me if Aidan's really okay. I need someone besides him to tell me that — a secondary source. There'll be time to feel guilty about it later.

Unfortunately, there's been no sign of Marla. Which is sort of strange, because the first time I met her, I got the impression she was in and out of here all the time.

My eyes are drawn to the cupboard above the phone.

Back home, we kept our list of phone numbers written in permanent marker on the inside of the cupboard. I get up, go over, and swing open the door. The list is short; only about six names and numbers are scribbled down. And there it is, second from the top, right under "Bar": "Marla."

I dial her number.

"Hello?" a voice says.

"Hi. Marla?"

"No, this is Jodi."

"Oh, sorry. Is Marla there?"

There are a few seconds of silence. "Uh ... no. Is there a message?"

"No. I'll try her later. Thanks."

As I hang up, I hear a noise in the hall. I'm about to go investigate when Aidan sticks his head in the kitchen door. "Just me," he says.

"That was quick."

"I forgot the keys to the cash box."

I follow him out. "Aidan?"

"Yeah?"

"Where's Marla? I haven't seen her since we had dinner. She's not staying away because I'm here, is she?"

"No." He laughs and shakes his head. "You being here wouldn't keep her away — more like the opposite."

"Oh, good," I say, relieved. "So everything's all right with you guys."

"Yeah." He narrows his eyes. "Why would you ask that?"

Did I hit a nerve? "No, I, uh, nothing. I wasn't implying anything, if that's what you thought."

His face clears. "She's just gone home to visit her folks. She's from Boston. You probably didn't know that."

"No, I didn't. When's she coming back?"

"Her grandfather's sick. So I'm not sure."

"Oh. That's too bad."

"Yeah. I hope she comes home soon." He picks up a set of keys off the front hall table and shoots me a lopsided grin. "I really miss her."

It's then that I get it. That's why he seems a bit off, a bit cranky — he misses Marla.

That explains everything.

Almost everything.

Chapter 18

Liam's sitting on the edge of my bed, stroking my hair. I feel so happy, like it's Christmas morning. A huge smile spreads across my face as I snuggle up under my blankets. I stay there for a long time, wanting the moment to last forever.

My eyes fly open, and I bolt upright, flinging back the covers. *Stop it, you idiot! Get a grip!*

Argh. Cradling my head in my hands, I let reality sink in. It leaves me with a cold, dull feeling.

The dream seemed so real. I touch my fingers to my hair just like Liam did. I could have sworn he was right here ...

I flop back across the bed. Whatever this thing is I have for Liam, I have to squash it. He's got a girlfriend — at least, he thinks he does.

From where I'm lying, I glimpse a flick of Bingley's tail. He's curled up in his favourite spot under the window, purring away.

My eyes go the door. It's open, just a tiny bit. I stomp over and give it a push. It squeaks closed, but I can tell it didn't catch. I'm about to give it another try when I turn to Bingley. "Why am I shutting you in here *with* me?"

He gives me a bored look and, maybe sensing the new vacancy, moves to my bed.

"Off!" I shout. Using both hands, I shove him over the edge. The thought of cat hair all over my bed ... *ew.*

"Aidan!" I can smell coffee, so I know he's here.

"What?!" he hollers back.

I wait a few seconds, assuming he'll appear. He doesn't. "Aidan!" I shout louder. This time he doesn't even bother to answer.

I sigh and thump down the hall. Now I know how Mom felt. I hear her voice in my head, *"When I call your name I expect you to come, not yell 'what?'"*

He's sitting in the living room, channel surfing. He stops on the *Today Show*.

"Didn't you hear me?" I demand, knowing he did.

"Yeah," he says. "Kinda hard not to."

I cross my arms.

"I'm trying to catch the news. I figured if it was important, you'd come find me," he says. "And now you've found me, so I'm guessing it's important."

I make a face. "You said you were going to get me a deadbolt for the inside of my door," I say calmly. "No matter how many times I kick him out, tell him to beat it, Bingley keeps trolling my room."

"So what you're saying is, he's not obeying you."

"Yeah." I nod.

"That's because he's a *cat*, Lyss." And he turns up the volume on the TV.

Just because his girlfriend's away doesn't mean he gets to act like a total dick. "Where's the closest hardware store, then? I'll friggin' go get one myself."

"Relax, would ya? You're kinda making a big deal over a stupid cat in your room."

"I —"

He puts up a hand and rolls his eyes. "I *know*. You don't like cats. FYI, I went to Canadian Tire the other day. They only had multi-packs, with like eight in them. I'll stop by later this week, okay?"

I smash my lips together and don't say anything.

"Look," he sighs. "I'm sorry. I don't mean to be such an asshole." He tilts his head and attempts a smile. "Forgive me?"

There's not much sincerity in his voice, but I say, "Fine. Whatever."

"Thanks." He smiles an actual, real smile.

As I turn to head back to my room, I see him get up and go to the window. I stop and watch him. He stands there, hands on his hips, staring outside. He looks so serious.

I backtrack a couple of steps. "You okay?"

He's as still as a statue. Maybe he's ignoring me again. Then he says, "Oh yeah. Just thinkin'."

"About?"

"Stuff."

THE SKY IS a steely grey. It's going to snow any minute. I look down at my feet. I should've worn boots. For a second I contemplate going back to the house, then I check my watch. No time, I'll be late for work.

Erin yanks open the service entrance door before I finish my first knock. "Back to apolo—" She sees it's me. "Oh, sorry. Thought you were Liam."

"Nope," I say, following her into the kitchen. I'm disappointed I missed him. He might have some info about the pill.

"Trust me. I'm glad," she snarls over her shoulder.

Curious, I ask, "Why would Liam be back to apologize?"

She turns the tap on full force. The water pounds into the sink. "Well, for some reason he felt the need to come in, even though he's not even *working*, and criticize every goddamn thing I did. From how I take the inventory, to how I fold the raisins into the muffin batter, right to my coin rolling technique."

I frown. "That doesn't sound like Liam."

"I've seen the signs before," she says, pouring a carafe of water into the coffee maker. "He's got *something* up his ass about *something*, and my guess is it's Princess — it's *always* Princess."

"Princess?"

"Oh, right. You haven't had the joy of experiencing full-on Rosalyn."

"Well, I've met her. She's ... um ... pretty." It's the only thing I can think of to say without getting into ... anything else.

"Pretty *bitchy*."

I try not to smile. "Really?" Who am I kidding? I'm loving the Rosalyn bashing. Scanning the room to check on the customer situation, I count two tables of women. Everyone has a coffee in front of them. "So you were saying?"

Erin putters around, putting things away, measuring out backup reserves of coffee. "Of course I'm only going by what I've seen, but she treats him like shit — like, takes him for granted, you know?"

I nod. I do know.

"I mean, she has him wrapped, and I can't figure out why. He trips all over himself trying to keep her happy. And let me tell ya," she stops and points at me, "she never is. I don't think I've ever seen her smile and thought she actually meant it."

"Oh?"

"And yeah, she's pretty, but seriously. Are guys that stupid? That shallow?"

If *my* experience is anything to go on …

"I'll tell you something else," she continues in a low voice. "And I'll deny it if asked, but comparatively speaking, Liam's a nice guy. I'll go so far as to say he *could* be considered 'hot' in a nerdy, slightly annoying kind of way."

Again, I try not to smile.

"Like, he'd be so much better off with someone else, someone … such as yourself, perhaps."

My neck seems to shoot up a few extra inches. "W-what? What?" I sputter.

"Oh, puh-lease." She gives me a knowing look. "I see how you are around him."

"No, no." I shake my head. "You've got it all wrong."

"Yeah. You keep tellin' yourself that."

"Nuh-uh." I'm still shaking my head. "It's nothing — you're way off base."

"Well, I totally ship it. So does Anna."

My eyebrows scrunch together. "You guys *talked* about us?!"

"Just once." She waves her hand dismissively. "You could probably get him, you know, if you put in a little effort. You're just as pretty as Rosalyn. In a different kind of way."

There's a compliment in there somewhere. "Thanks, but ..."

"Really, you are. You've got that whole ..." — she steps back, looks me up and down — "Bella from *Twilight* thing goin' on. And you *have* to be smarter than her — though that wouldn't take much," she adds.

I sigh and rub the back of my neck. "Weren't you off ages ago? Don't you want to get going?"

"Ha, ha." She shoves me, and I bang into the fridge.

"Go home." I shove her back.

While Erin counts out her tips, I peek into the front room again. Still the same ladies.

"All right," I say, slipping on my apron. "Everything seems to be under control."

"We're supposed to be getting a storm tonight," Erin announces, pulling on her jacket. "Janet might call and tell you to close early." She opens the back door. "Yuck. It's really starting to snow."

I stand behind her and look out. There's a thin layer coating the sidewalk, but not much on the street yet.

"Do you have a long walk?" she asks, glancing down at my sneakers.

"No. I'll be fine. Plus it's still big flakes, so there won't be much accumulation."

Erin has one foot on the back step and the other still inside the kitchen, as if she's hesitant to leave. "Right. Little snow, big snow; big snow, little snow. I dunno, though." She twists up her face. "They're calling for a lot."

A gust of wind whips up the deserted side street, swirling the loose snowflakes into tiny tornadoes.

"Go, would ya?" I say. "So I can lock the door. I have to get back to the front."

"Okay, but close if it gets bad. Janet won't care."

"I will."

Erin pulls the toggles of her hood tight until just her eyes and the bridge of her nose are showing. When she finally jumps off the step, she turns and says in a muffled voice, "Yep. There's definitely a storm a-brewin'."

CHAPTER 19

9:40 p.m., and the coffee shop is empty.

I can hear the *ting* of icy snowflakes hitting the window. They're no longer big, they're tiny. "Uh-oh," I whisper. "Little snow, big snow."

It's been a while since I've seen the flashing lights of a plow. I go to the front door. There's a lone set of tire tracks on the street quickly disappearing under the blowing snow, and a decent-sized drift is forming on the sidewalk, partially blocking the entrance.

Janet hasn't called to say close early. It's Friday night, so we're supposed to be open till 11:00. *If I don't hear from her by 10:00, I'll close.*

I'm refilling the sugar pack holders when I hear a rattling crash against the window. A tiny yelp slips out from between my lips, and I spin around.

It's Liam.

Goddamnit, Liam!

He's spread-eagle, both hands and his right cheek flattened against the glass. He looks like one of those Garfield cats you see suction-cupped to car windshields.

I laugh out loud, mostly with relief. Even though I want to smack him, I'm glad he showed up. I don't like being here all alone.

He seems to be struggling with the door, so I go help him.

Grinning, he points to the "push" sign on the door handle. "I was *pulling*!" he says. "Remind me to tell Mom that that English tutor place really paid off!"

I'm hit with a massive blast of beer breath. *Great.* I step back, away from the cold. And the smell.

"Lyssa!" he shouts, following me into the main room.

"Yeah?"

"Lyssa ... Lyssa ... Lyssa ..." he repeats, slowly but loudly.

I raise my eyebrows. "Yeah?"

"My tongue keeps pressing on the back of my teeth when I say your name! Go ahead. Try it!"

"Liam," I say patiently. "What can I do for you?"

"I'll bet ..." He leans in close and seemingly examines my face.

I wait for him to finish his sentence. It doesn't seem like it's going to happen. "You bet what?"

He scratches his chin. "Idonremember." It comes out as one word.

"You seem a little ... tipsy."

"Tipsy!" he exclaims as he bumps into one of the coat stands. He catches it before it falls. "Pardon me," he tells it, patting some abandoned jacket hanging on one of the hooks like it was a person.

I shake my head.

"Tipsy," he repeats. "That's for *girls*." His voice sounds like his tongue is too big for his mouth.

"Sorry," I say. "Is there another adjective you prefer?"

"Buzzed." He sits down heavily on the closest chair. "And I'm totally not."

His hair is wet with melted snow, and the front and shoulders of his coat are plastered with crusty ice pellets. I tilt him forward and tug it off, hanging it on the stand next to his new friend. Any thought I had about asking him about the pill goes out the window.

"I'll get you a hot coffee," I say.

As I head toward the kitchen he calls after me, "That's just an urban myth, you know. Coffee doesn't sober you up, if that's what you're thinking."

I reappear with a steaming mug. "Why would I be trying to sober you up? You said you weren't buzzed."

"Okay, you win," he admits. "I might be a little buzzed. Just a little, though."

I sit down across from him and watch him dump five sugar

packets into his coffee. He's on his sixth when he accidently drops the whole thing in, paper and all. "Ah, *man*," he whines.

"Settle down," I say. I grab a spoon and fish out the soggy paper. "There. All better." It feels like I'm babysitting a two-year-old.

He pushes it away. "I don't want it anyway. Caffeine's a stimulant, you know. It might actually increase my feeling of buzzedness." He pauses, stares up at the ceiling. "Buzzedness. Is that a word?"

"It is now." I smile. "So what's the occasion for your, uh ... buzzedness?"

He puts an elbow on the table, rests his chin in his hand. "Friggin' Rosalyn, man. She was supposed to go to the Seahorse with me. My roommate plays guitar in a band. We planned it like two weeks ago."

"And what, she couldn't go?"

"Noooo. She has some big biology lab or something. It's Friday night! She has all weekend."

"Biology?" A warning light flashes in my head.

"I've never seen anyone so ... so, like ... *obsessed* with their school work. And I'm in pre-med!"

I just nod.

"Every time I want us to do something, she's got an assignment. She's taking a B.A.! Not that there's anything *wrong* with that. But come on. It's a B.A.!"

He's talking way too loud. I nudge the mug of coffee toward him, hoping he'll pick it up.

"I dunno." He slides the mug back to me. "Maybe she wants to break up and doesn't have the guts. Maybe our relationship's run its course." Then he sits back and slaps his hand on the table. "I mean, should it really be this hard? Shouldn't the good outweigh the bad?"

I look around the room, everywhere but at him. I don't know how to answer his questions. It's obvious he's hurting, and if he was talking about anyone but Rosalyn, I'd probably be making up some lame excuse for her, hoping to make him feel better ...

"I'm the last person you should be asking for relationship advice," I finally say — my new escape clause. I said the same thing to Marla.

We both sit quietly for a few minutes.

"Did you end up going to the Seahorse?" I ask.

He shakes his head. "Wasn't in the mood. Me and Mr. Alexander Keith spent a quiet evening in."

"Uh ... then why are you out wandering around in a snowstorm?"

He doesn't answer me.

"I'm going to call Janet," I say as a blast of wind spatters snow against the window. I go to the counter and pick up the phone. All I hear is a clicking sound. "I think the phones are out."

"Here." He stands and reaches into his back pocket. "You can use my ... nope. Forgot my phone."

The lights flicker, and I freeze, expecting them to go out completely.

"Janet's not gonna care. Just close," he says. "You shouldn't be working the late shift anyway." He wags his finger at me. "No girls on the late shift. 'Cept Erin." He tries to muffle a burp. "Cuz who's going to mess with Erin?"

"It was last-minute. Someone called in sick. Zack, I think."

Liam mutters something unintelligible and then shrugs. "Well, suit up. We'll start walking. If we see a cab, we'll grab it."

I don't have a better idea. "Okay." And I rush around finishing up a few last things, shutting everything off, locking the front door, and flipping around the "closed" sign.

On the way out, Liam miscalculates and rams one side of his head into the door frame. "Ouch." He winces and rubs his ear.

"Good God, Liam." I lock up the back door, rattle it a couple of times to make sure.

"Told ya coffee doesn't do anything," he says, still massaging his ear. Then he links his arm through mine.

I don't bother to point out that he didn't drink any coffee.

The snow is coming down heavy. We can only see as far as the next corner. A few of the drifts are up to our knees. Somehow I don't mind.

We barely make it half a block when Liam slips on a snow-covered patch of ice. I feel him going down and try to save myself, yank my arm free. I don't make it and end up right on top of him.

"There's no way I wasn't taking you with me." Because of the cold, his words come out in little puffs of smoke.

"Gee. And after everything I did for you."

He smirks but makes no attempt to get up. Neither do I.

Our faces are only a couple of inches apart, the tips of our noses almost touching. His beer breath doesn't bother me a bit. All around us, it's so silent, like we're in a different world and we're the only people who exist. The snow collects on his hair. My head acts as an umbrella and shelters his face. We stare into each other's eyes, and a silence stretches between us. Does he feel my heart beating through my coat? One slight movement and our lips will touch. I hear myself swallow. He's going to kiss me. I know I shouldn't want him to, but I do. I want him to kiss me.

His head slowly lifts up off the snow toward mine.

My breath catches in my throat, and I close my eyes. I've seen this scene played out a thousand times on TV.

Then: "Uh-oh." Liam flips me off him and rolls onto his side. I see his shoulders heaving, hear him retching into the snow.

He's throwing up.

This can't be happening.

Feeling I should give him some privacy, I just lie there on my back. There's a scraping sound as a snowplow rumbles up the street. A second later I'm showered in a giant spray of slushy snow.

The scene on TV never ends like this.

I sigh and get myself up, start brushing myself off.

Somehow Liam is unscathed by the slush shower. He's off to the side rinsing his mouth out with clean snow.

He sees me, gives me a sheepish look, and comes over to help wipe me off. "Sorry about all that," he says, pulling some chunks of ice out of my hair.

I give my head a shake to get the rest out. I'm sure there are crystals of salt in there too. "It's okay. No worries." What else could I possibly say?

"Let's keep going," Liam says.

"Yup." It's like we've come to an unsaid mutual agreement to say nothing more about what happened.

Once again he loops an arm through mine, and we start off.

As we trudge up the street, the slipping and stumbling continues — Liam more than me. I hoped the fresh air would help sober him up ...

We keep walking, and after a while it seems to be getting easier, or maybe we're just getting better at it. The wind has died down and the snow is letting up. The flakes have gone back to being big and fluffy. With the plow gone, the street is still and quiet again. We see almost no one. No buses, no cabs, no traffic at all. A group of teenage types are across the street trying to push a car out of a snowbank.

"Dudes!" Liam yells and waves a fist in the air. "Be strong! Don't give up!"

They yell something back. I'm pretty sure it's, "Fuck off, asshole."

Finally we get to my house. We carefully make our way up the icy walkway.

Aidan whips open the door as we step onto the porch.

"Thank God. I was getting ready to go out and look for you." He stops, takes in me and Liam, snow-covered, our arms wrapped around each other — mostly because I'm holding him up. "I called the shop, but there was no answer."

I push past him, dragging Liam behind me. "The phones were out."

"Didn't you close early?" he asks suspiciously. "*We* did."

"Yeah, yeah. It just took me, uh —" I jerk my head in Liam's direction — "longer than usual to get home."

"And that's because you, like ... collected homeless people on the way?"

I glance at Liam. His wavy hair hangs in long, wet strings. His clothes are soaked, and he's swaying a bit. Cold and tired, I snap, "Oh, lighten up, Aidan. He's hardly a homeless person."

"Hey, maaaan," Liam says in a long drawl. "Why the beef?"

"Shush," I scold, elbowing him in the side. "There's no beef."

Aidan rolls his eyes. "Who *is* this clown?"

"You've met him before," I say through my teeth. "It's Liam."

"Oh, yeah," Aidan says. "Coffee shop boy."

Liam takes a step sideways, loosens up his shoulders. "Thems be fightin' words."

I sigh and steer Liam toward the sofa. "Here. Sit down." Then I go back to Aidan. "Ignore him. He's a little tipsy."

"Buzzed!" Liam shouts.

"I'm letting him sleep on the couch tonight," I tell Aidan in a low voice. "I can't let him walk home in this."

"He could call a cab."

"He'd have to wait forever. We didn't see *one* cab on our way home. It's no big deal, Aidan. A few hours."

He sets his jaw. "Fine." Then he looks over at Liam, who's already sprawled out, asleep on the couch. "Why is he half in the bag anyway?"

"Girl problems."

"Oh. He has a girlfriend?"

"Yeah. He has a girlfriend."

He nods as if he approves, like all of a sudden everything's okay. "Well, I'll leave you to it then." And he turns and heads down the hall.

For the second time that night I wrestle Liam's coat off him. It's harder this time, his body dead weight. Next, I go to my room, drag a quilt out of the closet, and take it back to the living room. I drape it over him, tucking it snugly in and around him.

Even though I'm exhausted, I don't want to go to bed yet. I sit on the edge of the coffee table and watch him sleep. He mumbles something and shifts so that his hair falls across his face. I gently lift it back from his eyes. It's still wet. Once again I notice his eyes, his lashes. "What a waste," I whisper.

One of his feet sticks out and hangs off the edge of the sofa. I get up and cover it, re-tucking the blanket in firmly along the whole length of his body until he looks like a giant egg roll.

He mumbles again, and my heart skips a beat. Did he say Lynnie?

He could have said Lyssa — they sort of sound the same.... Who am I kidding? No, they don't.

It feels like someone pricked me in the chest with a pin.

CHAPTER 20

The quilt is neatly folded on the end of the sofa. Liam's gone. I'm relieved. I can't help thinking it's going to be weird when we see each other again. My cheeks get hot at the memory of our walk home, our wipeout in the snow, our almost kiss. Then I cringe when I think about what followed. We'll probably continue on with our unsaid mutual agreement.

As I return the quilt to the closet, I can't ignore the tiny twinge of guilt that niggles at the back of my brain. I should tell Liam what I saw at Kyle's, put him out of his misery ... but then there's a whole new misery. No, I can't let myself be pulled into their mess. Stuff like that always comes out sooner or later. Figuring out what's going on with Aidan has to be my priority. Plus, if I was going to say anything, the moment would have been in the coffee shop when I first recognized her. And that moment has long passed. How do I explain why I kept my mouth shut? How do I tell him I'm a coward?

I check my watch. Is my next shift at noon or two? When I try to call the coffee shop, it just rings and rings — maybe the phones are still out, or even the power. I can't believe I never once thought to take down Liam's cell number, or Erin's for that matter. *Damn it.*

My only choice is to go and check the schedule myself.

If it turns out I don't work until later, I'll go up to Spring Garden Road — assuming they have power — and do some shopping. I need a pair of black pants for work.

Feeling a sense of accomplishment over the fact that I actually have a plan, I head to the kitchen. I find Aidan there.

"Coffee shop boy hit the road?" he asks.

I shrug. "Seems so."

"I didn't hear him leave. It must have been early."

"He might have had to work," I say, pouring some Cinnamon Toast Crunch into a baggie. Breakfast of champions.

Aidan nods. "Oh."

Pressing the Ziploc closed, I turn and catch him making a face. "What, Aidan?"

"Nothing," he says, looking all innocent.

I roll my eyes and go out to the hall to get ready.

He follows and watches me pack my bag.

My course calendar, in all its shredded glory, is lying on the hall bench. I put it there so I'd remember to take it to work. I thought I should leave a note for Janet, let her know my schedule for January, going on the assumption that she'll keep me on after the holidays.

Aidan picks it up and stares at it. "You all registered and everything?"

"Yup." I hold out my hand.

"It's quite a commitment, isn't it?" he says, passing it to me.

"What? School?"

"Sure you're up for it?"

Frowning, I shove the calendar into my bag. "Are you trying to say you don't think I should go? That I can't handle it?"

No answer.

"Didn't you, like, practically beg me to stay here *while I went to school*?"

"Yeah. I wanted you to stay …"

"But not go to *school*?" I finish. "That's nuts. That's the only reason I'm here."

"The only reason?"

I clear my throat. "Well, I mean, of course I'm glad to see you and that we're reconnecting and everything, but make no mistake, I'm here to go to university."

"But what if we want to go back home?"

"What is it with you? There's no *we* going back home. If *you* want to go, fill your boots. But I told you before, I'm not. Not while Vince is still around." I angrily zip up my bag. "Why do you keep bringing this up?"

He tugs on his chin. "I keep hoping you'll change your mind," he says quietly. "It's still our home, Lyss."

"Enough, Aidan!" I grab my jacket and head for the door. "I don't want to talk about this again."

"Okay, okay." He holds up a hand.

I'm about to reach for the doorknob when he says, "Wait."

I don't turn around. "What?"

"It's our Christmas staff party tonight at the bar. We have it early, before the Christmas rush."

"So?" He better not be asking me to come. I'm still pissed about the going home thing.

"I'm going in to work now, and I'll be gone overnight. They've rented some rooms for us at the Prince George. I probably won't be back until tomorrow afternoon."

"Great. Have fun," I say in a flat voice, and slam the front door behind me.

I stand on the porch for a minute, take a few deep breaths to calm myself down. The air is cold and crisp. My nose tingles. There's a lot of snow. Everything is white, even the street. The plow has made a pass, but no pavement shows through yet. I can hear the drone of snow blowers off in the distance. The sidewalks haven't been cleared yet either, so I try to follow along in someone else's tracks. It ends up taking me almost twice as long to get to the coffee shop.

The back service door is unlocked, so for sure we're open. As soon as I step in I can tell it's busy. I look through to the front room. Every table is full. Some people are even sitting along the window ledges. Erin's at the counter refilling coffee urns and setting up new ones. Liam is manoeuvring through the crowd with a tray.

Erin sees me. "Is this crazy or what?"

"Kinda."

"The power's out between part of Coburg and Jubilee," she explains. "Everyone's here for their morning fix."

"Do you want some help?" I ask.

"Nah. You're not on till 2:00, and it's actually under control now."

"You sure?" I crane my neck trying to catch a glimpse of Liam.

"Yes." She shoos me out. "Go play in the snow or something."

I go back outside and start off toward Spring Garden Road, fingers crossed that they have power there too.

Closer to the retail part of town, last night's storm hasn't seemed to affect anyone's morning plans. The sidewalks are crowded and the snow well trampled.

I wander up the street, taking it all in — one super trendy and expensive shop after another. People dodge around me and curse under their breaths. Guess I'm not moving fast enough.

As I walk, I think about Aidan. Why does he keep bringing up going home? How could he possibly think I would ever want to? I can't believe he actually *does*. I really want Marla to come back. I need to talk to her. Maybe she knows what's going on inside his head. I sure as hell don't …

Every time I come to a corner, I glance up the side street hoping to see a second-hand or consignment shop. No such luck. But when I check up the next side street, I see a bookstore. *Is that the bookstore Marla works at?* Standing still lets the cold set in. I hop up and down while I decide what to do. They'd probably know when she's coming back. And it's probably warm in there. Decision made.

Just like the coffee shop, it's an old converted house. The outside is bright yellow, with a lime-green door. It's obviously a children's bookstore. I don't remember if Marla mentioned that. No harm checking it out. Inside is comfy and homey, like your gram's living room. Pretty much the same size as your gram's living room, too. There are a couple of big armchairs, some benches, a tiny picnic table with building blocks, paper, and crayons. A giant dollhouse sits beside it on the floor. Every inch of the walls is lined with books. There's a whole other room filled with toys, puzzles, Lego, arts and craft kits. I would have loved this place when I was a kid.

There's a young girl kneeling on the floor, dusting the wooden shelves.

"Excuse me," I say. "Does Marla …?" I realize I don't know her last name.

"Marla Henderson?" she asks, standing up.

"Yeah." I nod. "I think so. I'm her boyfriend's sister. But I've only just met her," I explain, so it doesn't sound so sketchy.

"Oh. Well, Marla's not here. She came in last week, asked the owner for an indefinite leave of absence."

"She did? Did she say why?"

"Not really. All she said was personal reasons."

Aidan did say something about a sick relative. "So you don't know when she's due back?"

"No, but …" She looks confused. "Wouldn't your brother know?"

I raise my eyebrows. "You'd think so, wouldn't ya?"

The girl smiles and shakes her head. "She didn't give a return date, but if you're looking for info, talk to her roommate, Jodi. They share the upstairs flat in the green house at the end of this street. It has a red door. You can't miss it."

"Thanks," I say.

"I hope everything's okay," she calls after me as I leave.

The house is easy to find. It's exactly like the girl said — green, last one on the street, red door. I push the buzzer with the "2" beside it, hoping it's for the upper flat.

A few seconds pass, then I hear footsteps thumping down the stairs. The door opens.

"Yes?"

She's pretty. Long dark hair, dark eyes, brilliant red lipstick. It's freezing, and she has on super short gym shorts and a tank top.

"Hi," I say. "Are you Jodi?"

She looks closely at me. "Yeah …" Then her face fills with relief. "Are you Marla's sister?"

"No, I'm Lyssa. Aidan's sister?"

Her eyes narrow. She folds her arms and leans on the door frame. "So you're Lyssa. She mentioned you."

The intensity of her look is making me uncomfortable. "Um ... yeah ..." I swallow and forge ahead. "I was just wondering if you knew when Marla's coming home."

She holds out her hands, palms up. "How would I know?"

I try not to let on that I'm confused by her response. "Well, I thought maybe she's called or something. Aidan hasn't heard from her since she went away."

"Went away?" Jodi says. "Where *exactly* do you think she is?"

"Uh ..." I'm starting to get a bad feeling. "Visiting her parents in Boston? Sick relative?"

"Did that little shit Aidan tell you that?"

I open my mouth to say something, then close it again. I nod instead.

"I think you'd better come inside."

Chapter 21

I follow Jodi. With each step up the stairs, my stomach sinks a bit lower. At the top she uses her shoulder to shove open the door. "Come on in."

Now I know why she has hardly any clothes on. The apartment is about a hundred degrees.

Jodi puffs out a big breath of air and lifts the hair off the back of her neck. "The heat's broken — won't turn off. It's like living in a sauna."

"Oh."

"I was just on the phone with my mom. I have to go reassure her that it wasn't a serial killer at the door. She's probably freakin' out. Just give me a sec, okay?"

"Sure." I almost add, "Take your time," because though part of me is dying to know what she's going to tell me, the other part is dreading it.

I unzip my jacket and look around the room. It's messy, but not too messy. It's dark. The walls are painted a burgundy red. There are two front windows covered with faded purple velvet curtains. They match the sofa and armchairs. I can detect the faint smell of incense. All the lamps have fringed, jewel-toned scarves draped over them. *That's gotta be a fire hazard.*

"Do you want an ice water?" Jodi calls from the kitchen. "I have to constantly replace the fluid I sweat out."

"That would be great," I answer.

A picture on the mantle catches my eye. I go over and pick it up. It's of Aidan and Marla at Point Pleasant Park. I gaze off into space for a minute, thinking. Back home, there's a picture of me and Aidan at Point Pleasant Park too. Mom took us there for a picnic after a back to school shopping expedition to Halifax a few years ago. I study the picture more closely. It could even be the same bench, out on the point, overlooking the harbour. I set it back down just as Jodi returns with the water.

I flap the front panels of my jacket like wings. It's so hot in here. "So *do* you know when Marla's coming back?"

Jodi places the glasses on the coffee table, plants herself on the sofa, and tucks her long legs beneath her. She points to an armchair. "Might want to settle in."

I slip my jacket off, pick up a glass of water, and empty half of it in one gulp before sitting down.

"I guess Aidan forgot to tell you that he dumped Marla," she tells me.

"*What?* When?"

"Last week," she says. "Apparently he didn't see the relationship progressing any further, didn't see a future for them, so might as well cut the cord now."

"*What?*" I'm stunned. It makes no sense. Why didn't he say anything? Why did he pretend like everything was okay? That feeling in the pit of my stomach comes back. "Where *is* Marla?"

"Marla?" She pauses and tilts her head. "She's in the hospital. Psych ward."

I grip the arms of the chair with both hands. "Is she all right?"

"What do *you* think? Let's face it. She's not the most ... what's a good word ... emotionally *strong* person you're gonna meet. And your dickhead of a brother knows that." Jodi shakes her head, mouth all twisted up. "She totally lost it."

"Lost it. Lost it how?"

"I was here studying, she walks in looking like someone just died, and tells me Aidan broke up with her, tells me basically what I just told you. Then she sat right there," she points to me, "and barely moved. It was like she went into some sort of three-day crying coma. She wouldn't speak, wouldn't eat, wouldn't sleep, wouldn't *blink*. I don't even know if she could hear me. I tried getting in touch with her parents, but they're away on some kind of cruise. Left messages for her sister and brother. Never heard anything. I didn't know what else to do. I took her back to the hospital." She pauses, takes a mouthful of water. "She didn't fight me on it. I think she wanted me to."

I lean my head back on the chair, letting it all sink in.

"I never liked Aidan, you know. Never liked the way he treated her, talked to her. He was always bossing her around, controlling what she did. I thought he was a little fucker."

I can't think of anything to say. Should I be defending him? "How long will she be there?" I ask.

"No idea," Jodi says quietly. "Did she tell you about her last boyfriend?"

"Yeah."

"I'm afraid of what could happen, and I can't keep an eye on her 24/7."

"No, no of course not." I rub my forehead. "Listen, if I give you my number would you let me know how she's doing?"

"Yeah. I guess."

I root in my pocket and find an old receipt from Shoppers Drug Mart. She passes me a pen. I start to write down my home number then stop and scratch it out. "Probably easiest to get me at work," I lie, and put down the coffee shop number instead. "If I'm not there, leave a message with whoever and I'll call you back."

"Okay," she says, taking the piece of paper and propping it up against the picture of Marla and Aidan.

She walks me down the stairs to the door. At the bottom we turn and look at each other. We don't say a word, not even goodbye.

In a daze, I retrace my steps up Spring Garden Road. What the hell is going on? Aidan. What did he say he had? Mood swings? It's gotta be something more than that.

I pass a digital clock that's part of a bank sign. I have almost an hour left before my shift starts. I don't want to wait until after work. Picking up my pace, I turn and head toward home.

I'M STANDING IN THE hall, at the entrance to Aidan's room.

Bingley meows and winds his way in and around my ankles, leaving a smear of cat hair on the bottom of my jeans.

"Beat it," I sigh, and nudge him away with my leg.

It's not like I haven't been in Aidan's room before. I whip the vacuum around, drop off clean laundry, that sort of thing, but this feels different. It *is* different.

Bingley's watching me. It's like he knows I'm up to something.

Attempting to act casual, I slowly inch across the threshold. As soon as I do, Bingley hisses and pounces toward me.

"Oh, come on," I say. "Like you've never snooped around a room that wasn't yours."

Ignoring his disapproving look, I yank open the top drawer of Aidan's dresser.

Socks. They're all white, all the same. I shove them around, slide them from one side of the drawer to the other.

I move on to drawer number two. Underwear. They're all white as well. I never noticed, even though I've been doing his laundry.

Drawer number three, T-shirts and a couple of golf shirts.

Drawer number four, one lone American Eagle hoodie.

Drawer number five, empty.

What am even I looking for? A clue. A clue to what? I guess I'll know it when I see it.

Next I move to his side table. There's a novel by someone I've never heard of, and inside the drawer are a package of condoms, a library card, some random keys, a box of Vicks cough drops, a tie clip, some golf tees, and a deck of cards.

There's nothing unusual in his closet either. I sit down at his computer desk — that has no computer on it. Aidan says he has a laptop. It belongs to the bar, though. They bought it for him to use for work, so he mostly keeps it there. He told me he'd bring it home sometime so I can use it, but he never has.

The desk has a single, skinny drawer, and I pull it open.

My eyebrows almost touch my hairline.

"Well, looky looky. What have we here?" I turn as if in slow motion, and hold it up so Bingley can see. An eight-pack of door locks — the deadbolt kind — the kind that's on the outside of my door — the kind I've been asking for. "And it's open, Bingley. One missing."

Chapter 22

Bingley seems unimpressed by my dramatic announcement and skulks off down the hall.

I slowly lower myself onto the desk chair and flick the corner of the package with my fingernail. Is the missing lock the one that's on my door? If it is, then he's had these all along. He lied. So what do I do now? I can't bring this up without revealing I was snooping around in his room.

Sighing, I put the package of locks back in the drawer. My eyes land on something in the other corner. Aidan's Nintendo DS. The locks momentarily forgotten, a smile spreads across my face.

When Aidan became part of my family, besides two pairs of ginormous, smelly sneakers, he brought with him his Nintendo DS. I begged him to play with it almost every day. He always let me. Even if he'd been using it, he never said no.

One by one, I pull out the games, read the labels, and dump them into my lap. *FIFA World Cup*, *Need for Speed*, *NHL*, *Star Wars*, *Mario Brothers*, they're all here — even *Hannah Montana*. Mom gave it to me for my thirteenth birthday. I was pretty sure it had been Aidan's idea. I let him keep it with all the other games, teased him about playing it when I wasn't around.

A noise outside makes me jump out of my skin. It's the sound of a car door slamming. *Aidan's supposed to be gone till tomorrow.* I shoot up from the chair, sending all the game cartridges clattering to the floor. I gasp and drop to my knees, clump the games into a pile, and quickly throw them back in the drawer. I spread them out a bit, I'm pretty sure that's the way they were, and then place the Nintendo on top.

Giving the room a final glance, I take a deep breath and hurry out into the hall. My eyes are trained on the front door. A minute goes by, and nothing happens. It occurs to me that the noise I heard might have been from the neighbours.

I peek out the living room window. There's a cab parked right in front of the house. An old lady with steel-grey hair and a blue knit tam is sitting sideways in the back seat, her boots hanging out the open door, not quite reaching the curb. She's saying, or yelling, something at the cab driver, who's behind the car opening the trunk.

I think for a second. That must be Mrs. Collins, the lady who owns the house. I remember Aidan saying she was away visiting her daughter.

Grabbing my jacket and slipping on my boots, I go out to meet her. It wouldn't hurt to make a good first impression considering she probably doesn't know I'm living here yet.

"Hi," I say, opening the back cab door as far as it can go. "Mrs. Collins, right?"

She's doesn't move. I think she's stuck. She mutters something under her breath and holds out her purse, shakes it at me. I take it and sling it over my shoulder. It weighs about fifty pounds. Next she waves her arm in the air, indicating she wants me to pull her out. I do.

Once upright, she turns and squints at me with her apple doll eyes. "You're not Marla."

"No." I shake my head. "I'm Lyssa, Aidan's sister."

"Sister?" She sounds doubtful. "He never mentioned he had a sister."

"Stepsister."

She gives me a good look up and down.

"We, uh, kinda lost touch for a ... couple of years," I add.

"Hmmm."

"Hope it's okay, but I'm staying here for, well, I'm not really sure for *how* long. I'm starting at King's University. Aidan was, *is*, going to tell you, clear it with you or whatever. You were away, though," I finish lamely.

After a long, drawn-out moment of pinching and un-pinching her lips, she must decide I pass inspection. "I hope you're not noisy. I don't like a lot of banging and crashing around."

"I was a mouse in a previous life," I tell her.

She smiles. Her face scrunches into a network of a hundred wrinkles. "I'm Glady. Help me around back to the stairs, will you?"

"Sure."

The cab driver slams the trunk closed and sets a suitcase down on the sidewalk. "Fifty-two even," he says.

I pick up Glady's suitcase and wait while she pays the driver. She hands him three twenties. He whips out a wad of cash, peels off a five, gives it to her with some coins.

I try not to laugh as I watch her press a single loonie into his palm.

I hold her elbow as we head toward the driveway. I glance back over my shoulder. The cab driver is standing there, staring at his hand.

"Cheeky bastard," Glady says. "Wouldn't help an eighty-five-year-old woman out of a cab."

"I'm sure he would have, I just beat him to it."

She grunts.

Once we make it around back and to the top of the stairs, she hands me a key. I unlock the door and hold it open for her.

"Just put the suitcase in the hall," she says, unbuttoning her coat. "My God, it's good to be home. I couldn't take Ottawa one minute longer. You think it's cold here ... chilled to the bone, I was. Spent two weeks chilled to the bone." She goes over and jacks up the thermostat.

"But it must have been nice to see your family — your daughter, right?"

"Pfft. They had me drag my ass all the way there to have an early Christmas because *they're* going to Cuba for the holidays," she says sarcastically. "One of those all-inclusives."

I'm not sure what to say. "I hear you get sick if you drink the water."

One corner of her mouth goes up and she gets a sort of twinkle in her eye. "Yes, I've heard that too."

After Glady is all settled in, I tear down the back stairs. I've only got about fifteen minutes to get to work. I lock the front door and race up the street. I have to stop at the corner and wait to cross. That's just enough time to let everything start running through my head again — Aidan lying about Marla, Marla back in the hospital, and now the package of locks. The traffic light changes one, maybe two times before I notice the blinking "walk" sign. *Get it together!*

Finally I make it to the coffee shop. I rush in the service door, grab my apron, and slip it over my head at the same time I'm taking off my coat.

The place is a zoo, standing room only, so no one notices that I barely made it. I grab a tray and start collecting dirty dishes. From snippets of customers' grumblings and full-on rants, I conclude that the power's still out in part of the south end. People are pretty much camping out, in for the long haul.

Liam goes behind the counter and switches an empty coffee pot for a full one. He smiles when he sees me. "No one from Nova Scotia Power better drop in for a coffee. It'll be the apocalypse."

"No kidding." I rinse out his empty pot, place it in the coffee maker, and press "start."

I know Liam's shift is supposed to be ending. I hear him ask Erin if he should stay. "We'll be fine. Anna's coming in early. She has no power. She'd rather be here."

Liam gives me a nod and a wave on his way out. I nod back. There's no time for anything else.

I like that it's busy. It keeps me distracted — my mind has no chance to wander.

The customers are cranky. It's a student crowd, and it's a Saturday, so the majority of those students are nursing hangovers.

"I think I'm allergic to alcohol," one girl says as I top up her coffee. She plunks a bottle of antacid onto the table.

"Possible," I say.

"Bullshit," the girl sitting with her says. "It's called a hangover."

"Well, you're hungover too," the first girl accuses.

"No, I'm not." She puts her hand over her mug when I offer to refill it. "I'm just exhausted from being up all night."

"Yeah, getting white-girl wasted," the first girl snarls.

I roll my eyes, leave them to their bickering, and move on to the next table.

About an hour and a half later, someone gets a call on a cellphone and announces that the power's back on. The place becomes a ghost town in a matter of minutes.

Anna, Erin, and I all slump onto the nearest chairs. We take a good look around. It's like a bomb went off. Slowly we get up and start restoring order.

I'm wiping up the cream and sugar station when Liam reappears in the front door. What's he doing back? He's only been gone a couple of hours. He looks ... serious. Our eyes meet. He doesn't have to say anything. I don't know how, but I know the frown on his face has something to do with me.

Erin's pulling on her coat.

"You mind if I take a quick break before you leave?" I ask her.

She sees Liam and smirks. "Sure. Anna's got it. Knock yourself out."

He's at one of the tables by the fireplace. I wipe my hands on my apron and make my way over. What if he wants to talk about our almost kiss? He probably wants to set me straight, make it clear that nothing can ever happen. Was it so obvious that I wanted it to? Maybe it was only obvious to me. Or maybe he just wants to apologize for puking his guts out right in front of me.

He dumps his messenger bag on the chair and shrugs off his coat. He's just had a shower. I can tell by the way the hair on his neck is still damp and curling up. And he smells ... clean ... coconutty.

"Hey," he says. "Can you spare a minute?"

"No problem. I'm pretty much done." I sit down. Let's just get this over with.

He takes the seat across from me. "So Mia was there when I got home."

Oh God. Who's Mia? "Mia?"

"Sorry. Mia's my roommate's girlfriend. She's the one taking pharmacy."

The pill! I totally forgot about the pill! "Right," I breathe. "You were going to get her to look at the pill."

"Yeah."

"And ...?"

"Well, it's an antipsychotic."

"An antipsychotic?"

He nods. "It's called Olanzapine."

"Olanzapine." I let the word roll around in my head. It sounds foreign. In a way it is. "So, like, what's it for?"

"Bipolar disorder, dementia, some kinds of severe depression."

"Bipolar ... dementia ... depression ..." I repeat it like I'm memorizing a grocery list. I don't hear mood swings in there. "Okay ..."

"Um, yeah." Liam pauses, clears his throat. "But it's most commonly used for treating schizophrenia."

"Schizophrenia?"

He holds up a hand. "But that doesn't mean that's the reason Aidan's taking it. It could be one of those other things."

"Okay ..." I repeat.

"And even if it *is* schizophrenia," he continues. "Mia said this medication is a good one, that it works really well."

"Okay ..." It's like it's the only word I know.

chapteR 23

Tires screech. I jump back onto the curb. It's my fault, I wasn't looking. I give the driver a limp wave, hoping he can tell that I'm sorry. At this rate I'll be dead in the gutter before I make it halfway home.

I can't stop replaying my conversation with Liam.

I finally switched from "Okay" to "No. No, that's not what he has."

Liam raised his eyebrows. "I guess you forgot to mention you were an expert in schizophrenia."

"I'm not," I said, all defensive. "I just know he doesn't have it."

"It wouldn't be the end of the world if he did. I mean, as long as he takes his medication ..."

"Aidan's ... well ... there's nothing *that* wrong with him."

"Okay, Dr. Lyssa."

"Aidan's fine. He's just fine. But thanks. You know, for finding all that out. Oh, and say thanks to ... Mia? Yeah, tell Mia thanks."

I gathered my stuff and got out of there as fast as I could.

Thinking about it now, I realize maybe I should have reacted a bit differently — a little more toned down. Also, me saying "there's nothing *that* wrong with him" totally implies there's *something* wrong with him. And like Liam said, it could be just one of those other things. Maybe I should have asked him a bit about symptoms, or better yet, asked to borrow his laptop to do some research myself. *Shit.*

I must have been on autopilot because somehow I safely arrive home on the front porch.

It's after seven, dark. I should have left some lights on. The house is so quiet.

With Aidan gone for the night, I thought I might be creeped out at the idea of being alone, but I'm not. I'm relieved — relieved not to have to see or talk to him. At least not right now, not after the day I've had.

My stomach growls as I head for the kitchen, flicking on all the lights as I go. I should have grabbed something for dinner. I don't even remember if I ate today.

On the counter I find a box of Kraft Dinner. A piece of paper next to it says, "no groceries. found this in back of cupboard. expiry date good. don't get STUFFED." Under all the writing is a drawing of a happy face and Aidan's scribbled signature. He must have done it this morning, after I left.

I shake my head. A few years ago, Caroline and I were co-presidents of student council. We organized a year end fundraiser for the food bank — Stuff a Bus. It was really just an old donated minivan that didn't run anymore, but the goal was to stuff it to bursting with Kraft Dinner, which we did. The local news promised to come do a story about it, but it meant we had to wait a day before delivering the goods to the food bank. There was a rumour going around that the rival junior high was going to trash the van, steal the food. Since we couldn't move it, Aidan camped out all night with me and Caroline in the schoolyard and helped us stand guard. We played truth or dare, cards, twenty questions; he pretended to be enthralled by our gossip; we ate junk food till we were sick. We had the best night ever. No harm came to the van, and we all made the paper the next day.

I smile at the memory, but I'm still relieved Aidan's not here.

I cook up the KD, eat it right out of the pot. No point in dirtying a dish. I shoo Bingley off the couch and curl up to watch TV. I just want to tune everything out for a while. *Dateline* is on, but after jerking myself awake more than once, I give up and turn it off. My bed calls to me.

There's the sound of trickling water as I stand at the bathroom sink. It's coming from above me. Mrs. Collins. I'm not alone after all. Not really.

My bedroom feels cold. I pull an extra blanket out of my closet — the one Liam used the other night. I hold it to my nose, positive I can still smell him.

I close my door, throwing my hip into it. It squeaks loudly — seems extra loud in the empty house. I should try to fix that. Tomorrow.

Flopping into bed, I prepare myself for a long night of tossing and turning. I shut my eyes. The hamster wheel in my head is going around and around. After a day like today, how could I expect anything else? But about five minutes later, the hamster conks out and I sleep the sleep of the dead.

When I wake up, I notice that my door is still closed. I must have finally done it right.

I pull on my housecoat and thump down the hall.

Bingley is on the couch, pretty much in the same spot I left him last night. "Well, hello there. Did it cramp your style, being denied access to my room? Or did you even bother to try?"

His reaction is to hop off the sofa and dart toward the kitchen.

I follow him, refill his water dish, and top up his bowl of Meow Mix. Then I turn on the radio, pull out the Cinnamon Toast Crunch, and start eating it out of the box.

Ryan Seacrest's Top 40 Countdown is blaring, so I don't hear Aidan arrive home. He sneaks up behind me and jabs me in my sides with his fingers.

"What the!?" I spin around, swinging my arm. I get him in the neck.

He stumbles backwards. "Jesus, Lyssa! Settle down!" He rubs where I chopped him.

"Don't do that, *ever*!" I push my hair off my face and try to catch my breath. "You deserved that, you know."

"Just trying to have some fun. Call the cops, why dontcha?" He's still rubbing his neck.

I so want to bombard him with questions and accusations, but I don't. "How was your party?"

"Oh, the usual. Though let me state for the record, no good can come from attempting to invent new shooters."

"I'll bet."

"Hey. Could you do me a solid and put on a pot of coffee? I feel like hell."

"You *look* like hell." He really does.

"Great. I'm just gonna dump this stuff in my room."

He returns just as the coffee's sputtering its last sputter. "Oh, hey, I meant to tell you. I just said, screw it, and went back and got the big pack of deadbolts."

My back stiffens. I'm glad I'm standing at the counter so he can't see my face. I swallow. "Oh yeah?"

"Yeah. Mrs. Collins asked me to put one on the gate in the backyard. When it's windy it bangs, makes a lot of racket. Figured I'd better get it done. She's due back soon."

"She's already back." I turn and see him toss the package of locks on the table. I go over and pick it up. It's the same one from his drawer. "It's open," I say.

"I was going to do it but —"

"There's one missing." I cut him off.

"Let me *finish*." His eyes bug out. "I went to put it on the gate the other morning, but with all the snow, the gate wouldn't close tight. I couldn't level it up and —"

"I've been asking you for ages to get me a lock." I cut him off again.

"Yeah, I know."

"You kept saying you didn't have any."

He gives me a confused look. "And I didn't. Until I bought some the other day."

"But there's one missing," I repeat.

"*Again*, if you'd let me finish, when I was trying to get the gate levelled up, I dropped the lock in the snow. Couldn't find it." He shrugs. "Guess it's a good thing it's a multi-pack."

"Yeah. Good thing," I say.

His eyes narrow. I'm pretty sure he's picked up on my tone. "Wait a minute ..." He pauses for a second. "What? You think I already had them?"

I don't say anything.

"I'm right, aren't I? You think I've had them all along, and let me see ... that the missing one is the one on your door?"

I still don't say anything.

"Well, then, you're on to me," he says sarcastically. "You've figured out my diabolical plan — to force you to let Bingley sleep in your room. Because you know I'm such a *cat lover* and I need you to *bond* with him." He shakes his head and pours himself a coffee. "Christ, Lyssa. What the hell do I care if you want to lock your door and keep the cat out of your room at night?" He adds some milk. "Oh, and feel free to go stand at the bottom of the driveway and wait for the spring thaw. Trust me. There'll be a lock lying on the ground by that gate when the snow melts."

He's almost out of the kitchen when he spins around. "What the hell's up your ass, anyway? Coffee shop boy ask someone else to the prom?"

That does it. "Why didn't you tell me about Marla?" I blurt. "That you broke up with her?"

"And *there* we have it!" he shouts, slamming his mug down on the counter. The coffee sloshes over the sides, over his hand. "And how did you find out about that?"

"I went to Marla's apartment. I met Jodi."

"*Why* would you go there?"

"I wanted to find out when she was getting back," I explain. "You didn't seem to know. I wanted to do something nice for you guys, make you dinner."

"Jodi," he scoffs. "That bitch hates me. I suppose she made out like I was the biggest prick on the planet."

No point denying it. "How could you do that to Marla?" I say. "What were you thinking?"

"See? This is why I didn't tell you. I knew you'd react like this!"

"Like *what*?"

"Like all 'Oh, how could you hurt poor Marla? How could you be such an asshole?'"

"I never called you an asshole."

He crosses his arms, like he's challenging me. "I didn't love her. Am I supposed to chain myself to her for the rest of my life because she's ... not quite all right upstairs?"

I press my lips together in a straight line. I don't like the way he's describing her. "You were with her an awful long time considering you weren't in love with her."

"We met in the loony bin!" he shouts. "Honestly, neither one of us had a lot to choose from."

"Oh, that's nice," I spit. "Real heartwarming."

"Don't get me wrong. I cared, *still* care, about Marla. She helped me out a lot, and I helped her. But shouldn't a relationship be built on more than that? It's not my fault she thought we were going to walk down the aisle."

I refuse to agree with him. "Do you know that she's back in the hospital?"

He doesn't answer right away. "Yeah. Yeah I do. And I'm sorry about that. But there's no way I could have predicted that was going to happen. I mean, she's been really good, steady, for a long time."

I turn my head. I can't look at him.

"Lyssa," he sighs. "Marla's great, she really is. It's just ... well, she's a constant reminder of one of the worst times in my life. I had to end it. She deserves someone who can give her more."

I think about what he said, then I say, "Poor Marla."

He sighs loudly. "I have to say ... it's really, um, touching how torn up you are for Marla, considering you hardly *know* her. You've spent like, what? Three hours with her?"

I hate that he has a point. "I guess I just ... feel for her, because she didn't have a clue, never saw it coming. Not to mention, she was totally in *love* with you."

"And is that how it happened with Kyle? You never saw it coming?"

I suck in my breath.

"It doesn't take a rocket scientist to figure out that it all went in the crapper," he continues. "That whatever you'd planned, didn't go as ... planned. And you know what?"

I glare at him. I can't decide if I want to slap him in the face or kick him in the balls. I sniff and stick my chin out. "What?"

"I never asked you to explain *anything*. Didn't ask why you were showing up on my doorstep in the middle of the night — nothing. Do you want to know why?"

I shrug.

"Because you're eighteen. What you decide to do, the choices you make, they're up to you. And more importantly, they're none of my business!"

We have a staring contest, and all the bravado leaks out of me. What am I supposed to say to that?

He breaks the stare first. On his way out, he stops and punches the wall.

From where I'm standing I can see a mark. He broke the plaster.

Maybe now's not the time to ask him about the pills.

Chapter 24

Aidan and I pass the rest of the morning in silence. Neither of us works till later in the day. I focus all my energy on staying out of his way. I know he's doing the same.

I would have gone out, gone downtown or something, but it's snowing again. Since the big storm it seems as if it's hardly stopped for more than a few hours at a time. One mini storm after another, like aftershocks from an earthquake.

Aidan's pissed, offended, and I guess he has every right to be. No one likes getting the third degree, but he must know it's only because he's my brother and I care. I should probably go find him and clarify that, but I've never been very good at the olive-branch thing. I shove everything down inside, act like I'm right, even when I'm not. Even when I *know* I'm not.

I think I understand now why he didn't want to tell me about Marla. And the lock, well, he explained all that. It makes sense — the whole gate thing.

I should go apologize. My hand hovers on my bedroom doorknob, but I can't make myself turn it. I let my arm fall back to my side.

I hear him leave for work. He doesn't say goodbye.

Shortly after, I leave too and head off to the coffee shop.

"Hope you're ready for a giant snooze-fest," Erin says when I come in the back. "It's been like death in here."

"That's fine," I say, hanging up my coat. "Sort of suits my mood."

"Anything wrong?"

"Nah. Just in a bit of a funk."

"You sure? You want me to kick somebody's ass?"

I tilt my head to one side. "Is this place a front for the mob or something? Liam's made me a similar offer."

"No." She laughs. "We're just very protective of our staff."

"That's a good thing ... I guess."

"Damn right." Erin takes off her apron and pulls on her jacket. "Molly's probably running late as usual. She should be here any minute. In the meantime, try not to die of boredom."

"Okay, see ya tomorrow."

"No, I'll be back later. I'm closing for Liam. Warn Molly so maybe for once she'll keep track of her cash."

My heart drops, slips a little further down in my chest. "Oh? So, uh ... Liam's not working tonight?"

Erin raises her eyebrows. "God, Lyssa. I wish you could see your face."

"My face?" I scrunch up my nose. "Why?"

"You look like I just shot your dog. You're sooo obvious."

"What are you talking about?" I mutter, knowing very well what she's talking about. "I don't even own a dog." But she's already out the door and doesn't hear me.

After my shift, I trudge home, berating myself the whole way because apparently it's "sooo obvious" I have a thing for Liam.

Talk about hopeless, stupid. I mean, he has a girlfriend. Yeah, she's a lying, cheating whore, but *he* doesn't know that. I blast out a mouthful of air. I really need school to start so I can make some new friends. My world is a little too small right now.

my clock radio goes off at 7:05 a.m. I picked up a shift for Molly. I didn't sleep great, so I'm regretting it now.

Aidan's door is shut. He's still asleep. I don't know when he got home last night, but I was up around quarter after two to go to the bathroom and his bed hadn't been slept in.

I decide to skip breakfast, not wanting to crash around the kitchen and risk waking him.

It snowed again overnight. The sidewalks are slushy, and my

feet get soaked almost immediately. Trees line the street, all their branches coated with heavy, wet snow. Some branches are so weighted down they curve precariously over the power lines and almost touch the ground. One good gust of wind and it's lights out for the entire neighbourhood.

When I get to the coffee shop, I dig out Molly's key, but the service door's already unlocked. "Hello?" I holler and step inside.

Liam sticks his head around the corner. "Oh, hey. What are you doing here?"

My heart does a little somersault. "I picked up a shift. What are *you* doing here?"

He frowns. "If you're supposed to be the first one on, why would you say hello and come in when the door's already open? I could have been a burglar."

I take my apron off the peg. "I actually did think of that." I didn't. "But it was after I said hello. So what *are* you doing here?"

"I needed some breakfast before class. There is no food, I mean *no* food, at my place. Even the mice have given up and moved out."

I smile. "I'm going to put in a batch of muffins. How much time you got?"

"I grabbed a couple of day olds. I'm good. Just didn't want my stomach grumbling all through the lecture. That would be … awkward."

"Definitely."

"So, um …" He pours himself a coffee. "You blew out of here like a bat out of hell the other day. Did what I said upset you?"

"No." I shake my head. "I was just tired. I wanted to get home."

"I know you're worried about your brother," he says.

I get out the mixer and don't respond.

"I think you're worried he might be schizophrenic."

I still don't say anything.

"Where did you find the pill anyway?"

"Oh, just around."

"Do you know if he's taking them?"

I plop a brick of butter into a bowl. My silence gives me away.

Liam rips the tops off a handful of sugar packs and dumps them into his mug. "No matter what he's suffering from, if he's not taking his medication, that could be serious, Lyssa."

"He's fine," I say. "Just fine."

"Denial isn't just a river in Egypt, you know."

"What?" I think for a second. "Ha, ha." I smirk. "And I'm not in denial. Yeah, Aidan has issues, but we all do."

"So you don't see any ... red flags?"

"Red flags?"

"Well, like, is he different? You haven't seen him for a while, right? Is he acting different than you remember?"

I shrug and start measuring out the sugar. "It's been two years. I don't expect him to be the same person. People change."

He nods, stirring his coffee.

"They do, you know," I insist. "People. They change."

"I know," he says. "You're right."

We're both quiet for a moment.

"Listen, Lyssa," Liam starts. "I have an uncle who's schizophrenic."

"You do?"

"Yeah. He was diagnosed when he was sixteen — more than twenty years ago. He leads a totally normal life, is a teacher, has a family. Every summer we go backpacking in Newfoundland. He's, like, my favourite person ever."

"Oh, that's nice."

He opens his mouth, but I turn on the mixer before he can say anything else.

He watches me with an exasperated look on his face and drums his fingers against his cup. When I finish creaming the butter and sugar, there's another stretch of quiet, then he says, "Uh, totally off the topic. I broke up with Rosalyn last night."

My head jerks up. Did he just say what I think he did? Why is he telling *me*? I zero in on some random spot on the wall behind him. "Oh, yeah?" I ask casually.

"It was time," he says. "The weird thing was, neither one of us seemed that ... torn up about it. I think she knew it was time too."

"Wow." I can't think of anything else to say.

"There was no scene. We're not like enemies or anything."

"That's good. I mean, that's the best you can hope for, right? Like in these sorts of situations. It makes things easier, cleaner, when there's no drama." I marvel at how moronic I sound.

He smiles, probably *captivated* by my pep talk.

"Well, I better get to class," he says, draining his coffee. "And if you want to talk about your brother, I'm always available."

I give him a tiny nod. "Thanks."

"Anything you need before I head out?"

"Just flip the sign to 'open,' I guess."

"Sure." He goes to the door then stops, his hand on the push bar. "Listen," he says, looking back over his shoulder. "It's cheap night tomorrow at the movies. I always try to go if I'm off. There's usually something half-decent to see. Interested?"

I stare at him like he's speaking a foreign language. Is he asking me on a date? I mentally shake my head. He just broke up with his girlfriend — *last night*.

"Umm ...," I say, stalling.

He raises his eyebrows.

He's just asking me to catch a movie. It probably means nothing, because who wants to go to the movies by themselves? I'll offer to pay. He's done so much for me. Yeah, that's what I'll do, I'll offer to pay.

He's waiting. There's a strange look on his face. He probably thinks I'm having a stroke. I'm sure twenty minutes have passed since he asked me about the movie.

"Yeah," I croak, then clear my throat. "That sounds good."

from the front porch I can hear the phone ringing inside. I shift my takeout container of pad Thai to my other arm, unlock the door, and run to the kitchen. I don't make it in time.

I wait a second to see if the message light blinks. It doesn't. I reach for the receiver and press the back arrow to check the call display. It's a 351 number. River John. Home. But not my home. I know that number, though, I just can't place it. The phone starts ringing in my hand.

"Hello?"

"Lyssa? Is that you?"

I recognize the voice. "Yes, Mary. It's me."

There's a few seconds of silence, then: "My God. He was right."

"What? Who was right?"

"Vince. He said you'd end up with Aidan."

"I'm just staying here while I go to school." I don't know why I feel the need to explain myself to her.

"Is he there?" she asks curtly. "I need to talk to him. *Immediately.*"

It's like she's trying to brush me off. It brings back a flood of memories, her running Mom's funeral, her standing next to Vince greeting the mourners, her taking over Mom's kitchen as if she owned it. I don't think I'll tell her *immediately* that Aidan's not here. "How did you find him?" I say. "How did you get this number?"

"I looked it up in the phone book."

Right. That's what I did. Something occurs to me. "Have you known all along Aidan's been here in Halifax? Has Vince?"

She pauses, then: "Yes."

"Have you talked to him before? Called here?"

"No. Vince forbade me to make any contact."

"But —"

"Listen, Lyssa. I don't have time for this right now. Is Aidan in?" She's sounding extra curt now.

"No. Can I take a message?" I answer, syrupy sweet.

There's another pause. A sigh. A sniff.

"Vince is missing," she says.

"Missing. What do you mean?"

"He went off to check on the cabin after the storm, like he always does. You know how he worries about the roof collapsing when there's a lot of snow."

"Yeah, yeah. The hunting cabin. The love of his life. When was he supposed to be back?"

"Yesterday."

No point beating around the bush. "He's just probably face down, passed out drunk," I say.

She doesn't say anything. She's mad. I can feel it through the phone.

I realize that was a little harsh and make an effort to soften my tone. "You know, Mary, this is kind of what he does. He used to go on binges all the time, disappear for days."

"He doesn't do that ... as much, anymore."

"Trust me. He'll turn up. He always does."

There's a clattering sound — her earrings against the receiver. She always wears dangly earrings. "I know you don't give a flying fig about Vince, Lyssa. But he's Aidan's father, and I think he should know."

"Fine. But know what? We don't really know anything yet."

"I'm telling you, something's wrong. I can feel it in my bones."

What does she want me to say? Does she want me to agree with her? "If you're that worried, you should call the police, or the search and rescue, or whatever."

"They won't do anything," she snaps. "He hasn't been missing long enough."

"Okay then ..." So much for trying to offer advice.

"It's dark now," she continues. "First thing in the morning I'm sending Tommy and Brian out to look for him."

"That sounds like a good idea. Good luck then." I want to get off the phone. My pad Thai's getting cold.

"Could you please track Aidan down and tell him, tell him his father's missing?"

"He's at work. I'm not bothering him about ... this." I want to say, "Because it's hardly an emergency," but instead I say, "Because it might upset him and there's nothing he can do about it right now anyway. I'll let him know when he gets home." I leave out that he won't be home until well after midnight.

"Fine. Thank you for your *help*," she says sarcastically.

Rolling my eyes, I hang up the phone.

I stick my pad Thai in the microwave. As I wait for the beep I think about Vince, think about what if something really has happened to him. No. Mary's totally overreacting.

I come to the realization that I'm not so sure I care one way or the other.

I'm not so sure Aidan's going to care either.

chapter 25

"Lyss," a voice says. "Time for bed."

I drag my eyes open, blink to get rid of the fog. "Aidan?"

He unzips his jacket and kicks off his boots. "The one and only."

I yawn and swing my legs off the sofa. They feel heavy, like weights are attached to my feet. "What time is it?"

He sinks into the armchair and lets his long arms hang over the sides. His fingers almost touch the floor. "A little after one."

"Already?" I rub my neck to get out a kink.

"What are you doing out here?" he asks.

Then I remember. "Waiting for you."

He looks surprised and smiles. "That's a first."

I reach for the remote and turn off the TV. "Mary called."

His smile vanishes. "Mary? From home?"

I nod. "She, uh ... she says Vince is missing."

"Missing." He leans forward in his chair a little. "Like how?"

"He went to check on the cabin after the storm. He hasn't come home yet."

"So ... when was he supposed to be back?"

"Sometime yesterday."

He frowns. "Then he's really only a day late, right?"

"Yeah, I guess."

"Well, I'd hardly panic yet."

"That's basically what I said."

"I mean, we both know what probably happened, don't we?"

I raise my eyebrows. "According to Mary, he's not *like that* anymore."

"Really," he says, staring past me out the window. "Did she seem worried to you?"

"Yup." I pop the *p*.

Neither one of us says anything for a while. I dangle the fringe of the sofa blanket just out of Bingley's reach. He swats at it a bunch of times but doesn't make any real attempt to catch it. I keep doing it, letting it get really close then yanking it back at the last minute. He remains stubborn in his laziness and finally ignores me altogether.

Aidan moves from his chair to beside me on the couch, almost crushing Bingley, who hisses loudly but refuses to give up his spot. "What if she's right?" he says. "I mean ... maybe I should be worried. Should I be?"

I hope he's not waiting for me to give him an answer.

He slumps back and closes his eyes.

I study him. I think he *is* worried, and it surprises me. I thought he would say something blasé and indifferent, something like, "Keep me posted." But I was wrong. I give his arm a squeeze. "I'm sure he's okay."

"Mary should call somebody, don't you think?" he says. "The police or something?"

"She said she's sending Tommy and Brian back to the camp in the morning."

"Yeah. Give him some more time to resurface. She probably wants to make sure that ... it's not a false alarm. That would be embarrassing."

Not really. Small town. Everyone knows Vince, knows about his epic binges. But I bite my tongue. "Don't worry, they'll find him."

Without opening his eyes, he places his hand over mine. "Yeah, you're right."

"And you know how much snow we had, you can only imagine how much *they* got. He might just be snowed in or something."

He turns his head and looks at me. "Plus he has food out there, canned stuff, firewood and all that."

"Exactly," I say, smiling encouragingly.

"I bet you find it bizarre that I even care."

Again I bite my tongue. "He's your father."

"It's okay, I find it bizarre too. I think I'm just operating on not enough sleep." He stands and stretches. "I can't do anything now anyway, so might as well hit the sack."

I let him haul me off the sofa. "Yeah. I'm sure we'll hear something tomorrow."

He puts his arms around me and hugs me tight. I hug him back, all the friction of the past couple of days forgotten.

something wakes me, and for the second time that night I'm forced to drag my eyes open. I'm sure someone's in my room — sure I felt the breeze of a person walking by. It has to be a dream. I notice my door is open and Bingley's curled up on the bottom corner of my bed. *Bingley!* I do a scissor kick and push him off.

His paws thud onto the floor and he eventually settles on the rug under the window.

Not able to get back to sleep, I lie there for a while and try not to think about Vince. Because when I think about him, it makes me think about home, and Mom. Yeah, there are some happy memories in there, but they can't compete with all the bad ones. To turn my thoughts in another direction I start playing the alphabet game in my head. Aidan and I always played it, always tried to stump each other. This time I do candy bars. Aero, Butterfinger, Coffee Crisp, Dairy Milk, Eat More ...

Then I hear something. I sit up on my elbows and listen. It's not outside, it's coming from somewhere in the house. Voices? I'm sure I turned the tv off. I reach for my housecoat and get up. Down the hall I go and stop just outside the living room. Aidan's in there. He's talking to someone. I inch around the corner. It's dark except for the pale light shining in from the street lamps. I can see the outline of him standing in the front window. He's alone. I strain my ears, but I can't make out what he's saying.

"Aidan?" I whisper.

He doesn't move. Maybe he didn't hear me. "Aidan?" I repeat a little louder.

Slowly he turns. "Lyss. Sorry. Did I wake you?"

"Uh, no. I think it was ... " I look over at the black TV screen, "a bad dream."

He nods.

"Who were you talking to?"

"Talking to?" He sounds confused. "Oh. Ummm ... that. It was just Franco."

"Who's Franco?"

"The cleaner."

"What do you mean, the cleaner?"

"Huh?"

"Cleaner for what?"

"Oh, sorry. Bar cleaner. Franco cleans the bar. He called me."

I figure it out. The bar where he works.

"Franco comes in after closing," Aidan continues. "Usually on Sundays. He has a key."

That doesn't explain the call in the middle of the night. "So, what happened?"

"It's Monday. They had to change their night this week. Blake forgot and set the alarm when he locked up. Then Franco and his guys set it off when they arrived."

"Oh," I say.

"He was just letting me know so I'd call the security company right away and tell them not to send the police."

"So did you?"

"Did I what?"

"Call the security company."

"Oh. Yeah." He scratches the back of his head. "Yeah, I did. Just gave Franco the all clear."

I stand there for a second, rocking on my heels. "Guess I'll go back to bed then."

"Sure. Goodnight. And again, sorry if I woke you up."

As I make my way back to my room, I happen to glance down at the hall table. It's where we dump all our junk, spare change, keys, whatever's in our pockets, the mail. There, partially covered by a stack of grocery store flyers, is Aidan's cellphone. An impulse leads me to the kitchen. Our one and only cordless phone is on the counter by the fridge, the receiver resting in the cradle.

chapter 26

From the hall I see Aidan sitting in the armchair, fingers steepled and pressed against his lips. The cordless phone has moved from the kitchen and is now on the coffee table. Since he's staring at it like he's willing it to ring, I conclude he's heard nothing. I'm sure he's been there all night.

Seeing the phone reminds me of the whole fake conversation thing, Aidan and the cleaners. Could he have been sleepwalking or something? Could I? Maybe it never happened … No, it happened.

I take in Aidan's dishevelled hair, the dark circles under his eyes. He's obviously exhausted and strung out. I reflect on all that's happened to him lately. Me showing up, Marla, now Vince. Not to mention the medication that he may or may not be taking. It's a lot for anybody. It can only be making everything worse. Perhaps a few minutes of strange behaviour isn't that much out of the ordinary.

The sound of kids shouting out on the sidewalk interrupts my train of thought.

"Chances are Tommy and Brian haven't even left yet," I say, going over to the sofa and gathering up the blanket I used last night.

"I called Mary. She said she sent them out at dawn," he says without taking his eyes from the receiver.

"Yeah, well." I check my watch. "It's only nine-thirty. With all the snow, it'll take them forever to get back in there."

He doesn't answer.

"They're going to find him anyway. You know he's at the cabin doing …" — I search for the right word — "… whatever."

"I know." But he doesn't sound very certain.

"Are you off today?" I ask, changing the subject.

"I called in sick."

"Did you get any sleep at all?" Part of me hopes he'll make some reference to our encounter in the middle of the night. Offer up an explanation or something.

"I think I dozed at some point."

So that's that. "Okay then. I'm off to work." I get my coat, slip it on, then stop in mid-zip. "Look, uh, do you want me to stay here with you? Wait till you hear something?" I cross my fingers that he says no. Exam week is about to start, and there isn't a chance in hell I'll be able to find someone to cover for me.

"No." He smiles weakly. "You go. Someone's gotta bring home the bacon."

The circles under his eyes appear darker all of a sudden. "It's going to be fine, Aidan. Just fine."

He nods.

"You'll call me as soon as you hear anything?"

"Sure. When will you be home?"

"I'm working a double, but, um …" I chew on my lip. Tonight's the night I'm supposed to go to a movie with Liam. Is it wrong to still go when Aidan's sitting here all worried? Is it wrong to still *want* to go? Surely we'll know Vince is okay by tonight.

"We could make pizza for supper," he suggests, sounding a little brighter. "I've got a boxed kit. We could load it up with hot dogs, just like we used to."

"Actually, I, uh, I'm going to a movie after work." It *is* wrong to still want to go. At least it feels like it is.

"Oh," he says. He looks like a kid who's dropped his ice cream cone.

"It's cheap night." As if that somehow makes it better.

"Who with?"

"What?"

"Who are you going to the movie with?"

The word *Liam* gets stuck in my throat and won't come out. "Just some people from work." Not a complete lie.

"People from work," he repeats. "Coffee shop boy one of those people?"

"Yeah."

"Thought he had a girlfriend."

I don't bother answering him. "Promise you'll call me. You can get me at the shop all day."

"Until you go to the movie," he points out.

"I'm positive you'll hear from Mary way before then."

He sits back in his chair, not looking at me, a scowl on his face.

"I'll talk to you later," I sigh and hook my bag over my shoulder.

"Have fun at the movie," he says all sulky.

tHe wind cuts rigHt through me, but I don't care. Right or wrong, I'm thankful to get out of that house. When I arrive at the coffee shop, the place is full, seemingly all with students, textbooks and laptops covering every inch of table.

"Welcome to exam week," Erin says, tossing me my apron. "It looks like it's packed, but it's an illusion. It's actually a graveyard." She sweeps her arm in an arc. "They camp here. All day. And don't buy *anything*." She says the last part really loudly.

The phone rings. I listen when Erin answers. It's not for me, so not Aidan.

I get out the binder of recipes. "I may as well get a head start on the baking for tomorrow since it's so quiet."

"Okay, keener." Then she sidles up next to me. "So ... you and Liam have a date, huh?"

"What?" I slam the binder shut. "How did you know? Did he say that? Did he actually call it a date?"

"He *may* have mentioned something or other about it earlier this morning," she says coyly.

"You saw him? He was here?"

"You just missed him. He opened for me. I had a dentist's appointment."

"Well, it's not a date," I say, my face getting hot.

She crosses her arms and leans against the fridge. "I'm thinkin' maybe it is."

I shake my head. "Uh-uh. Just two friends going to a movie. It's cheap night," I add.

"Oh, I know all about cheap night." She gives me a smug look, as if there's some big secret about cheap night, like it's code or something.

"What's that supposed to even mean?"

"Do you get to pick the movie?" she asks without answering my question.

"I don't know." I shrug.

"If he lets you, then for sure it's a legit date."

"Then I guess he'll be picking the movie, because it's not a date," I insist.

"Listen. I think it's awesome. You and Liam. Five-ever."

She's making my brain hurt. "Five-ever?"

"It's longer than forever." She smiles.

"You're crazy." And I go off to assemble my baking supplies.

The phone seems to ring constantly all day. Every time it does, I stop what I'm doing, hold my breath, and wait. I should have heard something from Aidan by now. It's for selfish reasons I'm desperate to hear. I don't want my guilt hanging like a cloud over my time with Liam. I check my watch again. Four-thirty.

Erin's working the double with me. She's the only one who's answered the phone. "There haven't been any messages for me, have there?" I ask, thinking perhaps she forgot to tell me. But she says no.

I duck into the back kitchen and call home. It rings and rings. I try Aidan's cell. It goes straight to voicemail. Maybe he's finally sleeping, so ... everything must be okay? It probably just slipped his mind to call. Or maybe he tried and got a busy signal, which is totally possible. So yeah, everything must be okay.

My shift is almost over. I start grinding up a supply of coffee beans for Zack, who's on next.

"I'll do that," Erin says, pushing me out of the way. "Liam will be here soon. Go make yourself pretty."

"What?"

"You brought some makeup or something, didn't you?"

"Um, yeah."

"Well, time's a-wastin'. That mascara's not going to put itself on."

I grab my bag. It's easier to do what she says.

Liam's standing at the front counter when I come out of the washroom. He looks up and smiles. "Ready?"

"Yup," I say, taking my coat off the hook. "Let's roll."

"Wait." Erin disappears then returns a minute later with a handful of tiny pieces of paper that she presses into Liam's palm. "Here. On me. It's Monopoly time at McDonald's. They're all freebies. Put some meat on that girl's bones."

My jaw drops open.

"Uh ... " Liam squints as he tries to read the stamp-sized coupons. "Thanks?"

Erin herds us toward the door. "You two kids have fun now."

Liam shakes his head all the way to the car. "You must bring out the nurturing, motherly side of Erin."

"Is *that* what that is?"

He laughs. "Considering she's the same age as me, it's the only thing I can think of. She seems to like you, and, well, Erin doesn't like ... anybody."

we stand in front of the theatre, gazing up at the marquee.

Liam tries to muffle a burp. "I'm regretting that second Big Mac."

"I warned you it wasn't a good idea."

"Okay, smarty pants, what do you want to see?"

"You pick," I say. "Too much pressure."

"My only request is no chick flicks. Other than that, you can make the final choice."

"Okay." How would Erin interpret that? I study the start times, eliminate anything with a hint of romance. "Everyone seems to like that Sandra Bullock one."

He nods. "She is a chick, but it's about space, so yup, we're good."

Inside, Liam jumps in front of me in line and buys the tickets. I keep shoving money in his face, but he tells me to relax, it's only six bucks. I buy us frozen yogurt. It costs more than both our tickets.

We're early enough that we get our pick of seats — in the very centre of the theatre, in the very centre of the row. We sit close together but not touching.

The lights dim and the trailers start, my favourite part. But then there's one for a horror movie, and it shows a little girl in a nightgown walking down a dark hallway following some whispery voices. It makes me think of me, last night, and finding Aidan, talking to … himself? I shouldn't have left him today. I shouldn't be here. What if he gets, or has already gotten, bad news? Through the entire movie, my head is filled with all these thoughts.

I feel Liam looking at me as we walk to the car like he's waiting for me to say something, so I do. "What did you think?"

He shrugs. "It was pretty intense. The ending was kind of predictable."

It's a safe, generic answer — basically what I would have said. It makes me wonder if maybe he couldn't concentrate on the movie either. Was he thinking about Rosalyn?

"You wanna grab a coffee?" he asks. "There's a rumour going around that there are other places that serve coffee besides where we work. I never believed it till now." He gestures with his head. "There's a Starbucks over there in the bookstore."

I gaze longingly at the green and white sign. There's nothing I'd like more than to go with Liam for a coffee, but I know I can't. "I should really get home."

"Okay, Cinderella." He stops at the car and holds the door open for me.

As I crawl inside, I can see flakes beginning to fall, captured in the headlights of the other cars in the parking lot.

"It'll take a while for the heat to …"

He's talking to me, but it sounds fuzzy in my brain. I'm hypnotized by the snow. I should have made more of an effort to contact Aidan, found out for sure before I left with Liam. Maybe even called Caroline to see if she knew anything. Yeah. Why didn't I call Caroline?

After a while Liam's voice breaks through. "Lyssa. I'm going out on a limb here, but I'm thinking you're a little distracted."

I turn from the window. "No, I'm not. Why would you say that?"

"I just told you my favourite part of the movie was when Nicolas Cage stole the Declaration of Independence and you didn't bat an eyelash."

I scrunch up my nose. "Isn't that the plot of *National Treasure?*"

"Exactly."

"Oh." He got me. "I may have one or two things on my mind."

"Is it your brother?"

Why deny it? "Yes. Sort of. And some other stuff."

"Did you ever ask him about the medication?"

"It's … not really a good time," I say, shaking my head.

"Lyssa. We're talking about someone who's been prescribed an antipsychotic drug, and I can't shake the feeling that you think he may not be taking it."

"I never said that."

"You don't have to. I can tell by the way you repeatedly say he's fine."

I keep quiet.

"So, is he fine?"

Last night pops back into my head — not like it ever really left. But the thought of unloading all my crap on him, trying to make him understand my and Aidan's relationship, how much we depended on each other, protected each other, and now we have to again, because we have no one else, is overwhelming. "Everything's under control."

I know he doesn't believe me, but what can he say?

"Okay. Just remember I'm here. I'll help any way I can."

I stare straight ahead and nod.

"So … since we didn't get to have a coffee tonight, you want to meet up for one tomorrow?"

"Shouldn't you be studying for exams?"

"Did I forget to mention that I'm a genius?"

"No, I think you've mentioned that numerous times. But still, aren't you in med school? And isn't that, like ... *hard*?"

He taps his finger against the side of his head. "It's all up here, baby. All up here."

I roll my eyes.

He pulls up in front of my house and turns off the ignition. "Look. Joking aside." He rests his arm across the back of my seat. "I mean it about you asking Aidan if he's taking his medication. You need to find out what you're dealing with. Maybe it's not that serious."

I make a production of putting on my gloves, making sure each finger is snugly in its sleeve. "Okay," I say. "I'll think about it."

There's an awkward moment of silence.

"Well, thanks for the movie," I say, pushing open the car door.

"Hold on now." He opens his door too, runs around to my side, and helps me out and over the snowbank. "I'm not a caveman, you know."

"Oh, I know. But you don't need to do stuff like this. I'm quite capable of getting myself out of the car." My brain is screaming at me to stop talking. But no. "It's not like this is a *date* or anything," I continue, laughing nervously.

He laughs back. "What goes on in that head of yours?"

"You don't want to know."

We're on the sidewalk, facing each other, our toes almost touching. The street lamp shines down, enveloping us in a soft cone of light. He's so tall that he has to bend his neck to look at me and his hair flops in his face. My hand itches to brush it aside. He beats me to it.

"Would it be so awful?" he asks.

I stare up at his warm brown eyes. They're like pools of melted chocolate. "Huh?"

"If this was a date? Would it be so awful?"

I stop breathing. For at least ten minutes. "No, no. It wouldn't be so awful."

"That's good." He takes my hand and pulls me up the walk to the porch. Before I know what's happening, before I can get myself ready for it, he puts his arms loosely around my waist and kisses me lightly on the lips. One single, perfect kiss. I want to package it, seal it in a Ziploc bag, lock it in a safety deposit box, and keep it forever. Who am I kidding — five-ever.

"I'll see you tomorrow," he says.

Don't speak, I tell myself. *Don't ruin this moment.* I nod and watch him walk back to his car.

When I go inside the house, I'm feeling all dreamy and wobbly, as if I'm half-drunk. Then reality washes over me like a bucket of ice water. Aidan is still in the same chair, unshaven and looking even more haggard, still staring at the phone, or the floor, I can't tell. The only clue that he's moved are the six empty beer bottles lined up on the floor alongside his chair.

"Aidan?"

He ignores me. I dump my coat and bag, go over, and grab the phone. I press the back arrow on the call display. The battery's dead. "Did Mary call?"

Still ignoring me, he twists open the fresh bottle in his hand. His head bobs as he flicks the cap toward the fireplace. A bunch more are scattered in the same general direction.

"Well, did she?" I ask. "What happened?" I'm dreading the answer.

When he finally looks up, his eyes are empty and unfocused. I'm not sure he even sees me. "Vince is dead," he says. "That's what happened."

Chapter 27

"Here." I hold out a steaming mug of coffee.

Aidan looks up from his chair. "I don't want a goddamn coffee!" He sweeps it out of my hand, sending it smashing against the living room wall.

I just stand there and stare at the splatter of brown liquid soaking into the drapes. A puddle forms on the floor, slowly trickling its way around the broken pieces of china.

"Jesus. I'm so sorry, Lyss." He sighs and rubs his face with both hands. "I don't know what's wrong with me."

"Well, I can kind of *guess* what's wrong with you." I remind myself to not sound so flip. "I mean, no matter what went on between you and Vince, it still must … must be a shock."

He leans his head back and closes his eyes. "I'm so glad you're here. I can't imagine going through this without you."

I kneel down and start collecting the chunks of shattered mug. "Nobody should go through something like this alone."

"You did."

"Tell me what happened," I say, wanting to change the subject.

"Tommy and Brian found him."

"Where? At the cabin?"

"Outside the cabin. Over by the wood pile. They think he went out to get some wood, slipped on the ice, snow, whatever, and got knocked out."

"Oh God."

"Yeah. They said there was a huge gash on the back of his head. He didn't have a coat on or anything. Probably didn't take very long for him to freeze to death."

"Brutal ..."

"It took a while to find him. All the snow. No tracks to follow." He looks at me and shakes his head. "He was completely covered."

One giant, frozen Vince-sicle. "I'm so sorry, Aidan."

He attempts a smile. "At least he died in his favourite place. I guess that's something. I just wish ... we'd been able to patch things up, you know?"

"I know," I say, trying to sound sincere.

"I always thought there'd be time."

"I know," I repeat. Then I show him the debris in my hand. "I'm going to get rid of this."

"I'll come with you and get a cloth to wipe the floor."

As he gets up to follow me, I ask, "Do you think Mary will handle all the arrangements?"

"Probably. There'll be no *real* arrangements, no funeral. Vince didn't believe in God."

AIDAN'S UP BEFORE ME. I hear him rattling around in the kitchen. It took me forever to convince him to go to bed. I wish he slept longer. He's running on empty and bound to crash soon. I'm starting to feel a bit like that myself. Especially after checking the time and realizing I only slept for four hours.

I find him standing at the stove, cooking eggs. "Hey," I say.

"Hey," he says back.

"How are you doing?"

He shrugs.

"You're not going into work today, are you?" I ask.

"No. You?"

"I'm actually off." Then I remember that I'm meeting Liam for coffee later. If I didn't know better, I'd say the gods were conspiring against us.

"Good."

"So what happens next? Are you going to River John?"

He turns. "Why? Did you want to go with me?"

"No." I answer too quickly. I try again. "I mean, not really. But of course if you have to go ... and you want someone with you ..." Thankfully the phone starts ringing. The call display tells me it's Mary. I automatically hold it out to Aidan.

He raises both hands and shakes his head.

I have no choice. "Hi, Mary," I say.

She doesn't even say hello — she's already in mid-sentence. I open my mouth a couple of times to insert a word, but there are no pauses. I finally say, "Okay, I'll tell him." Then end with, "You should probably get some rest." My attempt at being nice.

"So what did she say?" Aidan asks as I hang up the phone.

"Vince's body is being brought to Halifax," I explain. "To the medical examiner's."

His eyebrows scrunch together. "What?"

"Apparently that's what they do," I say, pouring myself a glass of juice. "You know, when there's a mysterious death."

"Mysterious? He slipped, fell, then froze. What's mysterious about that?"

"I dunno. I'm just repeating what she told me. She's not happy about it. They'll do an autopsy. She knows Vince wouldn't want that. She hates the thought of them taking him away, cutting him open."

I watch Aidan take a seat, rest his elbows on the table, and hold his forehead in his hands. He's visibly upset. "How can I help?" I ask.

"I guess I agree with Mary, that's all. There's no way Vince would want this. Can't we refuse or something?"

"I really don't know. Do you want me to call Mary back?"

"Don't they have anything better to do?" he snaps.

It's like he expects me to have the answer. "Well ..." I try to think. "I'm sure they'll return him as soon as they can."

He stares at me for a second. "Yeah, you're probably right." And he gets up and goes back to his pan full of eggs. "Pass me a plate, would you?" he says. "They're kinda dried out, but there's a ton here if you want some."

"No thanks." I open the cupboard and take out a dish. As I set it next to him on the counter, I move the package of deadbolts. They're still lying there from the other day. "Where do you want me to put these?"

He glances at them. "Just put them on top of the fridge. Remind me to put that lock up for you. Things seem to keep getting in the way, don't they?"

"I wouldn't worry about that right now," I say. "Plus I think Bingley's growing bored with me."

He scrapes his eggs onto the plate, studies them for a while before saying, "I don't know why I made this. I'm not even hungry." Then he walks out without another word.

I decide to leave him be. There's nothing I can say or do that'll make him feel better anyway.

After picking at his abandoned eggs, I dump the rest in the garbage. I can't figure out what to do with myself. I decide to take a shower, wash my hair, and straighten it for a change. It takes forever. "Now I know why I don't do this anymore," I say to my reflection in the mirror. "It looks better wavy." I stick my head under the tap, soak my hair, then towel dry it.

Aidan's asleep on the sofa when I finally venture from my room. I reach for my jacket and bag and noiselessly slip out the front door.

I don't want Aidan to know I'm leaving the house. Because I know I probably shouldn't. But I want to see Liam. He's expecting me. I'll keep it to an hour. Likely Aidan will sleep the whole time anyway.

LIAM'S AT OUR TABLE by the fireplace, staring into his laptop, textbooks piled all around him. I slump into the empty chair and plant my head face down on the only bare spot on the table.

"Bad day?" he asks.

"You have no idea."

"Spill."

I upright myself. My whole body feels like it's filled with wet sand. "Um, well ... Aidan's dad died last night."

"*What?*" He closes his laptop. "What happened?"

"He fell. Hit his head." I keep it simple.

Liam nods thoughtfully, doesn't respond right away. "Are you okay?"

"Uh-huh."

"He's your dad too, right? Stepdad?"

"Yeah ..." Should I feel bad that I don't feel bad? "Let's just say we weren't that close. Long story."

"Wow. Still sucks, though. How's Aidan doing?"

I debate for a minute. Then another. "I think he's going to have a hard time." I pause and lick my lips. "Actually ... I think maybe he's ... been having a hard time. Like, before this even happened."

Liam stays quiet and waits for me to continue.

I sigh a giant sigh. "I caught him talking to himself, carrying on a whole conversation. Not like how you or I would talk to ourselves. This was different ... You see, there's a lot of crap that went down between him and Vince," I explain. "From a long time ago. I'm worried that me showing up, reminding him of home and stuff, may have brought it all back."

"And that's why he's talking to himself?"

I squeeze my eyes shut. "I don't know."

"Did you ask him about it?"

"Yeah. He said he was on the phone."

"But he wasn't."

I shake my head. "His cell was on the table. The house phone was in the kitchen."

Liam goes quiet again. "Anything else?"

"Just acting kind of distracted, the odd anger outbursts, that kind of thing." The stack of empty beer cases form a picture in my head. "He, um, I think he might drink, like more than I thought he did." I feel guilty telling Liam all this, like I'm throwing Aidan under the bus. "He's having girlfriend problems too ... add that to everything else, it could be all stress related."

Liam pushes himself back from the table. "I dunno, Lyssa, the behaviours you're describing ..."

"But it could be just stress, couldn't it?" I hear my voice, and it sounds a little desperate.

"I know you don't believe that. I think you believe the same as me, that there's something wrong and he's off his meds."

"And he's grieving now too. Don't forget that." I can't bring myself to admit that Liam's probably right, because I don't know what I'll do if he is.

"But his behaviour is already erratic. Who knows how the death of his father is going to affect him? Without medication, his behaviour could become even *more* erratic. He needs to be in treatment."

"You want me to gang up on him, and I can't. Not now when his dad's just died. I'm all he has."

"I get that you're scared, worried, but remember my uncle? Totally normal life." He leans in close. "But he has to take his medication to have that."

"I'm not scared. Or worried," I lie. "I'll just talk to him. He'll listen to me."

"Like an intervention?"

"Yeah, sure." I stick my chin out. "An intervention." I sound more confident than I feel.

"Do I have to remind you that you're not a doctor?"

I get up from the table. I don't want to talk about this anymore. "I gotta get back."

He must have gotten the message because he wears this pained expression like he's trying to stop himself from speaking. He pushes his hair off his face. "Look. I'll probably set up camp here tomorrow and study all day. I don't work till evening. Meet me and I'll buy you lunch before your shift starts."

I make him wait a bit before I answer. "And how do you know when my shift starts?"

"Oh, I have my ways."

"Would it involve checking the schedule that's posted in the kitchen?"

He slaps his forehead with his palm. "Why didn't I think of that?

I called everyone and asked if they were working. Figured it out through process of elimination."

I can't stay mad at him. "Since you put in all that effort, you're on. Big spender," I add. (We get forty per cent off food and free coffee.)

"Wait." He stands, seems unsure about something for a second, then pulls me into his arms and hugs me tight. "Let me help," he whispers into my hair.

"You just focus on studying," I whisper back. "I'll see you tomorrow."

"I'm not done with this, you know. We'll be talking about this again."

WHEN I GET HOME, Aidan's still asleep on the sofa. It looks as though he hasn't moved. I watch him for a while, imagine what I'd say if I *did* try some kind of intervention. It churns up an acid feeling in the pit of my stomach. Maybe I should listen to Liam. Maybe this is more than I can handle.

I check on Aidan periodically throughout the rest of the afternoon. He's so still, at one point I hold my hand in front of his mouth to make sure he's still breathing.

The next time I go in, he's sitting up, stretching. "You're alive," I say.

"Guess I needed that." He yawns and looks at his watch. "What did you do all day?"

"Oh ... read some, made a list of books I still need for my courses, had a nap," I lie.

He nods. "Sounds productive."

"Are you hungry?" I say before he can ask me anything else about my day.

"Starved."

I make us some grilled cheese sandwiches and tomato soup. We pretty much eat in silence, but at least he eats. When he's done he announces he's going to take a shower.

I stay in the kitchen, put some water in the microwave for hot chocolate. As I tear open a packet of mix, I hear a strange scraping sound coming from outside. Peeking out the window, I see Glady in a housecoat and winter boots, dragging a giant metal garbage can up the driveway. I zip up my hoodie and run out the door. "Glady! Stop! Let me do that." I grab the handle from her and haul it the rest of the way to the curb.

"Thanks, honey," she says, rubbing her back. "Aidan usually does it for me, but" — she frowns — "he must have forgotten. He always puts it out early in the day, before he goes to work."

"Well ..." I guess I should tell her. It's not a secret or anything. "You see, Aidan didn't go to work. His dad passed away."

"Oh!" Her hand slaps against her chest. "How awful. Is he okay?"

I steer her around to her door to get her in out of the cold. "Yeah, he'll be fine."

"Poor boy. And you too. Are you okay?"

"Yes, thank you." I help her up the stairs, back to the warmth of her kitchen.

She's still tsk-tsking, as she holds a kettle under the tap.

"Look, Glady," I say. "I know Aidan does little jobs for you and all that, but he's sort of got a lot on his mind right now, so I'll do those things, okay?"

"What a sweet girl. There's not much, only a bit of shovelling and salting, the garbage, maybe a hard-to-reach light bulb now and then."

"Sure, no problem." I go to leave, then I remember. "Oh, and Aidan tried to put on the lock, but the gate's frozen in place. He has to wait for the snow to melt some."

She takes a tea bag out of a tin. "What gate, honey?"

"The gate in the backyard. The one that bangs in the wind."

She gives me a blank look.

"You asked Aidan to put on a lock?" I gently remind her. "So the noise wouldn't bother you?"

"Sweetie," she says as she puts the tin of tea bags back in the cupboard, "I may be getting a little old and forgetful, but I never asked Aidan to put up any lock on any gate."

I get a prickly feeling all over my scalp. "Are you sure?"

"Yes." She nods. "I'm sure. My late husband, Murray, God rest his soul, who constructed that gate, fancied himself a bit of a handyman and overbuilt everything. It would have to be some bloody goddamn strong wind to flap *that* gate around."

"Maybe Aidan misunderstood or something ..." My voice trails off.

"That's probably all it is." She pats me comfortingly on the shoulder.

Outside, I lean against Glady's porch rail and stare up at the night sky. What the hell? She never asked him to put on a lock?

The stars aren't spelling out any answers for me, so I look down, down at the gate in question. Snow drifts halfway up its sides. No answers there either.

I trudge down the back stairs and up the side driveway, my heart thumping loudly in my ears the whole way. By the time I get to the kitchen, I feel nauseous. The microwave is beeping that my water is ready. As if in a trance, I press "clear," and sit down at the table. There's a faint humming inside my head, and it feels like something's pressing on my chest.

My eye catches a corner of the lock package sticking out over the edge of the top of the fridge. I think back to Liam and what he said at the coffee shop.

"His behaviour is already erratic. Who knows how the death of his father is going to affect him? Without medication, his behaviour could become even more *erratic ... I get that you're scared, worried ..."*

"I'm not scared. Or worried."

I think for a minute, go over, pull one of the deadbolts out of the plastic, and shove it in my back pocket.

Out in the hall the bathroom door is closed. Aidan must still be in the shower. I duck into my room, briefly study the door frame, and then head for the basement. I'm just reaching for the basement doorknob when from right behind me I hear Aidan ask, "What are you doing?"

It makes me jump. "Uh, I, uh … I'm putting in a wash," I answer, hoping he didn't hear my voice crack.

"Where's your laundry?"

I look down at my empty arms. "Right. I know, I was … um, checking first to see if there was detergent. I thought it was almost empty last time."

"No. There's a full bottle."

"Oh. Good." I glance at him over my shoulder. "Anything you want me to throw in?"

"No, thanks."

"You look tired, Aidan. You should try and have another nap or something."

"I can't. I've slept half the day away already."

"At least go lie down then — in the living room." *At the other end of the house.* "Watch TV, take your mind off things."

He twists up his face like he's thinking it over. "Okay." He starts off down the hall then stops. "You're not going out again, are you?"

Again?

"It's just, well, I don't want to be alone right now," he adds.

My mouth is dry, and I have to swallow. "No. I'm not going anywhere."

I wait for him to walk back to the living room, wait till I hear the creak of the sofa.

In the basement, I quietly rummage through the tool box until I find the right screwdriver. Back up in the hall, I stop and listen. Nothing but the muffled drone of the TV.

I carefully shut my bedroom door, cringing as it squeaks. I have to use all my weight to get it to close tight. As I stand on my desk chair fighting with the screwdriver, sweat drips down the side of my face. A drill is out of the question — too loud. My hands are killing me. The harder I try to keep quiet, the more noise I seem to make. Finally, after switching hands back and forth a thousand times, I twist the last twist.

"There." I wipe my forehead on the sleeve of my shirt and slide the deadbolt across. "Bingley can't get in. No one can."

chapter 28

Staring into the mirror, I tilt my head from side to side. The face staring back at me looks like it's a hundred years old. I put on some frosty white eyeshadow to brighten up the dark smudges around my eyes then add a couple of coats of mascara. I stand back, survey my work. "Better," I whisper. "But not much."

All night I kept dreaming that someone was trying to open my door. I don't know why I would dream that, because no one can. Not anymore.

The kitchen counter is littered with a new crop of empty beer bottles. There's no sign of Aidan. Probably sleeping it off. I shove the empties into the cardboard box on the back porch, turn on the dishwasher, and finish tidying up. Zapped of all energy, my movements are slow. How am I supposed to help Aidan — fix him? It all sounded so simple when I laid it out for Liam. Just have a little chat and everything will be peachy. What the hell was I thinking? God, we've got so much to talk about, so many issues, unanswered questions, it'll take days.

Gotta start sometime, I guess. Taking a deep breath, I knock lightly on Aidan's bedroom door.

There's no answer. I crack open the door and peer in. He's not there.

I check the hall table for a note or something. Nothing. I can see that the car isn't in the driveway. He didn't go to work, did he? It's too soon. Isn't it?

I GRAB my coat and head out to work. As I walk, I picture my brain. It's kind of pinkish, and all the little areas between the blood vessels are bulging out, like bubbles, because there's just too much shit in there. Can your brain burst like your appendix?

Even through the coffee shop window, I can see the frown on Liam's face. He's sitting at our table again. His hair falls across his eyes as he checks his watch. And for just a second I feel nothing else but a fluttering in my chest.

He looks up as I open the door. His expression immediately clears and breaks into a smile. I don't know how, but I manage to smile back.

"Hey," I say, draping my coat across the back of a chair.

"Hey. I was starting to worry you'd changed your mind."

"No. Just couldn't get my act together."

He takes in my bedraggled, sleepless appearance. "Is everything okay?"

I laugh as I sit down. I laugh because if I don't, I might cry. I laugh because I can't tell him. I can't tell him about the locks, about what Glady said. I don't even know *why* I can't. Is it because I don't want to be wrong? "Yup."

He squints at me like he's trying to see inside my head.

"You call this lunch?" I point at the plate of muffins and oat cakes on the table, trying to distract him. "Fess up. These are day olds, aren't they?"

"It's not like they're mouldy or anything."

I spread out a napkin, pick a muffin, and break it into pieces.

"So how's Aidan?" he asks. "How's he doing?"

"He's okay, I guess. I mean, it's not exactly an ideal time for him, right?"

"And how are *you* doing?"

"I'm fine. Just fine."

He can tell I'm not. It's written all over his face. "So have you given any more thought to your intervention idea? You know I'll help you if that's what you want to do."

I meticulously pick up every single stray crumb off the table, squishing down on them with my finger, then dropping them onto my napkin. "Well, I did kind of think of something." I don't tell him it literally came to me three seconds ago when I saw one of his medical textbooks, written by a Doctor so-and-so. It was the word *Doctor*.

"Shoot."

"What if I go to Aidan's doctor, tell him I don't think he's taking his pills, tell him what's been going on, how worried I am. Can I do something like that?"

Liam shakes his head. "His doctor isn't going to discuss anything like that with you. Aidan's the one who needs to do that."

"But I'm his sister. I'm family."

He shakes his head again. "Doesn't matter."

"But if I tell him everything, then he can go ahead and do something, make Aidan do something. He doesn't have to actually discuss anything with *me*."

"Yeah … I dunno. Do you even know who his doctor is?"

"No. Can't I just go to the hospital and ask?"

"They're not going to give you that information."

I sigh with frustration. "Why do they have to make it so hard?"

"You could just ask Aidan," Liam offers. "Tell *him* how worried you are."

"He's not going to tell me. He doesn't want to talk to me about any of this." I gnaw on a fingernail, try to think. Where do I go from here?

"I'm not saying the whole doctor thing is the *worst* idea. Just don't expect him to tell you anything." Liam looks like he's thinking too. "I don't suppose there would there be a pill bottle lying around the house or something that would have the doctor's name on it?"

"I haven't seen anything. Trust me, I've looked. Plus if he's decided to stop taking his pills, he's probably not going to hold on to the bottle."

"Anyone else you could ask? Does he have any friends?"

I lean back in my chair. "Aidan's never mentioned any friends. He doesn't seem to hang out with anyone. No one comes to the house, no one calls …" I sit up straight. "Except Marla. But she's kind of … indisposed."

"Who's Marla?"

"Aidan's ex-girlfriend. She would know who his doctor is. They, um ... sort of met in the ... mental hospital." I wince a bit. Is that what I'm supposed call it?

Liam doesn't correct me. "So he's actually been in a hospital before. In a treatment program. Why didn't you tell me?"

"Well, it's not exactly something that's easy to work into conversation."

He gives me a look. "Uh, it's not like we haven't discussed Aidan and his problems before. If he was in a treatment program, then he obviously suffers from *something*, and those kinds of *somethings* don't just go away."

"He said there was nothing wrong, and it was all made-up garbage anyway. He only ended up there because Vince and the doctor from home plotted against him." Hearing my words, it sounds like I'm trying to convince myself more than anything. "They wouldn't let him out of the hospital if there was still something wrong with him."

"Lyssa. I'm going to say this one more time, and I want you to listen. If Aidan's not taking his medication, all bets are off."

I don't say anything.

He's getting frustrated. "You're in over your head."

I'm so exhausted, I know I'm going to cry any second. I close my eyes, press my fingers into my sockets, just in case.

He keeps quiet for a minute, then: "I'm going home to P.E.I. next week when exams are over. My sister's visiting from Winnipeg with her kids. I'm taking them their Christmas presents. Why don't you come with me?"

It's so off topic I have to review in my head what he just said. "I can't. I've got too many shifts."

"Exams will be over. I'm sure you could find someone to cover for you."

"It's not a good time. I can't leave —"

"It is a good time, Lyssa," he interrupts. "I think you should step back from all this, take a breather."

I shake my head. "You only want to get me away from Aidan, to talk me into doing things your way."

"You mean the *right* way?"

I set my jaw. "I'm not ready to give up yet. I want to try it *my* way first."

I hear him blast out a mouthful of air. "I think you should consider coming to P.E.I."

Without answering, I stand and slip on my coat. "I've got a few things to do before my shift. I'll see you later."

He stares at the table, tapping his pencil against a binder.

No hug this time.

I know exactly what I'm going to do. I'm going to Jodi and Marla's. If Marla's still in the hospital, and I assume she is since I haven't heard otherwise from Jodi, then Jodi can tell me how I go about visiting her. Marla could hold the key. She probably has tons of insight into what makes Aidan tick.

In no time at all I'm standing in front of their bright red door. I knock and wait. There are no sounds from inside on the stairs. I knock again. Still no sounds. *Damn it!*

I jump off the stoop, out onto the sidewalk, and look up at their window. I'm about to turn toward the street when, for some reason, I take one last look. Those heavy velvet curtains. They move.

Should I try again? Knock louder? Something tells me not to bother.

Puzzled, and a little pissy, I walk back to Spring Garden Road. There's a wooden planter in front of some fancy ladies' clothing store. I sweep off the snow and sit, but I keep one eye on the door, expecting some snooty clerk to come out and bust me any second.

I lean my body forward and stare down at my boots. Pivoting my feet at the heel and making fan shapes in the slush, I think about Aidan and how it didn't occur to me that he doesn't seem to have any friends — not until I talked to Liam. He didn't have any friends back home, either. No best bud, no one he went biking with, hung out with, got into trouble with. Only me.

A noisy group of girls pour out of a doorway across the street. As I watch them laughing, hooking arms as they climb over the chunky snowbank, I realize it's where Aidan works. I recognize the name. I wonder if he's there. I should go see, and if he is, we could make plans to meet up later. We need to talk, *have* to talk. I dread it, though. The talking. I think I'm afraid of what he'll tell me, or what will happen after the talking. Maybe I'm the one who needs to be in treatment.

I cross at the crosswalk and make my way up the narrow stairs to the bar.

The lunch rush must be just finishing. There are only a couple of tables occupied, but loads that need to be bussed. A half dozen people sit on stools at one end of the bar watching a TV; a young guy wearing a black golf shirt and black apron is polishing glasses at the other end.

"Excuse me," I say.

He turns. "Hey. What can I do for you?"

"I'm looking for Aidan. He wouldn't happen to be here, would he?"

"Aidan Mackenzie?"

"Yeah."

"No." He slides the stem of one wine glass after another along an overhead rack. "I haven't seen Aidan in a while."

"Oh. I thought maybe he decided to come into work."

His forehead wrinkles into a frown. "Here?"

I mirror his look. "Um, yeah."

He stops what he's doing with the wine glasses. "Are you a friend of his or something?"

"Sister."

"Uh, well, Aidan doesn't work here anymore."

"*What?*"

"Sorry." He shrugs.

I slump onto the nearest stool. "Was he ... fired?" I whisper the last word.

"No. He quit."

His answer takes me by surprise. "He *quit*?"

"Yeah." He nods. "Said he was moving."

"*Moving?*"

"That's what he said." He goes back to sliding glasses onto the rack.

None of this makes any sense. "When? When did this happen? Today?" It has to have been today, because he told me just the *other* day that he'd called in sick to work.

The guy takes in my confused look and kind of cringes. "'Bout a week ago."

CHAPTER 29

I drag myself back down the stairs and out to the street. The sunlight is blinding after the darkness of the bar, and I stand on the corner blinking until my eyes adjust. At the same time I mutter a long string of curse words under my breath. I pick my three favourite and repeat them over and over.

The crosswalk light flashes "walk" and I follow a small herd of people across the street. *Moving? Moving where? What the hell is Aidan talking about?*

I clench my jaw and march up the sidewalk, determined to track him down. After about half a block, I stop. I don't even know where to begin, and my shift starts soon. There's not enough time to go hunting for Aidan now.

My eyes dart up and down the street. I decide to stick with my original plan. Jodi. She's home, I know it. She saw me. Why didn't she come to the door? I might not have enough time to get any answers from Aidan, but I have enough time to get some from Jodi.

I retrace my steps back to the bright red door. I knock loud, angry-like, and square my shoulders.

Jodi yanks the door open. She's out of breath from running down the stairs.

"Hey," I say smugly.

She looks surprised. "Hey," she says back.

"I was here earlier."

"Oh. I just got back from class."

I try to read her expression. I can't tell if she's lying. But she must be, unless ... wait a second ... "Is Marla out of the hospital?"

She picks at some peeling paint on the door frame. "Yeah."

My mouth falls open. "You said you'd let me know."

At least she has the decency to look embarrassed. "I know," she sighs. "I, uh, just haven't had the chance to yet."

This time I can tell she's totally lying. "When did she come home?"

"A few days ago."

My eyes bug out.

"Look. I've got school, work, plus I'm trying to take care of her."

"Take care of her? Why? Isn't she better?"

"Not really."

"Then why is she home?"

"It's all voluntary. She can come and go as she pleases. I think she thought she was fine. And she was. At first."

I get that sinking feeling again. "What happened?"

She flashes me a look that could kill. "She talked to your brother."

"She talked to Aidan?"

Glancing quickly over her shoulder, she says, "Don't talk so loud. I don't want her to know you're here."

"Why?"

She ignores my question. "Even though I threatened to tear the phone out of the wall, she still insisted on calling him. I don't know what that dick-breath said to her, but she's in worse shape now than when I took her to the hospital."

"Shit." I close my eyes for a second. "And she won't tell you what he said? What they talked about?"

She shakes her head.

"When did they speak?"

"A nanosecond after she got home."

"His dad just died, the day before yesterday," I say.

"Well, it was before *that*," she says, crossing her arms. "So don't try and throw that out there as an excuse."

"Don't worry, I'm not."

"Because that's what she did all the time. Made excuses for him, for the shitty way he treated her. 'Oh, he feels things so deeply,'" Jodi mimics, "'and he suffers from this, that and the other thing.' Fuck that."

I open my mouth to apologize. I feel like I should.

But she cuts me off. "I couldn't give two shits about what's wrong with your brother, I just don't want him around Marla."

At this point, I can't blame her. "I get it. But can *I* talk to her?"

"No," she says.

It throws me off. "What? Why?"

"I don't know, she won't say, but she was pretty clear. She doesn't want to see you."

"But I don't understand." I frown. "We always got along fine."

"I don't know what to tell you."

"And she said that," I persist. "Said that she didn't want to see me."

"She was pretty specific." Jodi positions herself in front of the doorway as if she thinks I'm going to take a run at it. "Listen," she continues. "I think it's for the best. A clean break and all that."

There's a moment of awkward silence, then she steps backwards through the door. "Bye," she whispers before closing it.

Feeling dazed, I stand there for a while.

My visit to Jodi's has given me no answers. Not one. If anything, it only created more questions.

I don't remember the walk back to the coffee shop, but somehow there I am, standing outside the service entrance.

There's no one in the kitchen. When I peek through to the front, I see Erin holding a coffee pot, talking to some girls at a table.

I shrug off my jacket and reach for my apron. As I measure out the coffee grounds into a filter, I notice Liam's not here. His laptop and books are still spread over the table, but he's nowhere to be seen. I'm disappointed. I want to talk to him, though I'm not sure what I'd say.

Erin joins me behind the counter. "Yay. I'm dying to get out of here." She pours the remains of the coffee in the sink and rinses out the pot. "Sometimes I think I should just set up a cot out back and live here. Save on rent."

"Good idea," I say, distracted. "Where's Liam?"

"He, ah ..." She swishes water around the pot again. "He ..."

I watch her, waiting.

"That bitch showed up," she finally hisses.

"Bitch?" *She doesn't mean...* "Rosalyn?"

She nods. "They were having some sort of deep convo. Looked serious."

I let the information settle. "Well ... it could be anything."

"I tried to eavesdrop by alphabetizing the magazines over by the fireplace."

"That's not too obvious."

"Yeah, Liam was on to me. That's when they left."

"They left?" I squeak. "Together?"

"I know, right?" Erin's eyes get wide. "Let's kill her."

Touched by her fierce loyalty, I can't help but smile. "Tell me again how this place isn't a front for the mob."

"I never trusted her," she says in a hushed voice. "There's just something about her."

We both lean against the counter for a second, thinking.

"You should call him," she says.

"No. He might think I'm checking up on him." I tug on my lip. "You know, maybe she just left some stuff at his place or something," I reason. "Or maybe they're studying together ..."

She opens her mouth, but then closes it again. "Actually, you're probably right. It's probably something like that."

"Yeah, totally." *Please let it be something like that.*

Erin gathers up her coat and bag. She gives me a little hug as she leaves.

All through my shift, I keep one eye on the door, but Liam never comes back. Ten minutes before he's supposed to relieve me, Anna appears.

"I'm in for Liam," she explains. "Something came up and he asked me to cover."

An uneasiness bubbles in my stomach. "Oh? Did he say what it was?"

"No," Anna says, twisting her ponytail into a bun. "And I could tell by his tone not to ask."

I look at all the stuff on his table, *our* table. I go over, intent on packing it all up for him, but just as I'm about to close the screen, I stop. I tap the touchpad, put in his password, go to Google, and type in "symptoms of schizophrenia." I click on the first website and start reading ... *first signs of schizophrenia usually emerge during adolescence or early adulthood* ... Though I read each symptom slowly, like I'm trying to commit them to memory, I feel my heart speed up. I go to a few more sites that basically say all the same things, then shut down his laptop, stack up his papers and books, and carry them into the back office.

"If Liam shows," I say to Anna, "just tell him I put everything in the bottom drawer of Janet's desk."

"Sure." She nods. "Anything else?"

"No. Nothing else."

there's someone standing in front of the house. Short, wide ... and fluffy. Not Aidan. As I get closer I make out who it is. Glady. Covered in fur from head to toe.

She waves when she sees me.

"What are you doing out here?" I ask. "Is everything okay?"

"It's my bridge night, honey. Just waiting for my ride."

"Oh. Okay." I shift my weight from one foot to the other, hesitant to leave her outside by herself.

She reaches a gloved hand out and touches my arm. "How's Aidan doing with all this? It must be terribly hard on him."

"Well, he ..." How do I answer that?

"This must be so hard. On *both* of you."

"We're ... surviving," I say, trying my best to look sombre. "Listen. It's freezing. Do you want to wait inside our door? You can still see the street."

"No. Estelle will be here any second. She's never late, not when there's sherry involved."

As if on cue, an ancient-looking gold Cadillac comes barrelling down the street, slams on the brakes, and stops beside us.

"Don't wait up," Glady calls, stepping toward the car.

I watch them squeal away from the curb, then I turn and head up the front walk. In the dark I can't tell if Aidan's car is down at the bottom of the driveway. He sometimes parks it there by the garage. I'm too tired to backtrack and check.

But the house is empty. I don't have to call out or anything. I know it as soon as I open the door. Though earlier I was all determined to confront Aidan, relief oozes out of me over the fact that he's not here. With my coat and boots still on, my bag still over my shoulder, I lower myself onto the sofa. I feel like I've just stepped out of the boxing ring. The loser. Battered and bruised.

I fall over on my side and shut my eyes. It's going to take a lot of effort to travel to my room. It's so far away it might as well be in another country. After a few minutes I force myself to get up. In my room I can lock the door. And that's what I want to do — lock myself in and not speak to *anyone*, because every time I do, they just end up telling me one more thing I don't want to hear.

I close my door, slid the deadbolt into place, and collapse onto my bed. That's when the phone starts to ring. And ring. I moan and pull the pillow over my head, tucking it in around my ears. The ringing doesn't stop. Why isn't the answering machine kicking in? Suddenly I sit up. It could be Liam. I run out to the kitchen. The call display tells me it's Mary. *Shit*. Taking a deep breath, I pick up the receiver. "Hello?"

"Lyssa?"

"Yes. Hi, Mary."

"Is this, um, a good time?"

I shrug. "Is there ever?"

"Pardon?"

"Nothing," I sigh. "What can I do for you? Aidan's not here," I add.

"I took a chance that you'd answer. I'm looking for you, actually."

"Oh?"

"Listen, I'd like to meet with you. We need to talk."

"Yeah, uh." I roll my eyes. I can't even begin to imagine about what. "I'm *really* busy with work right —"

"This is important, Lyssa. Do you think I would have called otherwise?"

She has that snarky tone again. It drives me nuts. "Listen, if this has something to do with your guilt over screwing around with Vince when Mom —"

"No," she says shortly. "It's about Aidan."

I wasn't expecting that. "Aidan?"

"I can't get into it over the phone, but something has recently come up, something you really need to see."

"Like what?"

There's a moment of dead air. "Are you going to meet with me or not?"

Chapter 30

Frustrated, I toss the phone onto the kitchen counter. It's saved by an oven mitt. You can't really slam down a cordless, all you can do is angrily press the "end" button.

Mary refused to tell me anything. She insisted we had to have this discussion face to face. I wasted I don't know how much time trying to get something out of her, but she wouldn't budge.

My mind works overtime as I crawl into bed. Like, did she have to sound so ominous? What could she have to tell me that was so important, so ... *serious*? Finally it comes to me. It has to be about the will. It was the way she said it had to do with Aidan. Mary tends to be overly dramatic — always has been. Mom called it "flair."

When Mom died, she left everything to Vince, her husband — pretty standard, I guess. She probably assumed Vince would look after me and Aidan, or would have assumed so at the time she put it in her will.

Well, we all make mistakes ...

Now that Vince is gone, logically everything should be split between me and Aidan — the house, the bakery, any money. But something tells me that's not how it's going to go down. Either there's nothing left, as in, all the money's gone (if there even was any to start with), or there's mortgages and debt out the yingyang, or Vince's will left everything to Aidan. He may not be that keen on Aidan, but he was definitely *less* keen on me.

And Mary, she was probably left out. Maybe she's pissed about it, thinks she's owed something, or maybe she just wants to see how I'll take it all, how I'll react.

But how would she know what's in the will? Then I remember: her brother Raymond, he's a lawyer, probably Mom and Vince's.

She wanted me to come to River John tomorrow morning. That is *not* doable. I've got too many shifts, plus I've got no way to get there except by bus. She kept pressing me — tomorrow afternoon, evening, the next day. We settled on three days from now. Her lawyer brother is coming to town for business. She'll come with him.

I'm looking forward to it like I look forward to getting my flu shot.

With all those comforting thoughts, I finally drift off to sleep.

I **wake up with** my hand clutching the edge of the mattress. My heart drums in my ears. *"They were having some sort of deep convo. Looked serious."* That's what Erin said. What if Rosalyn told Liam I knew about her and Kyle? That I saw her half-dressed in Kyle's apartment. That I knew and didn't say anything. Of course it would mean she'd have to confess to cheating ... would she risk it? She strikes me as the type who'd be able to talk her way out of anything.

All the possible scenarios play out in my head.

Liam said neither one of them had seemed that broken up about the split. But now that some time has passed, it's possible she wants him back. Or doesn't want anyone else to have him. Telling him I kept my mouth shut would definitely be one way to do it.

Could she be that much of a bitch?

I roll over, flip my pillow to the cool side, and stare at a crack in the wall until my eyes glaze over.

All along I knew this could happen.

I've got no one to blame but myself.

It takes every ounce of energy I have to get myself ready for work. I'm so stressed out, I keep forgetting what I'm doing halfway through doing it.

Aside from the fact that Aidan is still missing, my other concern should be my impending meeting with Mary, but it's not. I can't shake the vision of Liam and Rosalyn together and what might be going on.

On my way to the kitchen I pass Aidan's room. It's empty. I'm starting to worry. I come to a sudden stop when I see him hanging off the fridge door.

"We're out of milk?" he asks.

Stunned, I just look at him.

"Well, are we?"

I find my voice. "Are we what?"

"Out of milk."

"Where the hell have you been?" I exclaim.

He closes the door. "What? What's wrong?"

"You haven't been home since yesterday."

"Settle down, *Mom*." He shrugs. "I was with friends."

"Really?" I say, raising my eyebrows. *What friends?* I want to ask. But I don't. "None of these friends have phones? Come to think of it, why didn't you just call me on your cell?" I *do* sound like a mom.

"Sorry, Lyss. You know … I've lived alone for a while now. I'm not used to having to report in."

I lean against the counter and watch him riffling through the fridge. I can't keep putting it off.

"Aidan," I say quietly. "What's going on with you?"

He turns and gives me a blank look. "What do you mean?"

"I mean … you're not acting like yourself."

"And how would you know? We haven't been around each other for two years."

I don't say anything for a minute, then, "You can tell me, Aidan. No matter what it is, you can tell me."

"Lyssa," he sighs. "I seriously don't know what you're talking about."

"I stopped by your work," I say.

His face goes a little pale. "Why?"

"I was looking for you."

"Oh."

"The bartender," I say. "He told me you quit."

Aidan doesn't respond.

"He said you were moving away," I say.

I wait for him to explain, but instead he stares off into space, like he's deep in thought.

"And I talked to Glady. She doesn't know anything about a lock."

"That's right. Glady." Suddenly he strides across the kitchen and yanks open the drawer beside the stove. "Have you seen the tube of caulking?"

Caulking? What the hell? "The *what*?" I have no clue what he's talking about.

"For the windows," he says impatiently. "I told Glady I'd re-caulk the north-facing windows."

I shake my head. I'm at a complete loss.

"I'll check the basement," he says. "So if you hear a lot of banging and stuff around your window, it's just me." And then he leaves.

I feel Bingley brush against my legs. We both stand there listening to the tick of the kitty-cat clock.

Bingley meows.

I feel like crying.

my shift starts in forty-five minutes. I run to my room and grab my bag. Through the curtains I can see a shadowy figure. Aidan. Should I go over ... and do what? But then the hammering starts and makes the decision for me.

By the time I get to work, I'm so frozen I can barely feel my fingers and toes. The coffee shop is warm and toasty when I step inside the back door. This place feels more like home to me than Aidan's. Than anywhere.

"Hey, Molly," I say, coming into the kitchen.

"Hey," she says, reaching around me for the oven mitts hanging on the wall. "I just need to check that these muffins are done."

"Oh, sure." I move out of her way. "Anything I need to know?" I make it sound like I mean about what I have to do, but my fingers are crossed that she'll say something like Liam was in looking for me, or that he left me a message.

"Nope. All is well." She sticks the cake tester into the centre of one of the giant muffins. "Done," she announces.

"Great," I say in a flat voice.

"Once I flip these out, I'll wash up the pans."

"No," I say. "Don't worry about it. I'll do them. You go."

"You sure?"

"Yeah." The thought of trying to make small talk ...

Once I'm alone I pour myself a coffee, hoping it will help me get my head together. I doubt just one is going to do it.

I check for refills at the few tables that are occupied, put Molly's muffins in the case, grind some fresh coffee beans, top up the creamers, anything to keep me busy. Anything to keep all the crap in my head quiet.

I'm just about to individually wipe off the already spotless menus when Liam walks in the front door. It's all I can do not to grab on to something for support.

As he comes toward me, I study his face, searching for signs that he's angry. Because if he is, I'll know Rosalyn told him. But he stops and talks to some customers sitting by the fireplace.

And then he's at the counter, leaning on his elbows. His head drops forward. His hair follows and covers his eyes, so I still can't get a read on him.

"Hey, stranger." My words come out hoarse.

"Hey." His head stays down.

"I, uh ... I put your laptop and all your stuff in Janet's —"

"I got it. Thanks." He finally looks up, shoves his hair back. "Listen. I've got to talk to you."

He doesn't look angry. He looks ... wasted. Not the drunk kind of wasted, more like limp and lifeless, like everything has been sucked out of him.

"Okay ..."

"I know this isn't the time or place to tell you this," he says.

Whoosh goes my stomach.

"But I've got an exam later. I don't know when I'll get back in, and I wanted you to know."

I nod.

"Rosalyn ..." He pauses and licks his lips. "She came to see me yesterday."

I nod again, wanting to get whatever this is over with.

"She's pregnant."

Chapter 31

"Pregnant." I don't say it like a question or anything. I say it even, deadpan.

Liam's hands are resting on the counter. He flattens them out and pushes himself back, away from me. "Yeah."

My mind is blank as I stare at a lump of something next to the cash register. It's white-ish. Icing. I scrape it with my fingernail. It comes off in one piece, and I slide it to the edge until it falls to the floor.

All on its own, the word "How?" slips out of my mouth.

He makes a sound in the back of his throat. "The usual way, I guess."

"No, I ..." My face burns. "I meant more like, how can this be hap—" I stop myself. "Never mind."

"I know, Lyssa. I know what you meant."

We stand still, looking at each other until a guy comes up and asks for an espresso.

Liam shuffles off a few steps to the side.

I make the coffee as quickly as possible. I don't say a word except for the price. The guy pays. He doesn't leave a tip.

"So what now?" I whisper to Liam. "What are you going to do?"

"I dunno," he says, shaking his head. "I just ... I haven't figured that out yet."

"Oh. Yeah. Of course." I feel stupid for asking.

After a pause, he says, "My mom was a single mom. She did a great job and everything, but ..." — he stops and takes a deep breath — "I don't want that for my kid."

I nod and stare back down at the counter. There's water collecting in my eyes, and I don't want him to see.

"Well." I hear him sigh. "I should take off. My exam is ... though I don't know how I'm going to be able to —" He doesn't finish. His voice sounds so hopeless.

The urge to give him a hug, to comfort him, trumps whatever else I'm feeling, but the counter is between us, separating us. It's probably for the best.

Again we stand there looking at each other. I'm finding it hard to breathe. If he says something like "we can still be friends" ...

"I, uh, I'll see you around, okay?"

"Okay." Air leaks out between my lips. "Good luck."

He attempts a smile.

"On your exam," I add.

IT'S LATE IN THE day and quiet at the coffee shop. The time drags by. Each hour that passes feels like two. I've run out of chores to do, so I contemplate playing pick-up-sticks with the plastic stirrers. Thankfully, the milkman arrives at the back door. I sign for the order and lug the crates into the kitchen. I'm just finishing unloading all the milk and cream into the fridge when Erin shows up.

"Hey," she says, unwinding her scarf. Her cheeks are bright red. Snowflakes are melting into her hair. "It's colder than a polar bear's ass out there!"

I nod.

"Come on," she says, scowling. "That's funny stuff. What's wrong with you?"

"Nothing," I say, turning away and gathering up the empty crates.

She jumps around in front of me. "Liar."

I ignore her and focus on stacking the crates on top of each other.

"Tell me," she says, poking my shoulder.

When I still don't say anything, she pokes me again. "I'm gonna keep poking you till you tell me." Poke ... poke ... poke ...

"Oh for shit's sake!" I jerk my body away out of her reach. "Rosalyn's pregnant, okay? She's pregnant."

Erin's quiet for a minute. Then all she says is, "Hmph."

I was expecting more of a reaction. "That's it?"

She screws up her mouth. "Well …"

"Yeah … ?"

"I dunno. The first thing that comes to mind is, is she really even pregnant."

"*What?*"

"Yes, I'm suspicious by nature, and true, I don't like her, but I mean, look at the timing. Liam dumps her, begins to move on," she says as she nudges me in the side, "then suddenly, 'Oh, Liam, by the way, I'm preggo.' Kinda suspect, don't you think?"

"No." I shake my head. "No one would do that."

"Oh my God, woman! Have you ever watched TV? It's been done to death. Girl tells boy she's pregnant, girl and boy get back together, try to 'make a go' of it." She makes air quotes. "Then a few weeks later, girl trips and falls, or has some pains or bleeding, and conveniently *loses* the baby. And then girl is all, 'You can't leave me, I just lost your baby.'"

"Yeah, but that would never happen in real life!" I exclaim.

"You *are* from the sticks, aren't you? If I were Liam, I'd be getting her to pee on a stick right in front of me. And she'd bloody well better hope that thing lights up like a Christmas tree."

I raise my eyebrows. "I don't think it lights up. It's a plus sign, or two lines together, something like that."

"Whatever."

"You're out of your mind," I mutter.

"Hold that thought," she says and takes care of two girls approaching the counter. They order two medium coffees and two carrot muffins to go. Erin does the coffees, I warm the muffins, put them in a bag with napkins and a couple of pats of butter. After they pay and are on their way, Erin turns and says, "Okay." She crosses her arms. "We'll do it your way. Say she *is* pregnant. Is he sure it's his?"

Now it's my turn to be quiet for a minute. "Why would you say that?"

She shrugs and shoves the empty milk crates toward the back door.

I follow her. "No, really. Why would you say that. Do you know something?"

"No. But next to the old fake pregnancy, telling a guy he's the baby daddy when he's not is the oldest trick in the book." She spins around and squints at me. "Why. Do *you* know something?"

"No. I, uh … I'm just trying to figure out how your mind works." That part's true.

She takes a step closer, studies my face. "You do. You know something."

Am I that transparent? God, she should work for the CIA or something, be a professional interrogator. I think about denying it again, but can't find the energy. I tell her the whole thing. About the night I came to town, how I found Rosalyn at Kyle's, how Rosalyn turned out to be Liam's girlfriend …

"And you didn't tell him." There's no judgment in her voice.

I shake my head. "I couldn't. How do you tell someone something like that? And then, well, and then it was too late. I waited too long."

She nods. "My first job was cashier at a drugstore," she says. "The pharmacist was a sweet old guy. He called me Karen right from day one. I didn't correct him. It went on and on. Worked there for a year. As Karen." She sighs. "So I get it. It's sort of the same."

"Yeah." *Not really.*

While I count out my tips, Erin puts through a pot of hot water. A minute later she says, "Here," and she passes me a hot chocolate topped with a mountain of whipped cream. "I was so wrapped up in all my conspiracy theories, I forgot to say how much all this sucks, and ask how you were doing."

I look down at the mug in my hands, watch the whipped cream change shape as it melts into the hot chocolate. "We went to one movie," I say. "Shared a plate of stale biscuits."

She touches my shoulder. "Sometimes that's all it takes."

ERIN'S BOYFRIEND IS PICKING her up from work, so she lends me her scarf for the walk home. The snow is coming down heavily, but in the span of fifteen minutes, it turns to freezing rain, then to rain. I don't bother hurrying or flipping up my hood. What does it matter? I pass by the house with the stone wall — my thinking wall. I stop and sit, let the drops soak my hair and jacket.

I close my eyes and concentrate on making myself feel nothing, making myself not think. After a while it seems to be working. Or maybe I'm just turning numb from the cold.

My body starts to tremble. It's time to move on.

As I come down my street, I can see lights on at the house. That means Aidan must be home. I take a deep breath and brace myself for whatever's waiting for me.

I find him in the kitchen, seated at the table, a sandwich in front of him. I don't think he heard me come in. Unseen, I stand in the doorway.

Our kitchen table is square. One side butts up against the wall. There are three chairs, one for each of the other sides. Aidan is sitting in the middle chair, the one that's directly facing the wall. And he's just sitting there, staring intently ... at the wall.

"Hey," I call out and bustle over as if I've just arrived.

He answers, "Hey," but his eyes stay glued to the wall.

I slide out one of the chairs, angle it so it's sort of across from him, and with my coat and gloves still on, I sit. I don't say anything right away. I hope he'll initiate the conversation. He doesn't.

"You get everything done?"

He turns and looks at me.

"The windows," I say. "The caulking."

"Oh, that. Yes." Then he goes back to his in-depth study of the wall.

The kitty-cat clock ticks away.

"Aidan?"

"Yeah?"

"Do you think … I dunno, that maybe you might need someone to talk to?"

He turns again. "About what?"

"Um, like, stuff?"

"What kind of stuff?" He genuinely doesn't seem to have a clue what I mean.

"Stuff that's on your mind, that's bothering you, stuff you need help figuring out."

He smiles wide. "I've got you for that."

"But that's just it, Aidan. You don't really talk to me. Not about what you're thinking, or feeling, not the important things."

"Hmmm." He picks up a knife from the table, wipes one side then the other on a folded piece of paper towel. "I'll try to be more open."

"Good." *Sure you will.*

Kitty-cat keeps ticking.

"Aidan." I take another tack. "You never told me why you quit your job."

"It's no big deal."

"But people just don't quit their jobs out of the blue for no reason."

"Like I said, it's no big deal."

"Do you have a plan B? Aidan, please tell me you have a plan B."

He sighs. "I have a plan B."

I don't believe him. "And what about the moving thing? You didn't explain that either. Are you? Are you planning on moving?"

"Jesus. I didn't realize I was being held for questioning. Should I call my lawyer?"

I'm not letting him off the hook. "Where? Where are you moving?"

He cuts his sandwich in half, then into quarters. "Would you relax? It's all good."

"Okay." I sit back, fold my arms. "This is me being relaxed." And I wait.

"Fine." He rolls his eyes. "Originally, I was thinking of the waterfront. A guy I know has a wine bar down at Bishop's Landing. He offered me a job. Thought it would have been nice having a place close to work."

I absorb this new bit of information as I slowly pull off my wet gloves. I think about asking him about Glady's gate again, but figure it's better to deal with one thing at a time. And Glady is really old. It's possible she *did* forget.

He picks up a piece of sandwich. "Of course, I wanted you to move with me," he assures me.

"Um, sure ..." I notice he's talking in the past tense. "What did you mean by 'originally'?"

"Huh?"

"You said, *originally* you were thinking of the waterfront, you *wanted* me to move with you. What's changed?"

"Well, a lot's changed, hasn't it?" He takes a bite of his sandwich. "Lately anyway," he adds with his mouth full.

After a few seconds go by, it becomes obvious he's not going to reveal anything else. "That's not much of an answer, Aidan. You said you were going to be more open, remember?"

He chews and chews, and finally swallows. "I want to go home, Lyss. I want to go back to River John."

Not this again. I press my lips together, fiddle with my gloves, stretch out the fingers. "Then maybe you should, Aidan. If that's what will make you happy, do it."

"God, Lyss." He closes his eyes. "I've been waiting for you to say that."

It doesn't take me long to figure out he has misunderstood. "Oh. I'm not going with you, Aidan."

He frowns. "But I can't go without *you*."

"I'm staying here." I glance around the kitchen. "Well, not here, but in Halifax. I'm staying here and going to school." I look directly at him, carefully pronouncing each word.

The sandwich in his hand drops to the plate. "I don't get it. You said you'd never go back while Vince was around. Vince is gone. There's no reason for you to stay away anymore."

"My life is here now. I've got school, a job." I pause. "Friends."

"But you said …"

"I'm never going back there." I need to drill it into his head once and for all. "*Ever.*"

He clamps his jaw shut. His shoulders rise and fall with every breath.

It's like trying to reason with a child. "Aidan!"

"Okay," he says quietly.

"Is it?" I press.

"Yeah. I get it." He gets up and carries his dish to the sink.

"So … we're good?" I ask hesitantly.

Instead of answering he says, "Look, I gotta go out for a while."

"Where are you going? You're always disappearing."

"Down to that wine bar. Tell him I'll take the job, I guess."

I wasn't expecting that. "O-okay."

"He's got some books on wine I should pick up and start to study."

"I could help," I say, my attempt at an olive branch. "Quiz you or something."

"Super," he says tonelessly and walks out of the kitchen.

For a while I just sit there, my head held up by my hands. Once I hear the front door close, I get up, peel off my soaked jacket, and make my way to the bathroom. I turn the water on and let it run to get hot.

It's not until I'm undressed that I remember all the towels are in the dryer. I slip on my housecoat and run down to the basement. When I return, the bathroom is already thick with steam. Standing in front of the mirror I can barely make out my reflection as I pile my hair on top of my head — I'm just a ghost in the fog.

I step under the stream of water, let it hammer my neck and shoulders, run down my back. I keep the tap way over, arrow on red. My skin burns, but I don't care. If only the water could wash away the day, wipe everything clean and send it swirling down the drain.

I'm in there so long, the water temperature starts to cool. I've probably drained the tank. Finally I turn the tap off and fling back the shower curtain.

It takes a minute. I have to rub my eyes. There, staring back at me, drawn on the steamy mirror, is a giant happy face.

chapter 32

With the corner of the towel, I wipe my eyes again, as if somehow it will change what I'm looking at. It doesn't.

I wrap the towel tightly around me, tuck it in at the top, and open the bathroom door. "Aidan?" I call. Nothing. "Hello?"

I pad down the hall, leaving wet footprints on the hardwood floor. The driveway is empty, his phone and keys are gone from the hall table. It was him, though — it had to be. He must have come back for something.

I try not to make a big deal about it, try to ignore the creep factor, the idea that he came in while I was showering ... but that probably wouldn't have occurred to Aidan. He wouldn't have meant it that way.

A shudder ripples through my body as goosebumps burst out over my damp skin.

After I pull on a pair of sweatpants and a hoodie, I go to the kitchen and put some water on to boil for Mr. Noodles. The top on the pot begins to rattle. I dump in the package of noodles, add the seasoning packet, and set the timer.

I drain the broth off the noodles and start eating them out of the pot. They're undercooked, still a bit crunchy, just the way I like them. I reach for the noodle wrapper. A serving size is only half a package. I look deep into the pot for a second then eat the whole thing.

MY THUMB IS TIRED from channel-surfing. How can there be a hundred channels and nothing on?

I crawl into bed. The pillow feels extra hard, and when I lie on my side, my earlobe keeps bending the wrong way. I flip the pillow, punch it a couple of times, and roll onto my other side ... then back again. It's no use. No matter how tired I am, what position I contort myself into, sleep won't come. My head swirls with so many thoughts I can't even begin to sort them out. Liam, Rosalyn, Aidan, Marla, Mary, Glady ... the list is endless.

I strain my ears for noises in the house, any sign that Aidan's come home.

Because I have to, *have* to talk to him.

I look up at the lock. If Aidan has noticed, figured out I did it myself, he hasn't said so. Exhaustion finally triumphs, and I drift off.

Not before I check that the deadbolt is slid into place.

AIDAN'S NOWHERE TO BE found the next morning. Big surprise. I'm not sure he even sleeps anymore. Where the hell does he go?

Maybe this job at the waterfront is a sign. If he finds a new apartment, that would probably be a good time for me to go my own way, move onto campus like I planned. Hopefully the timing will work out, a room in residence will open up or someone will answer my message on the bulletin board. It's not like I'm abandoning him or anything — I can still be his sister, still help him and be supportive without sharing the same bathroom.

I promise myself I'll stop by the university and see if anything's changed, see if I've moved up the list.

Tucking a Ziploc of Frosted Mini-Wheats in my coat pocket, I head out for work. At the door, I pause and rummage around my bag for a pen and a scrap of paper. I eventually find a crumpled Thai menu. On the back I scribble, *Aidan. Hope you're around 2nite. Wanna talk. L.* The "wanna talk" is going to make him cringe, I know it, so I stick an "xo" at the bottom.

When I get to the coffee shop it's pretty full for late morning.

"It's a whole bunch of English Lit today," Erin says. "So a ton of people are writing." She turns on the dishwasher. "Don't worry, the place will be empty by twelve-thirty. Afternoon exams start at one."

Erin's right. By 12:25 the place is a ghost town, with only a half a dozen people scattered around, no one under the age of twenty-one.

I'm counting muffins in the display case when Liam schleps in looking like a flu victim. My heart stops. I checked the schedule just before I started. I know he isn't on it.

Erin nudges me on her way to do coffee refills. "No one told me *The Walking Dead* was shooting around here."

I can see his bloodshot eyes from across the room. I watch him as he comes toward me then around behind the counter. He's in the same clothes as yesterday and his hair is flat on one side, sticking up on the other.

"Hey," he says, reaching for a mug and pouring himself a cup.

"Hey," I say and slide him four sugar packs.

"Thanks. Um, you don't know if, uh, if Janet dropped the cheques off yet?" He keeps his head down, stirring his coffee, not making eye contact.

He's standing close enough I can feel the cold from outside coming off his jacket. "Oh, I, uh, don't … I didn't see any …" I look all around, make like I'm searching for anything that might be labelled "cheques."

"Janet usually has them here by … or most times anyway, uh, yeah, by noon."

"Maybe … Erin knows?"

"Maybe. Because, well, that's why I came … so …"

"Yeah, I didn't see your name on the … like when …" *Shit*. I take a deep breath and hold it, hoping nothing else stupid comes out.

He sighs and gives me a half smile. "Can you sit for a couple of minutes?"

I glance over at Erin. She crooks her finger, beckons for me to come. I do. Barely moving her lips, she says, "You're not here to be his shoulder to cry on."

"I know." I try not to sound offended.

"I only mean, well, it's obvious you still like him."

"No, I —"

"*Please.* I just had the pleasure of overhearing your last bit of witty repartee. The both of you. *Painful.*"

I follow him to our table by the fireplace. When he pulls out a chair for me I say, "Do you mind if we sit over here?" I move to a different table in front of the window.

"Yeah. Sure." He doesn't ask why.

We sit there facing each other.

"This. This feels a little weird, huh?" he says.

"It shouldn't," I say, not denying it. "I mean, we were friends before, we'll be friends again. We're friends now." I feel like choking over the word *friends*. At least I'm the one who said it, not him.

He seems to be thinking about this. Then he says, "I came by here last night. I was hoping you might be working."

"Oh?"

"But it was Zack and Molly."

"I kind of wanted someone to talk to." He shoots a look at Erin. "Instead I got you-know-who. She was here studying, and couldn't wait to give me advice."

I wince, realizing there's no way Erin would have kept her mouth shut. "Sorry. I told her. It kinda just came out …"

"It's okay," he says. "Everyone's going to know eventually, aren't they?"

"Um, yeah, I suppose so."

"You'll never guess what she said — Erin."

I shrug. *Oh God.*

"She said I should get a paternity test. Said I was almost a doctor and should have thought of that first thing. She practically bit my head off."

Oh God, oh God. I clear my throat. "But that's just Erin's MO. She kind of speaks her mind, doesn't waste time beating around the bush."

He rolls his eyes. "I'll say."

"Did she, uh," — I nervously scratch my neck — "say why she thought you should? Um, you know, get one."

"Said you can never be too careful about these sorts of things."

"Oh. So ... are you?"

He scrapes the stubble on his unshaven face. "Lynnie's a lot of things — hard on the head and all that — but I never thought of her as someone who'd cheat."

I can only nod as guilt burns in my stomach like lava.

"It's just ... it doesn't make for a very good start, you know?" he continues. "It basically says I don't trust her. And I mean, trust is the most important thing, right?"

He looks at me so innocently, all I want to do is throw up. I may not have cheated on him, but I lied to him. Is there really much difference?

After a moment he says, "Every time I try to picture me and Lynnie, picture our lives together ..." He pauses and shakes his head. "Tell me what to do, Lyssa. I need someone to tell me what to do."

There's a gob of thick phlegm that's stuck in my throat. I cough to dislodge it. "I can't tell you what to do, Liam."

He sighs, defeat written all over his face. "I know. I'm sorry. That wasn't fair."

"It's okay."

"No, it's not. I'm being a self-absorbed shit."

"Really, it's okay."

He gives me another half smile. "How are things with Aidan?"

"Oh, you know ..."

"No, what does that mean?"

"We're fine. He's fine," I lie. "Tell me how your exams went."

But he's not ready to let it go. "Have you asked him about his medication, suggested he see someone about his treatment? Maybe they can offer up another option that he'd be more open to."

"I'm working on it," I sigh.

"Well, I still think taking a break is a good idea. When I go home to P.E.I., you can stay at my place. I know it's only for a few days, but ..."

"Don't you live with three guys?"

"Yeah." He makes a face. "Never mind. They're totally disgusting."

"Liam." I smile, reach over, and pat his shoulder. "It's not your job to look after me."

He looks down at the table. "But I want to. And it might have been my job had things ..."

"I should get back to work." I slide my chair back and stand. I need this conversation to end.

"You know you can still come with me," he says.

"Where? To P.E.I.? Um ... isn't Rosalyn going with you?"

He shakes his head. "No, I told her I needed to — I needed some space."

My turn to shake my head. "No, Liam. That wouldn't help anything. Thanks, but no."

"Yeah." He sweeps his hair off his forehead. "You're right. I know you're right."

"I'll see you around, k?" I say softly.

He looks back down at the table and doesn't answer.

The burning lava in my stomach flares hotter as I slowly walk back to the kitchen. I have to tell him. If he never speaks to me again, well, I'll cross that bridge when I get to it. He has to know about Kyle, know that there's a fifty-fifty chance that the baby's not his.

I stop in front of the counter, focus my eyes on the blue thumbtack on the bulletin board, and take a few deep breaths. But when I finally get my courage up and turn around, Liam's gone.

Chapter 33

I'm still standing in the same spot staring at Liam's empty chair when Erin waves her fingers in front of my face.

"You okay?" she asks.

"I was going to tell him," I whisper.

She pats my back sympathetically.

Her touch causes a bunch of emotions to stir inside me. "I'm a horrible person!" I cry. "I totally suck!"

The few people scattered around the room look up.

"Simmer down, woman," Erin says, pushing me into the back office.

"But it's true. What was I thinking?" I drag my hands through my hair. "I should have just told him. I shouldn't have been such a coward."

"Look, I know. Woulda, coulda, shoulda, but it's —"

"Really?" I cut her off. "Great words of wisdom. Makes me feel loads better."

Erin folds her arms. "I'll choose to ignore your shitty attitude. What I was going to *say* was, it's not too late. They haven't sent out wedding invitations or anything. If you really want to tell him, find him and tell him."

I stare at the floor for a second, my mind racing. "Yeah, that's what I'll do. I'll go find him and tell him." I grab Erin's shoulder and squeeze. "Thanks."

"No problem." She smiles. "It's kinda what I do."

"Where do you think he went?" I say, yanking the ties on my apron. "Do you think he went home? Where should I look?"

"Good question," she says thoughtfully.

"You know him." My emotional roller coaster gears up again,

and my eyes fill with frustrated tears. "You must have *some* idea where he'd be."

"Just calm down. Let me think. Okay, he's finished exams, so he wouldn't be at school or the library ... he's a simple guy." She stops and looks at me. "I don't mean in the head, I mean like his wants and needs, you know?"

I nod.

"So if he's not at the university or here, he's either home, at Dalplex — he runs the indoor track — or ... maybe down at Taz Records."

"Taz Records?"

"Yeah. Picture the comic book store on *The Big Bang Theory*, but with records. He spends hours down there. He thinks he's a hipster."

I close my eyes and press my fingers against my temples. "I don't know where any of these places are."

"Relax." She reaches for a napkin and pulls a pen from her apron. "I'll draw you a map."

I stand behind her and watch.

"Worst-case scenario, you come back later tonight. He has closing shift."

"He does?" I shake my head. "I don't want to wait that long."

"No problemo. You go. I'll cover for you." She keeps drawing. "You're lucky I'm an expert map-maker."

When she's finished, she hands me the napkin. "Okay, so this is the coffee shop, here." She points. "Walk up to Robie —"

Just then the bell on the front door jingles. We both glance up from the drawing to see Rosalyn coming in. As she strides across the room, she keeps pausing and looking back over her shoulder. "Is Liam here?" she asks, her tone curt, her mouth barely moving.

"Darn. You just missed him," Erin answers, mock sad.

Rosalyn checks over her shoulder again. "I really need to find him," she says.

Erin tilts her head and squints at Rosalyn. "Hey ... you look different. Did you change your hair? Your makeup?"

"No ..." she says hesitantly.

"Because you're positively *glowing*!"

Rosalyn's eyes get really wide. She breathes in deeply through her nose, then turns to face me. "Did he say where he was going?"

I crumple up the napkin map and shove it into my pocket. "No. He didn't." I don't bother to hide the dislike I'm sure is plastered all over my face.

Rosalyn gives me a look like she doesn't believe me. "He said he was coming to pick up his cheque."

"They're not ready," I say. Our eyes lock, long enough that it becomes uncomfortable.

She drops her gaze first and begins to dig through her purse. I see her hands are shaking. "I'll take a medium Colombian to go, then," she says.

"Decaf, I presume?" Erin asks sweetly, punching it in on the register.

"Never mind," she snaps. "Cancel my order."

As she spins around to leave, the bell on the front door jingles again. When I see who it is, I let out a tiny gasp.

"Shit!" Rosalyn hisses.

Erin sidles up closer to me, sees the look on my face and Rosalyn's face, sees the guy coming in the door. "What? What did I miss?"

"Kyle," I say.

"*That's* Kyle?" She gives him a once-over. "Not bad."

Meanwhile Rosalyn's head is whipping around like the kid from *The Exorcist*. I know she's looking for an escape route.

"Rosalyn!" Kyle yells, stomping toward us.

"I *knew* it!" she yells back. "You're following me, aren't you?"

"Yes!"

She seems thrown that he openly admits it.

"I don't have much choice now, do I?" he continues. "You won't return my calls, answer my texts!"

"Then take the hint!"

The people sipping their coffees try to pretend they're not listening, but they totally are.

He glances over at me. We make eye contact. Red starts to creep up his neck. "Rosalyn, can we please go someplace private?"

"No," she says, stepping closer to the counter, closer to us.

She better not be thinking I'm gonna protect her.

"I know you're ..." Again Kyle's eyes meet mine before swinging back to Rosalyn. "*Pregnant*," he says in a whisper.

"Wow." Erin leans sideways till our heads are touching. "Did not see this one comin'."

Rosalyn puts her hands on her hips and faces Kyle. "Oh, and I suppose Heather told you that."

Kyle sticks his chin out. "Yeah. As a matter of fact she did."

"Christ, Kyle. Heather's been trying to get with you since frosh week. Don't be such an idiot."

He looks confused. "How is telling me you're pregnant going —" He puts up a hand and takes a deep breath. "It doesn't matter. You know that this baby is probably mine, Rosalyn."

Erin leans sideways again. "You just can't make this stuff up."

Rosalyn violently zips up her purse. "Stay away from me, Kyle."

He steps between the counter and Rosalyn, turning so his back is to me and Erin.

"Can we please go someplace that's not *here*, and talk this through?" He fights to keep his voice low, but we can still hear him.

She shakes her head. "Liam's the father of this baby."

"Really? Are you positive?" he says sarcastically. "Because I'm pretty sure you were having sex with me a hell of a lot more than with him."

"Liam's the father of this baby," she repeats firmly. Is she trying to convince Kyle or herself?

"Are you fuckin' kidding me? You have no way of knowing that." He tries to grab her arm.

Flinching, she shrieks, "Don't touch me!" And practically runs out the front door.

Kyle makes a move to follow her but then stops and comes back to the counter. He swallows. I see his Adam's apple bob up and down. "Where's Liam?" he asks me.

"I — I don't know," I stutter.

He curses under his breath and then leaves too.

The room is filled to the brim with an uneasy silence.

"Well, *that* was entertaining," Erin announces loudly. She picks up a coffee pot, goes out, and circulates around the tables as if nothing happened.

But something definitely did happen. Something that makes me realize I'm not the only one who's desperate to talk to Liam.

I snatch my coat off the hook, reach for my bag, and loop it over my head. "I'm outta here," I call to Erin. "I'll be as quick as I can."

"Good luck."

THE NEXT HOUR AND a half is a total bust. There's no answer at Liam's apartment, no sign of him at Dalplex or that Taz Records place either.

My feet are aching. It feels like I've walked a marathon.

I find myself sitting on my stone wall again. I wonder if the family inside ever notices me, notices there's some strange girl with a weird attachment to their front yard.

I rub my hands over my face. My gloves are wet, and I see traces of mascara on the leather tips. I must look like crap. Staring at the streaks of black, I fight to organize my thoughts.

My suspicion is that Rosalyn knows Kyle is going to tell Liam everything. Kyle seems pretty sure that this baby is his. Rosalyn is going to be hell-bent on getting to Liam first so she can spin it to her advantage. There's no way she can squirm her way out of this unscathed, though. I can't even *imagine* what her defence will be. Unfortunately, I can't ignore the fact that if she goes down, there's no doubt in my mind she's taking me with her. Why wouldn't she? I would.

A group of people come down the sidewalk carrying coffees from Tim's. I tuck my legs in closer to the wall, out of their way, and watch the parade of brown cups go by. Later tonight I'll go back to the coffee shop, get there before Liam's shift starts. I'll talk to him. Tell him everything. It'll be what it'll be. Maybe for once things will go my way. Maybe Rosalyn or Kyle won't get to him first. But if they do, it's not going to matter what I say. The shit will have already hit the fan.

An ugly thought creeps into my brain. In all my strategizing, it's like I've forgotten who's going to be most affected, most hurt by all this. Liam. It only reinforces the things I said to Erin earlier: I'm a coward, and I suck.

When I finally gather enough energy, I get up and head for home.

I DON'T REALIZE HOW tense and on edge I am until I round the corner and see the empty driveway. My muscles relax, my body goes limp. I know I left a note for Aidan saying I wanted to talk, but I'm just not sure I have it in me anymore. I unlock the door and go directly to the kitchen to put the kettle on for some tea. The light on the answering machine is flashing. I notice it right away — mainly because no one ever calls here. I listen to the recording.

"*Hi. This message is for Aidan Mackenzie. This is Dr. Evans's office calling. Aidan, you missed your last appointment. As this is the second time, Dr. Evans would like to reschedule as soon as possible. Could you call us back at 420-4408, extension 135, to set something up? Thanks.*"

The tea forgotten, I take the phone into the living room, curl up on the couch, and wait. The fact that I don't feel like facing Aidan at the moment doesn't matter anymore — I don't have much of a choice. Some time later I wake to the jingle of Aidan's keys being tossed on the hall table.

I sit up, wipe some drool from the corner of my mouth.

"Hey," he says.

The phone is still clutched in my hand. For a second I can't figure out why, then I remember the message. I jump right in. "Your doctor's office called," I say.

"Oh?" He shuffles through the mail and doesn't look up.

"Yeah. They say you missed some appointments."

His head stays down, seemingly enthralled by some grocery flyer.

"Well?" I demand.

"It's nothing," he says.

"Are you sure?"

Turning slowly, his face all tight, he says, "Yeah, I'm sure. Why? Were you and her talking about me? Was she telling you stuff?"

I frown. "Who? Your doctor?"

"Yeah."

"Of course not. It was a message on the machine."

"Because she doesn't know what she's talking about. These so-called therapists — I think most of them are just trying to work out their *own* problems."

I don't say anything.

He takes a deep breath. "I told you. There's nothing wrong with me. Never was."

"I don't buy that anymore, Aidan." Time to cut the crap. "You wouldn't be under a doctor's care if there wasn't anything wrong with you."

"I explained all that. I go through the motions, do what they want, tell them what they want to hear, whatever it takes to keep me out of that hospital."

I grind my teeth together and just stare at him.

"What?" he says. "You think I'm some kind of *psycho*?"

"Of course not!" I snap, a little too loudly.

He gives me a long, hard look. It makes me uncomfortable.

"You came into the bathroom when I was showering," I blurt out. "You drew a happy face on the mirror."

"So?" He shrugs. "I came back for my phone, saw the steam pouring out of the bathroom. It's obvious you don't pay the water bill, by the way. I thought it'd be funny." He slams the stack of mail onto the table. "Apparently I was *wrong*."

"It's not right," I say. "It's not ... appropriate."

"Oh my God, Lyssa. Do you hear yourself?"

I take some breaths through my nose. I so want to kick him. How dare he. How dare he make it like I'm the unreasonable one.

"You need to take a chill pill," he says, shaking his head.

"Funny you should say that, Aidan. I found some pills. I saw them on the bathroom floor."

He looks up at the ceiling, as if he's thinking hard. "Pills?"

"They were by the toilet, like maybe you flushed them, *a whole bunch of them*," I add pointedly, "and some spilled."

"I don't know what you're talking about. Maybe it was Marla. Maybe they were hers."

"Marla's?"

"She kept a lot of her stuff here."

I've never seen anything, but hearing Marla's name makes me think about Jodi, which makes me think about something Jodi said. "You told me you had to do whatever it took to keep you out of that hospital. Weren't you in the hospital on a voluntary basis? Couldn't you leave if you wanted?"

I can tell it throws him off that I know the hospital rules. "Vince was pressing charges. Said I tried to burn down the shed with him in it. I had to stay to get them dropped, finish the so-called treatment."

There's no way I'm stopping now. "Those pills I found were ..." I try to remember the actual name, but I can't. "They were antipsychotics. Is that what you're taking?"

"And who told you that?" he asks quietly, almost ominously. "Coffee shop boy?"

"You don't take antipsychotics for mood swings, Aidan."

"He just knows everything about everything, doesn't he?"

"It wasn't him," I lie.

"Don't listen to that guy, Lyss. He's trying to turn you against me."

I press my fingers to my temples. "Aidan, you're not keeping your appointments, not seeing your doctor. I don't think you're taking your pills. You wouldn't be acting like this if you were."

A darkness falls over his face like a veil. "You nosy bitch!" he shouts. "I don't have to explain anything to you!" Then he immediately clasps his head with both hands. "Sorry. That was too loud. I — I didn't mean to yell at you."

I feel a prickle of fear. I force myself to ignore it. He's my brother. "I'm only trying to help you, Aidan," I whisper.

"I know, I know, I know …" He sighs. "But really, I don't need any help."

Telling him I disagree isn't going to have any effect. I check my watch. *Shit!* Liam's closing shift starts in a half-hour. "I can't deal with this right now, Aidan."

"If you're worried because we're fighting, it's no big deal. It's what brothers and sisters do," he explains.

I'm out of things to say. I go over and put on my boots.

"You're going *out*?" he exclaims. "*Now*?"

"Yeah." I scoop up my jacket. "I have to do something."

"Have to do something?" He blocks my way. "Let me guess. It has to do with coffee shop boy."

Frustrated tears fill my eyes. I'm so tired I want to scream. I swear I can hear the second hand on my watch ticking away. *I gotta go.* When he doesn't move, I push him hard into the closet door.

"You're coming back though, right?" he asks, rubbing his elbow.

He sees me hesitate and reaches for the note on the hall table. "I read your message. You said you wanted to talk. We'll talk all you want. We'll figure this out."

I check my watch again. "I told you," I almost yell. "I can't deal with this right now."

"Please, Lyss." He sets the note back down. "You're all I have left."

For a moment I see the fourteen-year-old Aidan who crawled out of Vince's car the day they moved in. He stood by himself, hanging back behind the passenger door, looking shy and afraid.

My shoulders fall, my chest slightly caves. "I'll be home later."

"Are you just saying that?"

"Where else am I going to go?"

IT'S RAINING. THE DROPS freeze as soon as they hit the ground, making running pretty much impossible. I end up doing a mix of tiptoeing, jumping, and swerving — sort of like a never-ending game of hopscotch. The whole way, I keep my fingers on both hands crossed.

There's a patch of ice on the sidewalk right in front of the coffee shop. I almost wipe out but manage to save myself by slamming my entire body into the door. While pressed against the glass, I can see Liam putting some wood in the fireplace. He must have heard the noise. He looks up at me.

Even through the window, his face tells me that I'm too late.

chapteR 34

Liam immediately lowers his head, goes back to building the fire as if he hasn't seen me.

I lick my lips, smooth my hair, and step inside. The place is empty except for a few students over at the chalkboard reading the menu. I stand there for a minute, unsure what to do next. Do I hide behind the coat rack or wrap my arms around Liam and beg for forgiveness?

Molly's bussing a table near me. "Hope you didn't drop by for some friendly conversation." She jerks her head in Liam's direction. "Mr. Personality is in a craptastic mood."

"I can imagine," I breathe, not taking my eyes off him.

I tentatively make my way over and tap him on the shoulder. "Hey," I whisper.

"What are you doing here?" he says stiffly, keeping his back to me.

"I thought, um …" I let out a mouthful of air. "Maybe we should talk."

"We don't have anything to say." He drags a wooden match along one of the fireplace bricks. It breaks in half.

"Okay." I nod. "Correction. *I* have something to say." I watch him destroy three more matches before one finally ignites. He throws it onto the pile of wood.

"Don't want to hear it," he says, staring at the flame as it catches on some crumpled newspaper. "Whatever you have to say, I don't want to hear it."

I manoeuvre myself around so that I'm facing him. He refuses to meet my eyes. "Who told you?" I ask quietly.

"Lynnie, I mean, Rosalyn. *And* Kyle. Almost simultaneously."

He shakes his head. "It was quite the display. Rosalyn, clawing her way over Kyle to get her story out first. Guess *that* love affair is over," he says flatly.

"I'm so, so sorry."

Finally he looks at me. "Oh, that's good. That you're sorry. Now everything can go back to normal."

He's mocking me. I hate it, but I deserve it. "I don't expect that," I say. "I know that's not going to happen."

"I really liked you, you know? Really *trusted* you," he almost shouts.

My eyes fly to the students. Now they're at the counter. Molly's taking care of them. "I —"

But he cuts me off. "And you didn't think enough of me to tell me your douchebag boyfriend was screwing my girlfriend!"

His words are like a punch in my gut. He doesn't really believe that, does he? "That's not true. I think ... *everything* of you. You're the best, nicest person I know."

"Yeah, right." He grabs a rag hanging from his belt and starts wiping down a table.

"Liam," I plead. "You don't understand."

He stands up straight and squints at me. "Oh? I don't understand? Enlighten me, then."

"I — I wanted to tell you," I say, stumbling over my words. "I almost did, the other day."

"What a coincidence," he says, snapping his fingers. "Too bad someone beat you to it."

I press my lips together to stop them from wobbling. "I know I should have told you right away. But think about it. I hardly knew you back then. And God, Liam. I had, *have* so much of my own shit to deal with." Hot tears pool behind my eyes. "And Rosalyn said it was a one-time-only thing. She said she loved you."

"Well, if she said it, it must be true," he says sarcastically.

He's so mad and hurt. I sniff and blot my nose on the cuff of my jacket.

"And everyone deserves a second chance, right?" he adds.

"Um ..." I'm not sure how to answer. *I want a second chance ... but it feels like a trap.* "Maybe. Depends."

"How about you give Kyle a second chance?"

It *was* a trap. I look away.

"That's what I thought," he says, and returns to violently scrubbing the table.

I whip my head back. "You guys broke up," I defend desperately. "And then there didn't seem to be any point. Like, what would it have mattered?"

"Yeah, well, it sort of really *did* matter, didn't it?"

"Look! It's not my fault your girlfriend cheated on you!" I regret it as soon as I say it.

The conversation hits a wall, and we both stand like statues, staring at each other. Then Liam says, "I gotta get back to work."

WHEN I COME DOWN the street, the house is ablaze with lights. I was hoping Aidan wouldn't be home. I come to the realization I hope for that pretty much all the time now. My heart hurts, and all I want to do is crawl into bed. I touch my forehead. It feels hot, feverish, but it might just be from the good cry I had on the walk home.

I linger on the porch, sitting on the rail. Why am I crying over some guy I went on one and a half dates with? I went out with Kyle all through high school. Did I ever cry over him?

Not that I can remember.

I'm a mess.

The smell of beer greets me as soon as I open the door. Aidan is sitting on the couch attempting to build a pyramid with empty Moosehead bottles.

"Cans would work better," I say.

He grunts something nonsensical as he tries to place a bottle in the last top spot. It all comes crashing down. One lands on the brick hearth and smashes to pieces.

"Jesus Christ, Aidan."

He doesn't move.

I throw my coat and bag on the bench and go over to start gathering up the scattered bottles. It's when I pick up the first one that I notice a Post-it note stuck to the label. There's a happy face drawn on it. Crouching, I reach for the other bottles that rolled away. They all have identical Post-it notes.

"What the hell's this?" I hold one up.

He blinks like he's trying to focus, then he grins. "Face. Happy one."

"You're trashed," I say, and collect the rest of the empties and set them back on the coffee table. "I wasn't gone that long. How did you get so drunk?"

Shrugging, he says, "I drank a beer for every happy face I ever made you."

His words are all slurred together, no break in between. It reminds me so much of Vince that I actually feel sick inside.

"I only got to eight and then I couldn't remember any more, or I got too drunk. I forget," he rambles. "Do you want some spaghetti?"

"Aidan. Why?"

"Because I'm *starving*."

"No." I close my eyes for a second. "Why were you trying to remember all the happy faces? More importantly, why did you feel the need to drink a beer for each one?"

"Because you're so *pissed*."

"Um ... okay ..."

"I wanted to remind you of all the times happy faces made you — you know — happy. That's their job." He shakes his head sadly. "Last time they *sucked* at their job."

I sigh. "What?" My patience is non-existent.

"The mirror? Remember that?"

"Yeah, I remember."

"I just want you to be happy so you won't leave."

"Who says I'm leaving?"

"Jackie says."

Jackie? "Who's Jackie?"

"Said their roommate isn't leaving until February, but whatever, you can call if you want."

It takes me a minute to figure out what he's talking about. The bulletin board at King's. "Aidan. Did someone named Jackie call? When? When did she call?"

"I dunno. Last week. But you can't leave, you just can't."

"Last week? Was there a message? You never gave me any message."

"Didn't take one."

"Goddamnit, Aidan! You knew I was planning to move onto campus eventually!"

"My bad." His head rolls around like his neck can't support it.

"You little shit," I say through my teeth. I can't even look at him. "I think maybe you should just go to bed for now." I hook my arm under one of his and try to ease him up. Guess I should be thankful he's drunk or I might never have found out about Jackie.

"No." He pulls away. "We're supposed to talk. That's what your note —"

"I can't talk to you right now."

"I don't want you to be pissed at me, Lyss." He sticks out his bottom lip like a sulky toddler. "I *hate* when you're pissed at me."

At this moment I'll say anything to get him to go to bed. "I'm not pissed at you, Aidan."

He tilts his head back. "Good. Now some spaghetti."

"Spaghetti tomorrow." I sigh.

This time he lets me help him up and lead him down the hall to his room. He does a face plant onto his bed. I turn out the light and close his door.

My first inclination is to go back and clean up the mess in the living room. Halfway there I stop, backtrack to my room, and do my own face plant onto my bed. With my nose mashed against the bedding, I admit defeat. Liam was right. I'm in over my head — I can't do this myself. But what *do* I do? I can't knock him out and drag him to a doctor, I can't pour the pills down his throat. Though if I just give up and walk out on him, what does that say about me? I must be able to go somewhere for advice. A hospital, or a clinic. Yeah, tomorrow I'll look into that.

I pull myself up and go slide the lock into place.

I DReaM ONe BaD dream after another. I force myself to wake up, if only to make them stop.

As I lie there waiting for the rest of my body to come to life, something tugs at my brain. Is today the twelfth? I fling my arm over, grab the clock, and slide it toward me. *Shit!* I'm supposed to meet Mary. With everything that's been going on, I totally forgot. I wonder if it's too late to cancel. I check the clock again. No, she's probably already left.

I roll out of bed and get dressed. When I come into the kitchen Aidan's there. Any other time, there's no sign of him for days, now I can't get rid of him.

He's pouring a glass of Coke. A bottle of Advil sits on the counter.

"Hungover?" I ask loudly.

He winces at the sound of my voice. "No."

I smirk with satisfaction.

"Look, about last night," he says. "I was drunk. I'm not even sure what I said. I'm really sorry —"

"That's okay." I cut him off. I don't want to get into anything. I open and close the cupboard doors, making as much noise as I can. He cringes each time I move. I fill a Ziploc with Frosted Mini-Wheats and throw it in my bag. "I'm outta here."

"You've been working a lot," he comments.

"Yeah." But not today.

"If you wait until I jump in the shower, I can drive you. I'm going to the unemployment office."

"Unemployment? I thought you had a job at that wine place."

"Nah. The guy is a total asswipe. Thinks he knows everything. I can't work for someone like that."

I squeeze my eyes shut as the beginnings of a headache ping against my skull. I can't worry about this right now. "Oh. Uh, no thanks. I need the fresh air."

I'm about to leave the kitchen when he says, "Wait. You know, I meant to ask you something last night."

"What?"

"Well, I noticed on the call display that Mary called."

"Oh yeah?" I say casually.

"Yeah. A few days ago."

"You make a habit of going through the call display?"

He smiles, but it's not real. And he doesn't answer either.

"I don't know what to tell you, Aidan." And I start digging around in my bag to hide my face.

"Did you take the call? Talk to her?"

"No," I lie.

"And she didn't leave a message?"

"I guess not."

He frowns. "That's weird. Do you think it was about the autopsy or something?"

"I've no idea." I pocket two Advil from the bottle and fling my bag over my shoulder. "I'm sure she'll call back if it's important."

I pass by the phone, then I stop, stare at it for a second, and pick up the receiver. I press the CID button until I find what I'm looking for, "Jackie Nelson." I tear off a corner of the cable bill and jot down the phone number. I leave without saying goodbye.

THE WIND IS RUTHLESS. It whips up the fresh snow that fell overnight, causing mini whiteouts. It feels like I'm walking through a blizzard even though it's not even snowing.

It takes all my willpower not to veer off course toward the coffee shop. Is Liam working today? Who am I kidding? He probably wouldn't talk to me anyhow.

I pull out a scrap of paper from my bag. There's an address scribbled on it — where Mary wants to meet me, some bakery café place called The Gingerbread Haus. I've never been, or even heard of it, which is fine by me. I'd rather go there, someplace unknown, than *my* coffee shop. The thought of trying to introduce Mary ... "*Oh, this is Mary, my mom's best friend, who was sleeping with Vince, my stepfather, while my mom was lying in bed dying of cancer. Did I mention the part about her being my mom's best friend?*"

As expected, the whole place smells like freshly baked gingerbread. Mary is already there, seated at a table in the far corner reading a newspaper. I take a deep breath and walk across the room to join her.

"Hello, Mary," I say.

She glances up and smiles a thin smile. "Hello, Alyssa." She motions with her hand toward the other chair. "You look well."

I look like hell.

She looks older than I remember. I guess living with Vince will do that to you. "Yeah, uh, you look ... well yourself." I can lie too ... I shrug my coat off, drape it over the back of the chair, and sit down.

"I ordered coffee and a piece of cake," she says. "Do you want something?"

My stomach rumbles. It was too windy, so I couldn't eat my Mini-Wheats. "No thanks."

She arches one eyebrow. "I can tell you're *thrilled* to be here," she says.

"Could we maybe just get on with it?"

Just then the waitress drops off Mary's order. "Nothing for me," I say as she opens her mouth to ask.

I impatiently wiggle my foot as I watch Mary add cream and sugar to her coffee then proceed to cut her cake into nine equal bite-size pieces.

"Look, Mary," I sigh. "If this is about Aidan getting everything in the will, you could have just told me that over the phone. And news flash, I don't care. He can have it all."

She slowly sets down her knife. "This has nothing to do with any *will*. And trust me, you might want to lose the attitude and get comfy, because what I have to tell you is going to take a long time."

chapter 35

I can't believe she's sucked me in, made me curious. I hope it doesn't show. "Okay then, let's do this."

Mary studies me over the rim of her coffee cup. "God, you look so much like your mother." She takes another sip before she sets it down. "That's as far as the similarities go though, isn't it?"

I shrug, wondering what this has to do with anything.

"You're your father through and through."

It doesn't sound like a compliment. "Thank you," I say.

She goes back to studying me, then puts on this forlorn sort of look. "I wish you had been kinder to your mother."

My eyebrows shoot up. "Like you were?"

She leans across the table and practically hisses, "I don't think you should be sitting there all holier-than-thou."

"I'm not."

"You were horrible to your mother. Just horrible. Do you think she didn't know?"

"Know what?"

"That you wished it was her who had died in that car accident instead of your father."

"That's not true," I say a bit too quickly.

She sits back in her chair, smiles a fake smile as the waitress tops up her coffee. Then she adds a splash of cream and stirs, leans back in. "You pushed her away. It broke her heart."

I want to deny it. But instead I just stare down at my hands in my lap.

"Do you have any idea what it was like for her knowing you couldn't forgive her for being the one who survived?"

This time it's me who leans in. "The only thing I couldn't forgive her for was bringing Vince into our house."

"You," she says, pointing her spoon at me, "are wrong about Vince."

I clench my hands into fists until my nails dig into my skin. "Is this what you wanted to talk to me about?"

"No," she says. "Seeing you ... brought back some memories, that's all."

"So is the walk down memory lane over?"

She narrows her eyes. "If I were you, I'd be a little nicer to me."

"Oh really. And why is that?" *I can't wait to hear this.*

"Because if it weren't for me" — she bends sideways and rummages around in her big purse hanging off the corner of her chair — "God knows if and when you'd have ever come across these." She places a small stack of flat, magazine-size books on the table.

I recognize them immediately. "My yearbooks?"

She nods. "Three junior high and one high school, grade ten. They were in a duffle bag, shoved under the eaves in your attic."

I frown. "The attic?"

She nods again. "I was looking for boxes. I know you and Aidan haven't decided what to do with the house yet, but I thought at least I'd send some of Vince's clothes off to the Salvation Army."

I pull the books toward me, open the one on top and start turning pages. It takes me a second to figure out what I'm seeing. When I do, my heart jams up into my throat. Every single picture of me is cut out — teams, student government, class, committees. Some perfect squares, others full body or head silhouettes. I go through one book then the next. All the pictures. Gone.

"I'm assuming you didn't do that yourself," Mary says dryly.

I say, "No," but it comes out silent.

"There were newspapers in the bag too."

"Newspapers?"

"The local paper. From when you and Caroline did that Locks of Love, Stuff a Bus, when your soccer team won provincials, things like that. Every picture was cut out. Well, every picture of *you*," she clarifies.

There's a lightness in my head, in my whole body, like I might float away any second. "I ... I ... don't ..."

"It has to be Aidan," she whispers.

I sit there trying to get my head around it, trying to get it to make sense. But I can't. It doesn't.

"Why would you say that?" I ask.

She gives me a confused look. "Well, who else could it be?"

I can only stare back at her.

"Seriously, Alyssa. Who?"

She becomes annoyed by my silence. "Your mother? Vince? The family of squirrels living in the attic?"

Sighing, I drag both hands down my face, pulling on my skin. "But why? Why would he do something like that?"

"I don't know, but I've seen enough *CSI*, *Criminal Minds*, *Law and Order* to know there's something wrong here."

"Something wrong with *him*, you mean."

She squishes a tiny piece of gingerbread with her fork. I watch the cake ooze up between the tines. "I don't know Aidan, not really." She looks up at me. "You lived with him, live with him now. What's he like? What's he like when he's around you?"

My eyes dart around the room, avoiding hers. She's the last person I see myself confiding in.

"Because you're the one who's closest to him," she presses, as if she senses I'm holding back. "You know him best ..."

"Yeah, well, it's not really like that," I admit.

"Oh?" She tilts her head. "What's it like, then?"

"Um ... " Should I tell her the truth? Protecting him isn't going to do him any good. "He's not the Aidan I used to know. He's different, acts different. He suffers from ... something. Some kind of mental illness, I think." There, I said it. But I don't feel the need to share anything more.

She rubs some red lipstick prints off the edge of her cup with her thumb. "Those yearbooks," she says. "You realize he would have had to have done that years ago, back when he was still living at home."

My imagination conjures up a vision of Aidan in a darkened room, hunched over a desk. A lamp shines a pool of light onto his hands. He's holding scissors. And he cuts, and cuts, and cuts. A shudder ripples through me as I gaze blindly out the window over Mary's shoulder. My ears feel clogged, and all the noises around me sound muffled.

"You two were inseparable when you were younger," she says. "Did you ever notice anything? Anything out of the ordinary?"

I shake my head. Quick, tiny shakes.

She gives me a doubtful look.

"I mean, I'd have to think about it," I say. "But no, I — I don't think so." My voice doesn't sound very confident.

We sit back in our chairs as the waitress stops by to check on us. Mary asks for some more cream. Then the waitress turns to me. "Sure I can't get you anything?"

"For God's sake. Would you just order something?" Mary says.

The thought of putting anything in my stomach makes me physically ill, but I look up and say, "I'll have a tea, I guess."

At that moment someone at the table behind us slides their chair out and bumps into our waitress, who's carrying a tray of dirty plates. The dishes crash onto the tile floor. Everyone except Mary and me breaks into applause.

They're so loud I want to stand and scream, "Shut the hell up!" But like a robot, the inner waitress in me forces me to go over, kneel down, and help her pick up the broken plates.

"Thanks," the waitress whispers. "They don't pay me enough for this shit."

I don't have it in me to even fake a smile. I slide all I've gathered onto her tray and slip back into my chair.

"Mary?" I say.

"Yes?"

"What would you consider to be 'out of the ordinary'?"

"I've no clue. And like I said, I never really knew Aidan. Though I have to say, my first impression of him was that of a strange sort of kid."

Our waitress returns and sets my tea and Mary's cream on the table.

Once she's gone I say, "But look at his childhood. Dead mother, Vince for a father, uprooted from his home. I'd be a strange sort of kid too."

"Maybe." She sighs and rips open a packet of Equal. I can tell she's thinking. "Do you know anything about Aidan's mother?" she asks.

"No. He never talked about her."

"Never?"

"No. All I know is she died in a house fire when he was thirteen. Mom told me that."

"I don't know anything either. Except that her name was Claudia. That's about it. The only time Vince ever mentioned her was when he was drinking, and that was seemingly only to badmouth her."

"Badmouth her? She's *dead*."

Mary rolls her eyes. "Trust me. There was no love lost there. He'd go on and on about Claudia being his downfall, all *this* — whatever *this* means — was her fault, and that Aidan was just like her. Nothing he said really made any sense. It was just drunken gibberish."

I tug on my tea bag string, dunk it over and over. My eyes fall on the yearbooks. "You're sure they were *hidden*."

She nods. "Oh yes."

My eyes are still on the books. "Who do you think hid them?"

She follows my gaze and frowns. "I never really thought about it. I just assumed it was Aidan."

"If it was Vince, he would have had to have known there was something wrong with Aidan, would have known for a long time."

A troubled look crosses Mary's face. "But if it was Vince, wouldn't he have just gotten rid of them?"

"Yeah ... yeah, I guess so."

"Not to say Vince didn't know there was something wrong with Aidan." She goes silent. Again I can tell she's thinking. "You know, Alyssa. A few days before Vince passed, he was desperate to get a hold of you."

"Why?"

"He wouldn't say. He called you several times, though, even left messages."

"At Aidan's?"

She nods.

"But how did he know I was there? I didn't tell anybody except Caroline. And I know she wouldn't tell him."

"I don't know. I'm guessing you didn't get any messages?"

"No." Then I remember what Aidan said in the kitchen this morning.

"... I noticed on the call display that Mary called."

"You make a habit of going through the call display?"

He never did answer.

"Aidan would have deleted them," I say.

She presses her lips into a straight line. "Yes. Vince probably knew there was a good chance of that. Perhaps he hoped that one time he'd luck out and you'd answer, or maybe you'd get to the message first."

"Do you know what the message was?"

"No." She shakes her head. "When he was drunk, he wouldn't shut up. Nothing made sense, mind you. And when he was sober, it was like getting water from a stone. I will tell you, it must have been important. Twice I found him stumbling out to the truck, wasted out of his mind, bound and determined he was going to drive to Halifax. I finally had to hide his keys."

"So you have no idea what it was all about."

"No. And now, we never will." Sniffing, she reaches for a napkin and dabs her nose. I avert my eyes until she's pulled herself back together. She smiles weakly and says, "It's kind of like the blind leading the blind here, isn't it?"

Re-stacking the yearbooks, I slide them back to her using only two fingers, as if they're poisonous, as if I'm afraid of them.

"I wonder where they are ... all the cut-out stuff."

She blows out a mouthful of air. "I don't even want to think about it."

Again my imagination kicks in. I watch TV too. Collages, shrines, hidden in some room, or some closet, behind a wall panel ... in an old shed ...

A knot tightens in my stomach. "What do you think it means?" I ask softly.

Mary takes her time answering. "Well, if I had to guess, I'd say that either Aidan really, really loves you ..." — she pauses and motions with her finger for me to come closer — "or really, really hates you."

chapter 36

I'm back at the place I always seem to go to when my life goes to hell. My stone wall feels extra cold today. The damp is seeping through my jeans. I glance down at my hands. They're shaking.

I have only a vague recollection of how I got here. At some point Mary and I must have said goodbye. Did I thank her? Thank her for what? Heaping more shit on me? All I really remember is feeling claustrophobic and needing to get out of that bakery.

I rest my elbows on my knees. My pulse throbs in my ears. I'm sure it's racing twice as fast as it should.

What just happened? I force myself to go over the conversation with Mary, but it's all jumbled inside my brain. The only thing I can focus on is, "He either really, really loves you ... or really, really hates you."

So which is it? Love or hate?

Again I think back to that first time I saw Aidan, standing in our yard by the car — all lanky and awkward. In the beginning I treated him like shit, didn't want him anywhere near me. Maybe he never forgot, never got over it.

No. I shake my head. It can't be that. My meanness didn't last. We became best friends. I was closer to him than anyone. And I told him that all the time — how much I needed him, how he was the only one I could count on, the only one I trusted.

I hear the echo of Mary's words, *"really, really loves you ..."* So ... could he have gotten things all twisted up? Goosebumps break out all over me that have nothing to do with the cold. "I'd rather he really, really hated me," I say out loud.

I jump off the wall and start pacing up and down the sidewalk, shaking my hands at the wrists like a rag doll. "Okay," I breathe. "What's my plan? I need a plan." I try to calm myself, but it's not working. I feel the panic rising inside, about to strangle me.

Just then, I see a guy coming up the street, keys dangling from his fingers. I hop back up onto the wall to get out of his way. He gets into a car parked at the curb in front of me. As he pulls away, the car sticks on some ice. He guns it and proceeds to spray me from the knees down in chunky, wet slush. I stare at the darkness spreading up my legs. My nose begins to tingle. I won't let myself cry.

When I finally look up from my drenched pants I notice a pay phone, down the block on the other corner in front of a sub shop. "A friendly voice," I whisper.

As I hurry to the crosswalk, I dig for my change purse, which is always crammed with coins thanks to my share of tips. At the phone I dial the operator then feed some money into the slot.

It rings and rings, then a recorded voice says, *"I'm sorry, the person you are trying to reach ..."* Caroline's cell. I disconnect.

Again I feed in more money, try another number. This time someone picks up.

"Hi," I say. "Is Caroline there?"

"No, she's — wait, is this Alyssa?"

"Yeah, it's me. Hi, Mrs. Dobson."

"Oh, she'll be so sorry she missed you. She's away in the States on a ski trip with the Andersons. You know, the family she works for?"

"Right." I feel my shoulders droop.

"She's looking after their kids," Mrs. Dobson adds. "They'll be home Christmas Eve day."

"Right," I say again.

"How are you doing, honey? Sorry to hear about Vince."

"Yeah, uh, thanks."

"Is there a message?"

"No ... I'll try her ... after Christmas, I guess."

"Okay, sweetie. Take care. I'll tell her you called."

"Thanks," I say.
"And Alyssa?"
"Yes?"
"Since I won't see you, Merry Christmas from the Dobson family."
I try to say Merry Christmas back, but the words catch in my throat and come out all garbled.

I hang up the phone, shuffle sideways, and sit on the ledge of the sub shop window. The wind whips some sandwich wrappers, straws, and other assorted garbage in and around my feet. A piece of foil sticks to the toe of my boot. When I reach down and pull it off, it leaves behind a glob of some kind of white sauce. I feel something in me snap. There's a trash can less than a metre away. "Goddamn lazy, shithead assholes!" shoots from my mouth as I scoop up all the mess and throw it in the can. When I finish, I realize there's an icy wetness coating my cheeks. I'm crying. And I didn't even notice.

I look longingly back up the street. Part of me wants to return to my spot on the stone wall until I get myself together and work everything out, but I'm freezing, I need to keep moving. I start walking and eventually pass a caramel-coloured house with a turret. It looks familiar. It dawns on me that I'm close to Liam's. Did I subconsciously head this way?

It doesn't matter if I did or didn't. All I know is I have to see him. He's really the only one I can talk to about all this. There's a chance he'll slam the door in my face, but I'm going to try anyway.

It doesn't take me long to find his building. I press the button by his name and wait. The buzzer sounds without anyone asking who's there, then there's a click and I pull on the handle.

Music vibrates through the entire hallway. Every few seconds I hear a yelp or shout of some kind. The unmistakable smell of marijuana hangs in the air. I marvel over the fact that it's only mid-afternoon and make my way toward Liam's apartment, all the while hoping I'm wrong, but as I get closer, I know I'm not — it's all coming from behind his door.

I stand there for a minute, contemplating turning around and leaving. *To go where, though?* Squaring my shoulders, I knock loudly, one, two, three times. I raise my hand for a fourth when the door swings open. A cluster of guys fill the doorway. One has a hand on the top edge of the door frame, seemingly to hold him up.

"Hey," he says.

I take in his bright blue T-shirt with "Nova Scotia Drinking Team" emblazoned in yellow across the front. "Um, is Liam here?"

"Nope. Will I do?" He jams his thumb into his chest.

"Uh, do you know when he might —"

"He went to P.E.I.!" shouts some guy from the back, jumping up and down like he's on a pogo stick.

"Oh." I don't bother to hide my disappointment. It's not like anyone would pick up on it.

The jumper moves to the front of the group. That's when I see he actually *is* on a pogo stick. He's also wearing a T-shirt that says "Drink. Refill. Repeat." "Can you believe he left early and missed the party?"

"Loser!" someone calls out.

"I know, right?" the jumper answers. "It's the end of exams, man!" Then he bounces away.

"Since you're kind of hot," the guy hanging off the door says, "you can wait for him if you want."

"Won't he be gone for, like ... a few days ... ?" I say.

"Uh-huh." He nods. I think he's trying to wink at me, but he's so buzzed, it looks more like he's having a spasm.

"Thanks, I'll, um, catch him later." As I head back down the hall I hear someone yell, "Dude! Use a coaster!"

Holding on to the stair rail, I slump down onto the bottom step. *What now?* I press my forehead against the metal railing and take a couple of deep breaths.

The only thing I know for sure is, if I wasn't afraid of Aidan before, I sure as hell am now. I have to get away from him. It feels like I'm betraying him, but I can't help it. So there's just one option. I'm going to have to stay in a hotel, at least till I can figure something out. I'll burn through everything I've saved in no time, probably have to start taking from my student loan. *Shit.*

My feet start toward the coffee shop. The cold makes my face sting, and I zip my jacket up to my chin, hold my gloved hands over my ears.

A blast of coffee-scented heat hits me when I pull open the service door. It's a delicious feeling, and it makes me shiver as I begin to thaw. I hang my coat on the hook, go over and stare at the schedule.

"What are you doing here?" Erin asks, coming around behind the counter. "You don't work today."

I have nowhere else to go. "I wanted to see when I was on next."

She gets closer. "Your eyes are red."

"The wind."

"Right, the wind." She points to a stool. "Sit. I'll make you a hot chocolate." Then she calls out to Molly, who's clearing a table by the fireplace. When Molly comes over with a tray of dirty dishes, Erin takes the tray, hands her a coffee pot, and says, "Trade ya. Can you check on table five for me? We're low on cranberry muffins, so I'm going to mix up a batch."

Molly glances over at me, then back at Erin. "Sure. No problem."

Erin dumps some chocolate powder into a mug, adds hot water, and stirs. She tops it with her signature obscene mountain of whipped cream and sets it in front of me. "Down the hatch," she says.

I poke at the cream with my finger. "Can you pass me the phone book? It has the Yellow Pages, right?"

"Yup." She takes it from a drawer and slaps it on the counter.

"Thanks." I flip it open, turn to H.

She bends at the waist so that she's practically lying across the counter, her nose all crinkled up. "Why are you looking up hotels?"

"I, uh ..." *What should I say?* I lower my head, letting my hair cover my face. "I need a place to stay."

"Come stay with me," she says immediately. "Problem solved."

I look up. "That's really nice of you, but —"

Waving a hand in the air, she takes out her cellphone and dials.

"Yo. Me. We're having a guest for a bit so I need you to get all your shit out of the living room." Pause. "Lyssa." Pause. "Yeah, and clean the bathroom too." Pause. "No, I'm off at six." Pause. "Um ... check the freezer." Pause. "K. Love ya." Then she hangs up.

"Listen," I say. "This is way too —"

"Stop. Ever since Josh finished exams he's been horizontal on that couch drinking beer and watching Netflix." She shakes her head and mutters, "Party's over, big boy."

I sit quietly for a moment, feeling not so completely alone anymore, and watch her break eggs into a bowl. "Thanks," I say.

"No worries ... Now, I should warn you, he's offered to make dinner, so I hope you like chicken strips and fries." She rolls her eyes. "It's the only thing in his repertoire."

"I love chicken strips and fries." My voice sounds all gravelly because I'm about to cry again.

She gives me a long look, pulls her phone out again and dials. "Hey. Forgot something. Liquor store." Pause. "I dunno. An assortment." Pause. "Yeah, that'd be good. Maybe some Baileys for coffee after your gourmet feast." Pause. "K. And don't forget the bathroom."

Their conversation makes me smile.

Erin leans over closer to me and says in a low voice, "You said you need a place to stay ..." She waits a bit, like maybe she thinks I'll fill in the rest of the sentence. When I don't, she continues, "So I assume you can't go home ..."

I still don't say anything.

"Okay." She nods. "What about all your stuff?"

"Yeah." I tug on my bottom lip. "I'll have to figure that out."

"You can borrow whatever you need from me for now. I'll get Josh to take you to your place when you're ready."

I love her for not asking for any kind of explanation.

"Actually ..." I check my watch. "Can you pass me the phone?"

She passes it to me and I dial the house. No answer. I think for a minute, and then I flick through the phone book again. "Collins, Collins ..." I punch in the number. "Hi, Glady? It's me, Lyssa." I go on to ask her if she knows if Aidan's home. I tell her I tried calling downstairs, but there was a busy signal. She says she hasn't seen him all day and that the car's gone. I make up some story about how Bingley must have knocked the phone off the hook. I thank her and hang up.

I think some more then dial Aidan's cell number. It rings and rings. Perspiration blisters along my hair line. He finally answers. "Hello?"

"H-hey," I stutter. "It's just me."

"Hey," he says. "What's up?"

"Nothing. Is this a bad time? You're not driving, are you?" I try to make myself sound normal.

"No. I'm in a parking lot."

I grab on to that. "Oh? Where?"

"Down by the Split Crow. I'm meeting a guy I used to work with."

"Sounds like fun," I say, full of fake enthusiasm.

"You could come join us. Are you still at work?"

I clear my throat. "Yeah, uh, that's why I'm calling." My eyes flit around the room and land on Molly. "Molly's not feeling well, so I'm going to stay and work for her. I wanted to let you know so you wouldn't worry, like if you got home before me."

He's quiet for a second. "Didn't you just work all day?"

"Yeah."

"They can't make you work all those hours if you don't want to."

"It's fine, I need the money."

I hear him sigh. "Okay then. I probably won't make it home before you. Brandon likes to party."

As soon as I hang up, I let out a huge breath. *Okay, so at least I know where he is.*

Erin is looking at me strangely. Who could blame her? I still can't believe she doesn't demand to know what the hell's going on. "My brother's not home," I say. "I'll whip over, get everything I need, then I don't have to worry about it later." I begin to slide off the stool, but she grabs my arm.

"Now, I'm not one who likes to get involved in other people's business." My mouth drops open. She doesn't notice, or pretends not to. "But I watched you on the phone when you were talking to him. I heard it in your voice. You sounded scared."

"No." I shake my head. "We haven't been getting along lately, that's all." I can't get into this with her. Not right now.

She raises her eyebrows.

"I really need my stuff," I explain. "My last cheque, my wallet with my bank card and all my ID. I know for sure Aidan's not home. The place is empty. So, in-out. Piece of cake."

"I'll call Josh." She reaches for her phone.

"No. It's fine. I'll leave right now. And like I said, Aidan's not home. Plus Glady will be there, upstairs. She owns the house."

Erin frowns.

"You're going to be here for at least a few more hours," I point out. "I'll go do my thing. And actually, that will give me time to track down this girl who's looking for a roommate. Maybe she'll want to meet up. It's all good." Just hearing myself say my plan out loud makes me feel better.

"Okay," she sighs. "But if you get there and your brother's come home, turn back. Josh will take you over later."

"Deal," I say, slipping on my coat. "Maybe jot down your address, in case I get tied up, like if this girl wants me to come see the apartment or something. I don't want you to have to wait for me."

She writes on her order pad, rips it off, and hands it to me, but there's still worry all over her face. "I put down my home and cell number in case you need me."

"Thanks." I tuck it my pocket. "Oh. And I like plum sauce with my strips and fries," I say lightly.

"Redneck," she snorts.

As I head up the street, I check my watch again — tons of time. Plus I only need about ten minutes. Everything I own fits in one bag.

Yeah, ten minutes should be *more* than enough time.

CHapteR 37

I hover on the sidewalk, a few doors up from the house. The driveway is empty — no sign of Aidan's car. Still I hang back.

Stop being an idiot. He's not in there.

As I get closer I see Glady coming around the side yard. She waves. I wave back.

"Hi, dear," she says.

"Hi." I notice she's holding a small suitcase. My stomach does a little dip. She's obviously on her way out. "Are you going somewhere?"

"My sister-in-law just had hip surgery. I'm going to help her out until she's back on her feet."

"Oh. That sounds ... fun."

"Now, when I told Aidan, I forgot to let him know that Scotia Fuels is coming to clean the furnace on Friday. Someone needs to be here, okay?"

"Sure," I lie.

A cab pulls up beside us. I open the door for her, hold her suitcase while she gets in. "I hope your sister-in-law gets better soon."

"You and me both," she says, rolling her eyes. "See you in a few days."

Smiling weakly, I shut the door. There's a good chance this is the last time I'll ever see her.

I dig out my key and unlock the front door. The house seems extra quiet. It feels as though I'm breaking and entering. Leaving my jacket on, I head directly to my room.

My hands are sweating. I wipe them on the back of my jeans, grab my wallet and paycheque off the dresser, and stuff them into my bag.

Not wasting any time, I haul my duffle bag from under the bed, scoop everything out of the drawers, and shove it all inside. I can hear my heart thumping the whole time. I check the closet. Only my housecoat, a hoodie, and an extra pair of sneakers. I jam them in the bag. My textbooks are in a recyclable tote on the desk. I quickly loop the handles around my wrist, take one last look around, and lug my stuff down the hall, stopping at the bathroom to snatch my toothbrush and makeup bag.

Kitchen, dining room, living room — as I go by, I quickly scan them for anything that's mine. Nothing. It's as if I was never here.

I pause at the hall table. My course calendar. I forgot it. I scribbled down all my student loan information, a bunch of phone numbers, my temporary student ID number. I need it. *Shit.* Dropping everything, I rush back to my room, trying to visualize the last place I saw it.

It's nowhere in sight. Then I remember. I was reading it in bed. Lying on my stomach, I inch my way under the box spring. There it is, wedged down behind the headboard. I stretch my arm out as far as it can go. My head's on its side, and a droplet of sweat finds its way into my eye. It stings like crazy. Finally I'm able to get a hold of a corner of the cover. As I pull it toward me, I feel something on my leg. My whole body freezes, paralyzed.

"Hsssss."

"Damn it, Bingley!" I slide myself out. "You, I am not going to miss!"

The calendar is coated in the dust bunnies that live under my bed. I sweep them off, my fingers feeling the jagged slashes courtesy of Bingley. I know I should get out of there as fast as possible, but I can't help glancing over at Bingley, at his tiny little paws, and then back to the calendar, the deep, widely spaced gashes. "There's no way ..." I whisper.

A squeaking noise from behind makes me flinch and jerk my head around. The door is swinging closed. Then I hear it, the sound of metal scraping on metal. The deadbolt.

I jump from the bed, run to the door, try to open it. It won't.

"Aidan!" I pound with my fist. "Is that you?"

Silence.

With both hands, I tug on the knob. "Aidan!" I scream. "Open the door!" I keep twisting and turning until it feels like the knob might pop off. "What the hell are you doing!?"

More silence.

"I know you're out there! Answer me!"

"You're leaving," he says quietly.

I take a step back. "Uh ..." *Shit!* "No. No I'm not."

"Your bag. It's all packed. In the hall."

My mind races. "I'm just staying overnight at a friend's, that's all."

"With your textbooks?"

Shit. "I, I ... "

"Don't bother!" he shouts.

"Aidan. For God's sake. Let me out. I'll explain everything."

"There's nothing to explain!"

I start slapping my palm on the door. "Aidan!"

"How's Mary, by the way?"

My hand stops in mid-air. "What?"

"You guys looked pretty buddy-buddy."

"What are you —?" I drop my arm. "Were you *following* me?"

"I knew you were lying this morning when I asked you about Mary. It was all over your face."

"So you *spied* on me?"

"Bet she had a ton of juicy stories."

Think, think, think ... "It was about the will. I'll tell you everything she told me. Just unlock the door."

"You lied to me about working, too. You didn't work today. You were in there less than an hour."

"Aidan!" I give the knob another yank. "I can explain that too."

"I knew sooner or later you'd try to leave. You wouldn't shut up about school. About living on campus."

"Aidan!"

He carries on as if he doesn't hear me. "And then there was that loser," he says. "Coffee shop boy. You were here for what? A day? Before you started sluttin' around with him? Got over Kyle pretty fast."

What the hell? "You piece of —!" I kick the door.

"You never learn, Lyssa. You choose poorly every time. And they screw you over every time."

"Asshole!" I start kicking the door again. Once, twice, twenty times.

"You might want to calm down. You're only going to wear yourself out."

His words make me kick even harder. "Open this goddamn door!" Pain shoots up my leg. I have to stop. Now soaked in sweat, I peel my jacket off and toss it on the bed. He's right. Stay calm. It's not like he can keep me in here forever. "Aidan!" I yell. "What about Glady? She must hear me screaming my head off."

"She's away. Gone."

Damn it. Of course. He knows. "You dick!" I limp to the window, try to slide it open. It doesn't budge. I jiggle the wood frame, hoping it's just stuck. It moves a bit, but it's like it's catching on something. I flatten my body against the wall, turn my head sideways, and try to see the outside of the window. Though I'm looking from an almost impossible angle, I see it. There it is, a nail, hammered down between the top and bottom frame. A memory flashes through my brain — Aidan with the hammer.

"I told Glady I'd re-caulk the north-facing windows ... So if you hear a lot of banging and stuff around your window, it's just me."

"Bastard," I breathe as I run my fingers along the frame. Both panels are made up of eight paperback-sized panes. Even if I could find something to break the glass, I'd never fit through ...

I fly back across the room. "You bastard! You planned this!"

No answer.

"You did! You nailed the window shut!" I pummel my fists on the door. "Aidan!"

No answer.

Frustrated, I crumble in a heap against the door. Bingley, unaware of, or not caring about, what's going on around him, pads over and plants himself next to my leg. Once again I look at his paws, and I know I'm right. "Bingley didn't trash my calendar, did he?" I shout.

I wait. And wait. I start thinking Aidan might be gone. Bending sideways to look under the door, I see something dark blocking the space in the middle. He's sitting on the floor as well, leaning against the door. "You just needed a reason to put up the lock."

Still no answer.

I drive my elbow into the door. "How long? How long have you been planning this?"

Nothing.

"Aidan, why are you doing this?"

I feel the vibrations of movement, and he finally speaks. "Because. Because I love you." His voice is muffled, like maybe he has turned and his mouth is touching the door.

I shudder, thankful he can't see me. How should I respond to that? "Well, of course you do. You're my —"

"Don't! Don't give me some brother-sister bullshit. You know that's not what I mean!"

"But —"

"I have *always* loved you!" he yells. "*Always!*"

He sounds so angry. I crawl away from the door, huddle closer to the bed.

"And I know that you love me too. I just have to help you realize it."

"No!" I shake my head.

"It's okay. You don't have to deny it anymore. Let go. Let yourself feel it."

"There's nothing to feel. I don't love you ... like that, Aidan. I'll *never* love you like that." I say it as gently as I can, but still loudly. He needs to hear me say the words.

He pounds back on the door, so hard it makes me jump. "You will!" he orders. "After everything I've done for you, you will!"

"What do you mean? What have you done for me?"

"You're such a liar," he whispers. "You said you'd go back home ..."

I can barely make out what he's saying. I slide over, press myself right up to the door. "What?"

"You said you'd go back home if Vince was gone."

"What? I never said that."

There's a sniffling kind of sound, and I mash my ear against the wood. "Are you crying?"

"Why can't you remember how it was?" he says hoarsely. "We were so good together."

There's a *scritch-scratch* as something pokes its way under the door. I pick it up. It's a piece of what seems to be cardboard, folded a bunch of times. I open it. It's the photo of Aidan and me at Point Pleasant Park, the one on the bench, the one like at Marla's. The folds have made deep creases, and the edges are worn and ragged. I flip it over. There's a happy face drawn in blue marker.

"I carry it in my wallet," he says. "One of the best days of my life."

"But we spent the day shopping for school clothes."

"I know. And after, your mom bought us fish and chips, took us to the park. You told me you were so happy I'd be there at high school to look out for you."

Did I say that? "Um ..."

"You wanted me to take care of you. You knew, even back then. I'm *supposed* to take care of you."

"Aidan, you misunderstood."

"I tried to recreate the day with Marla, you know. It wasn't the same."

The hairs on my arms stand up. The picture at Marla's ... it was on purpose. I hold my head in my hands. "Aidan, why?" I whisper.

"I got her to cut her hair like yours. Coloured it the same too. You stopped wearing it like that, though," he says sadly.

Her hair. She told me Aidan was behind it. I knew there was something strange about that.

"I bought her your perfume for Christmas," he continues. "You know, that Vera Wang stuff you like?"

He wanted her to smell like me? "I don't use that anymore."

He sighs. "Yeah, I noticed."

My head still cradled in my hands, I dig my fingers into my scalp. I think back to when I first met Jodi. She thought I was Marla's sister ... "I can't believe you tried to make Marla into me."

"She's not you."

No fucking kidding! I close my eyes and try to process everything. My mind keeps going back to something he mentioned earlier. "Aidan, you said you did something for me, but you didn't tell me what."

"I did it *all* for you," he whispers.

"What are you talking about?"

Silence, then: "I swallowed my pride."

"What?"

"I called Vince. Told him you'd come back to me, told him about our plans."

"What? What plans?"

"That we were coming back. That we were still in love, that we were going to reopen the bakery, have a life. That he needed to leave, get out of our house."

Still *in love? What?* "Aidan ... why? Why would you tell him that?"

"He said I was crazy, that once you found out, it would all be over."

"Found out what?"

"So I had no choice, I went to see him."

"To River John? When?" I'm sure Aidan hasn't gone home since I've been living with him. "When did you go?"

"He was going to tell you everything, make you hate me."

"What's everything? What was he going to tell me?"

"He wouldn't listen."

Uh-oh. "Aidan? What did you do?"

"He hadn't changed. Same ol' bastard."

I don't ask any more questions. I'm afraid of what he'll say next. Something hot and liquid travels from my stomach into my mouth. I wince as I swallow and force it back down. *This is insane!* He really thinks we belong together ... that we're going to have a life together ... that I want it too. How can he possibly believe that? What's he willing to do to get it?

Is it me? Did I say something? Do something? I think back to that day in the park. I don't remember what I said, but even if I did say that ... I didn't mean it the way he thinks. Could it have been something else?

No. It's not me. It's all him. He's twisted everything up.

I wipe my face with both hands, tighten my ponytail, and take a deep breath.

I've got to get out of here.

Come on, Lyssa, you're smarter than this.

No more fighting. Tell him everything he wants to hear. Sell it. Whatever it takes to make him open that door.

"Hey," Aidan says, knocking. "You still awake in there?"

As if I would let myself sleep. "Uh, yeah. Just thinking."

"About what?"

"I was, uh ..." I survey the room, searching for something to use as a weapon. "I was, uh ... thinking about everything you said." The curtain rod is plastic. So are the coat hangers. Can I gouge his eye out with a pencil?

"Yeah?" His tone is suspicious.

"Yeah." I struggle to keep my voice steady. "I mean, I suppose there are worse things than going back home." My eyes land on the lamp. The lamp's my best bet.

"Really?"

If I can convince him to open the door, I can catch him off guard and make a run for it. I only need to disable him for a second. He's bigger, but I'm faster.

"Lyssa?"

I'm so focused on my plan, I let the conversation drop. Frantically, I backpedal. "Um, sorry ..." *What did I just say? Right. Home.* "I think I might be ready to talk about going home."

There's a long pause. "You mean that? Because you said —"

"I know, but," — on my hands and knees, I move slowly toward the dresser — "well, now that Vince is gone, we might actually be able to make a go of it — and, like you said, we've got the bakery."

"We could make it work, you know. We only need each other."

"Uh-huh. Each other." As I reach along the wall to unplug the lamp, my elbow bumps the back of the dresser, causing a thud.

"What are you doing in there?"

Distract him. "You know, you were right," I say quickly. "About Kyle and Liam. About every guy I care about screwing me over." I pause and lick my lips. "Except for you."

"I'll never hurt you, Lyssa."

"I know that." I get to my feet and pick up the lamp by the base. Carefully, I remove the fabric shade and place it on the bed. Then I examine the area around the door. The corner is too small to hide me. "I think maybe we just need to spend some more time together."

"Things will be better when we get home." He sounds all eager, like a puppy dog. "The feelings, they'll come back to you then."

Whatever's in my stomach curdles. "Home." I practically gag. "I want to go home, Aidan."

I hear a shuffling on the other side of the door. It sounds like he's getting up. "You don't know how long I've waited to hear you say that."

I almost feel guilty, but it passes quickly. I grip the lamp tighter and position myself against the wall, next to the door.

"Aidan," I say. "You don't have to keep me locked in here. I'll go with you. If you want we can even leave right now."

He falls silent again. I don't like it when he does that. It gives him time to think.

"Aidan?"

"What about school?" he asks. "Your job?"

Shit. I wish I could see his face, read his expression. "Maybe I'm not meant to go to university. Maybe there's a reason why the timing is off."

"But wasn't it your dream?"

He's not buying it. "I can always go later. Like after the bakery makes some money." I keep talking while I make myself flush to the wall, praying I'll magically become invisible. If he opens the door, there's a chance he won't see me right away and I'll have enough time to pounce. "No student loan then. What if this was how things were supposed to work out all along?" Hopefully he'll step right into the room and I can hit him from behind.

Just silence.

"And my job," I add. "I'll call Janet from the road." *Please, please.* "Honestly, Aidan. Let's just do it. Let's go tonight. There's nothing keeping me here anymore."

The floor squeaks over and over. He's pacing? Or rocking? "Why should I believe you?" he says. "Why should I believe that suddenly you're on board with this?"

While I try to think of an answer, I wrap the cord around the lamp base so it's out of the way — nothing to trip me up. "Because, Aidan. Because when you get down to it, we're all that's left of our family. We only have each other."

The squeaking stops. I hold my breath. The bones in my back dig into the plaster until it feels as though they're going to pop through my skin.

Every heartbeat sends a tremor through my body. I glance down at my hands clutching the lamp. They're slippery with sweat. My knuckles are white. I don't move a muscle. Finally I hear the deadbolt slide. I watch the knob turn, the door start to open.

But he doesn't step in. He stays on the other side. "Lyss?" he says softly. I'm out of his sightline.

I hold my breath and don't answer. He still doesn't come in. He must suspect something. Then I see his head slowly emerge through the doorway, then immediately jerk to the side. Our eyes meet. It's like he knew I was there all along. *Fuck!*

It happens fast. I sweep the lamp through the air in an arc, smashing it against his head. The bulb breaks. Startled, he stumbles, holding on to the door frame for balance. I make another sweep and jam the socket with the broken shards of glass into the side of his face. He stumbles again and lands on his knees. As I watch the blood drip from his cheek down his chin, I'm so shocked by my own violence that I forget to run.

He touches his fingers to the gash. His eyes widen as he lowers his hand and he sees the blood.

I drop the lamp and rush forward, desperate to squeeze past him. But he's back on his feet before I even get there. I waited too long — I missed my chance.

"I knew it! You lying bitch!" He grabs me by the wrist and twists my arm behind my back. The pain makes my eyes water. "I won't make *that* mistake again!" Then he shoves me hard, hard enough that I end up sprawled on the floor. It feels like I've been bashed in the chest with a block of cement. I can barely catch my breath. I lift my head, look back over my shoulder.

He's gone.

The door is shut.

I hear the deadbolt slide back into place.

Chapter 38

Gently I run my fingers along my rib cage. *Shit, that hurts.* I crawl back to the door, careful to watch out for pieces of the shattered light bulb. It's not easy because my arms and legs are trembling — I'm beyond scared. Aidan's rage is like nothing I've seen before. I can't believe he pushed me like that. Then I think about what I did to him ...

Unable to stand, I stay on my knees, wrap both hands around the knob, and turn. The door still doesn't open. Why did I think it would?

"So what now, Aidan?" I cry out.

No answer.

"Aidan!"

Nothing.

Tears pool in my eyes. "People know I'm here. Somebody's going to come looking for me." The only problem is, no one knows where "here" is. Except Liam. And he's in P.E.I.

"I'll take my chances." He knows I'm lying.

I sigh and close my eyes. "Aidan. Please let me out."

He doesn't reply.

Fresh tears leak from my eyes, but they're tears of frustration. I'm so pissed. "You know, for someone who hated Vince so much, you turned out just like him! Locking me up the way he did!"

"It's the only useful thing he ever taught me," Aidan shouts back.

It feels like a slap in the face.

"You don't get it, do you?" he says.

I slump against the door. "Get what?"

"Vince was locking you up to keep you away from me. He found out we used to meet up at night."

"How? He never caught us."

"He suspected. He asked, and I told him."

"What? Why would you do that?"

"There was no point denying it. He already knew how we felt about each other. That's why he kicked me out of the house in the first place."

I ignore the *how we felt about each other* part, and the nauseous feeling it creates. At least I have another piece of the puzzle — the cause of the big fight. "And you moved into the shed," I say.

"He didn't expect that. He thought I'd just leave."

Now I get it. "That's why he burned it down. To drive you away."

There's a long pause. "I burned it down. I locked him in, but he got out."

"*You? Why?*"

"He found something. He was going to ruin everything."

"Found something," I echo. "Found what?"

"You won't understand."

"What did he find, Aidan?"

Silence.

Resting the back of my head against the door, I can't help but think what Vince found were the cut-out pictures, or the cut-up books ... or, God forbid, something worse. "I was right. Vince knew you were messed up a long time ago," I say to myself.

But Aidan hears me and smashes his fist on the other side so hard it makes my skull bounce. "I'm not crazy!"

"I know," I say quickly. "*I* never said you were." I have to keep him calm, keep him talking. It's the only thing I can think of to do. "I mean, what would Vince know, right?"

"They kept trying to convince me I needed to be hospitalized, needed to be medicated."

"They?"

"The doctors."

"You didn't believe them?"

"No. They're all idiots."

"They gave you pills. You took them, didn't you?"

"For a while."

"And didn't they make you feel better?"

He smashes his fist on the door again. "Better than what? There's nothing wrong with me!"

"Then why did you take them?" I snap, all my patience shot to hell.

He snorts. "Don't try to get in my head, Lyssa. You can't."

Prick. "I'm just trying to understand, that's all."

Silence, then he says, "I took them because they helped take the edge off — you know, of life. Then when you came, showed up at my door, everything changed. I knew I didn't need them anymore."

"Why would me showing up make you think that?"

"Because I knew you were all I needed. And each day I didn't take a pill, I felt better, everything around me was clearer, I was more myself, the Aidan you love."

Once again I'm glad he can't see my face, the horrified look.

"After a while, I knew I was all better, and yes, I flushed the pills." He laughs. "Guess I was sloppy, like you were with the games."

"Games? What are you talking about?"

"I found *Hannah Montana* on the floor by my bed. You should be more careful when you're going through other people's stuff."

Shit. The Nintendo games. I must have dropped one, I was in such a rush. He knew I'd found the locks, made up that story about Glady's gate … "I was only looking for something that would help me figure out what was going on with you."

"Yeah, you're a damn Nancy Drew in training, aren't you?"

I take a deep breath. "Aidan. Maybe you shouldn't have stopped taking your medication."

"Maybe you should shut your fucking mouth!"

Either he really, really loves you, or really, really hates you …

"Please, Aidan," I say. "Let me get you some help."

"I don't need any *help*," he spits.

Think, Lyssa. "Okay, what if we try it your way? I'll do whatever you want. We'll see if we can figure it out together, just us." I ooze just the right amount of sincerity. I almost believe what I'm saying.

"It's too late."

I'm not sure I want to know what he means by that. "It's never too late."

"I've done terrible things."

I swallow. "We've all done terrible things."

Silence.

"Did I ever tell you about my mom?" he finally says.

"No."

"She died in a fire."

I see an opening. "Tell me about her."

"Now *she* was crazy."

"Crazy how?"

Silence.

"Aidan?"

"She said voices talked to her through the TV, told her what to do. I mean, *that's* crazy, isn't it?" Thankfully, he gives me no time to respond. "One night I overheard her telling Vince she was leaving, and that she wasn't taking me with her."

"I'm sorry. That must have been hard to hear."

"Why couldn't she have been more like *your* mom?"

I think about my complicated relationship with my mom, how we always seemed to butt heads. "We had our issues ..."

"I know. She tells me about them all the time, how she wishes you two had gotten along better. She tells me to take you back home, make you happy. She wants us *both* to be happy."

"Um." I need a minute to absorb his words. "Um, she *tells* you, or she *told* you ...?"

"Hell, *my* mom," he goes on as if I hadn't spoken, "she didn't give a shit about my happiness. I mean, how can a mother leave her son?"

I try to concentrate. "Uh, she might have felt she had to leave." My thoughts are still back on his comment about *my* mom telling him stuff — present tense. "You know, for a while anyway, until she was better."

"No. I could tell. She wanted to go. But I never gave her the chance ..." His voice trails off, leaving another long space of silence.

There's something about the way he said that. "What does that mean?"

"It was easy. Vince was at work ..."

My back stiffens. I sit up straight. "What are you saying?" But I already know.

"I can't give you the chance either."

Oh God. All is quiet except for the thumping inside my head, as if somehow my heart is sitting behind my eyes.

I give the door another bang. "Aidan? Are you still out there?"

Nothing.

And then I hear it — a scrape, a whoosh, a fizz. I know that sound. That's a match.

CHapteR 39

"Aidan!" I try to shout, but panic grips my throat and allows no sound. My eyes ricochet around the room. There's got to be a way out of here. If Aidan thinks I'm just going to sit here and let him torch me alive, he can rot in hell. I scramble to my feet and tear to the window. It's dark outside. There are no lights on in the house next door, and their driveway isn't shovelled. They must be away. I try the window again, prying with my fingernails until they snap off and become smeared with blood. The window doesn't budge.

I run across the room, press my ear to the door, and listen — nothing.

I mash my nose against the door jamb and sniff — nothing.

Rushing back to the window, I yank off my hoodie and twist it around my hand. I hold on to the ledge for support and crash my wrapped fist against the glass. The shock of impact shoots up my arm, filling my eyes with water. I pound on the window over and over, but the panes are too small and I mostly come into contact with the wood. I have to give up because it hurts too much.

Again I return to the door to check for sounds and smells. This time I smell it — smoke.

Shit. "Aidan!" I kick the door because my hands are so sore. "Don't do this!"

He doesn't answer. I'm not even sure if he's still there. Then I hear a *beep, beep, beep*. The smoke detector. My heart does a little jump. Is it loud enough that someone might hear it? Especially if it keeps going off? Just as I finish my thought, there's a clatter and the beeping stops. Aidan must still be out there.

"Aidan," I plead softly. "Please, *please*, don't do this." Waiting for him to respond, I notice the air in the room. I can see it. I can fan my fingers through it. There's a haze. I glance down at my feet. Little wisps of white are coming in under the door, drifting and whirling along the floor then floating up.

Jesus Christ. Ignoring the pain, I slap my hands on the door. They leave behind bloody prints. My fingernails are still bleeding. "Aidan! Let me out!" I grab the doorknob and tug and tug. My arms feel like they're going to pop out of their sockets. I scream his name until I'm hoarse. Nothing. I slide down the door to the floor and hug my knees to my chest. *Shit.*

The white curls of smoke working their way in are getting thicker. I push down the fear because I need to be able to think straight. I remember the rug by the window, the one Bingley spends most of his time on. I get to my feet, scoop it up, roll it tight, and jam it under the door. "There," I breathe. "That's something."

I survey the room for the hundredth time. My eyes swing back and forth between the window and the door. One of them is my way out. Because I'm getting out of here. There's no other option.

And then I notice the lamp base partially sticking out from under the bed. I grab it and race back to the window. Holding it with both hands, I aim the metal socket at the glass and start pounding. It's less clumsy than my fist, and I can feel it, hear it, hitting dead centre. The window still doesn't break, but I don't give up. My breathing becomes laboured, and I finally have to stop for a second. I tell myself it's just from exertion, but glancing behind me, I see the smoke. It's changing, getting denser. It's leaking in around the rug, through the seams of the door, and filling the room.

I set down the lamp, hurry to the door, and tuck the rug in tighter. My eyes sting, and I blink furiously to clear my vision. I can feel heat through the wood, and I can hear noises on the other side, like leaves rustling in the wind, but I know that's not what it is. And whatever the rug is made of, it's creating its own smoke that's black and smells terrible. It's in my mouth — I can taste it.

Staying close to the floor, I crawl over to the bed and pull off the quilt. My plan is to switch it with the rug. I yank out the rug and, using my heels, stuff the quilt into the opening under the door. Then without thinking, I reach for the doorknob to haul myself up. I yelp and jerk my hand back. There's a red blotch burned onto my palm.

Fuck. Tears dribble down my cheeks as I cradle my hand to my chest to ease the pain. It doesn't work.

The heat from the door is so intense, I have to move away. On my knees and one good hand, I head back to the window. My discarded hoodie is in my path, and I pick it up and drape it over my head. The smoke still manages to find its way underneath. I start coughing, so I hold part of the sleeve snug against my mouth. But then I have to breathe through my nose, which is too clogged up. I toss the hoodie aside.

Defeated, I lean against the wall, feeling my chest heave up and down. All that bullshit I kept telling myself about Aidan not getting away with it, about me getting out of here, that's all it was — bullshit.

The air is heavy and thick. I let the last bit of energy drain out and lay myself flat on the floor. This is the way they'll find me. My throat burns, and my eyes feel like they're on fire. I close them — close them against the smoke, and to block out what's around me. But that doesn't block the sounds. I hear the crackling and snapping of the flames, the creaking of the house. I try to imagine where the fire is, how close, the flames licking up the walls, everything that's happening on the other side of the door. There's a whistling and then a pop, like when I broke the light bulb.

I'm so hot. It's becoming almost impossible to breathe. I roll over on my side so my lungs aren't so squished.

This is it. No one's coming.

Was it like this for Aidan's mom? What was her name? I can't even remember.

Then I think about Mom and when she died. Did she feel it? Did she know when she went to sleep that night that she wouldn't wake up?

I feel it. I know I'm not waking up.

Shouldn't my life be flashing before my eyes? Maybe that comes later, in those seconds right before the end.

Please let me die from the smoke before the fire gets me. The thought of my skin sizzling, bubbling, and melting off my bones ... I start coughing again, dry hacks. I have to sit up to stop from choking.

From out of nowhere Bingley lands on my lap, meowing, nuzzling his head under my chin. I totally forgot about him. How is he still up and about? He seems to be his usual indifferent self. He leaps from my lap and walks a circle around the lamp base that's still on the floor where I left it. I watch him. His meowing is louder. I know it doesn't mean anything, that it's only coincidence, but something makes me get to my feet and reach for the lamp.

Once again I grasp the base tightly. It slips and slides because the burns on my hand are weeping liquid, but it's my stronger hand and that's what matters now. I don't feel the pain anymore anyway. This time I drive the bottom of the lamp into the glass as hard as I can. The window splinters into a starburst. I cry out with joy and strike one more time. I hear the tinkle of glass hitting the floor.

The outside acts like a giant vacuum, and for a second I'm mesmerized, staring at the smoke as it's drawn out the hole. I clean away more of the shards and hold my face to the opening, oblivious to the jagged edges digging into my forehead and chin. I suck in the fresh air. My head doesn't fit through, but it's okay. Right now, the cold night air is all I need — an injection of adrenaline.

I yell, "Help!" but my mouth is dry, as if coated in chalk. All I can manage is a bark. I back up and stick my arm through the hole. I get it out up to my shoulder. Miraculously, the nail keeping the window shut is within my reach. I try jiggling and twisting it, but it doesn't take me long to figure out it's in there way too deep.

Next, I wave and wave, whipping my arm around like a propeller. Maybe someone walking by will see. I grab my hoodie, stuff it out. Flap it like a flag. Minutes pass, and my arm turns to rubber. I have to pull it in.

To create some saliva, I run my tongue around my teeth and

gums. Once again I stick my face against the frame of broken glass and scream for help. This time sound comes out. I scream at the top of my lungs. All of a sudden I feel arms around my waist, lifting me up and away from the window.

Someone finally saw me! Heard me! *I'm rescued!*

Before I have a chance to turn my head to identify my saviour, a hand is slapped over my mouth and my bruised and battered ribs are squeezed so tight, I can't draw in a breath.

And I know. It's no saviour. It's Aidan.

He's got me mashed against his chest. I thrash and squirm, try to slip through his arms. It only makes him grip me tighter. I try to pull away the hand covering my mouth. I can't get any leverage because it's gloved or wrapped in something. I try biting, but I can't get my teeth through. I have to keep at it. His hand is blocking my nose and barely any air is getting in. It feels like forever since I've taken a breath.

I reach up behind me, feel for his face. He can't control my arms without letting me go. I dig whatever's left of my nails into his cheek, hoping to make contact with his fresh wound, and drag them over his jawline and down his neck. I feel his flesh tearing, so I must be doing some damage.

"Bitch!" he yells, and his hold loosens.

Wrenching myself out of his arms, I think I'm free, but then I'm instantly snapped back. He's got a handful of my hair. My scalp stings, so do my eyes. He pulls me close, still holding my hair. Then he smacks me across the face with the back of his hand. It knocks me to the floor. On my way down, my knee catches the corner of the bed frame and I hear a crack.

I lie there on my stomach, waiting for the splashes of light to clear from my vision. There's a metallic taste in my mouth. I know it's blood. All at once, something heavy covers me. It takes me a second to realize it's Aidan. He's laid his body on top of mine.

"Shhh," he whispers into my hair. "I forgive you."

It's so hot, I'm soaked. My clothes are plastered to me. The thought of his sweat mixing with mine — it makes me want to throw up. But if I did, I'd probably drown in my own vomit, because his chin is resting in the nape of my neck, pressing one side of my face to the floor. The pressure of him on my back ... I can't inhale. "Is this what you really want?" I ask, my words muffled. "For me to die like your mom?"

"Shhh," he whispers again. "Don't talk about her."

"Did Vince know? Did he know what you did?" My mouth is filled with blood and God knows what else. I can barely talk, but I have to know.

He ignores my question. "It's okay, Lyss. Don't fight it. It's happening. We're going to be together forever."

I buck my body, try and flip him off, but he weighs too much. He has me completely pinned.

"Just close your eyes and relax," he says.

"Like hell." I flail my arms out sideways, curving them around behind me, hoping to claw his back, but all I get is his jeans.

There's a crashing sound from the hall, something smashing to the floor. It reminds me that the door is open, and it's only a matter of time before the fire finds its way into this room.

I start to whimper, my body trembling beneath his. "Aidan, please."

He strokes my hair. "Don't cry, Lyssa."

"Don't cry?" The fact that he's trying to comfort me suddenly fills me with rage. But there's no way to let it out, no way to scream. I'm talking to the floor. "Why can't I cry? What difference does it make?"

"It breaks my heart."

"Like I give a fuck about your heart." I shouldn't have said that.

He goes quiet. I worry about what's going through his mind.

With my one exposed eye, I see Bingley under the bed. He meows, blurs in and out of focus as the smoke drifts by. I mouth the word *shoo* and hope that for once he obeys me.

"It didn't have to be like this," he finally says. I feel his lips moving against my ear. "Why couldn't you have just been happy with me?"

"Because you're a fucking psycho!" I can't seem to stop myself.

"Hey!" Again he grabs a handful of my hair, then lifts my head and smashes it back onto the floor. "That's not very nice."

Pain explodes through my cheekbone. "Bastard!"

"Watch your mouth," he scolds and nestles his head next to mine so our cheeks are touching. I don't fight back. I know I have to conserve my energy. I'm not sure I'd be able to anyway.

As a result of the head slam, my line of sight has changed. Under the haze of smoke, I'm now able to see out the bedroom door. Flames. In spite of the heat, I shiver. Even if I could get away, would I be able to survive what's out there?

Guess I won't know until I try.

I make my body limp and slow my breathing to almost nothing. Maybe he'll think I've passed out. Maybe he'll think I'm dead.

I wait. But it's torture. It's already hard enough to breathe without actually trying not to.

"I love you, Lyssa." He goes back to stroking my hair. "Tell me you love me too."

I don't move. I just keep waiting, my eye trained on the doorway. There are sporadic pops and crackles that are so loud, if I closed my eyes I would think there were fireworks going off right next to me. I watch sparks shoot from the flames and catch on the ancient wallpaper. Some of the pieces burn off and float through the air like snowflakes. All the while I take the shallowest of breaths, making sure my body barely moves.

"I *said*, tell me you love me," he hisses.

My lungs scream for air. *Turn to stone, like your garden statue. Stone can't burn.*

"Lyssa?" The pressure of his chest on my back lets up. "Lyssa?" I feel his hand on my shoulder as if he's about to turn me over.

Time! Like a slippery eel, I flip myself around and knee him in the groin.

He groans in pain, curls himself into a ball, but his body is still lying across one of my legs.

I have to get him off. Sitting up, I brace myself against the dresser, jam the heel of my free boot square into the middle of his face, and grind. He groans again, covers his face with his hands, and rolls off my leg. I'm free.

Coughing and spitting out gobs of blood and black goo, I pull myself to my feet. I want to run, but I'm lightheaded and my eyes and throat are burning. I head for the bedroom door. I'm almost there when something goes wrong and my knee gives out — the one that cracked when I fell. I end up right back flat on the floor.

I look behind me. Aidan's starting to come around.

I scramble up and limp the rest of the way to the door. Every step is like a hammer to my kneecap. I'm about to cross into the hall when suddenly the flames flare up, as if someone poured gasoline on them. They're more than waist high — a giant blazing hedge blocking the threshold. The intense heat causes me to shrink back. *Shit.* What now? My plan was to lock Aidan in once I got out. But even if I make it through these flames, there won't be time. I'd have to stand in the middle of the fire to lock the door.

Just go.

There's scuffling behind me. I glance over my shoulder. Aidan's on his feet, but he's stumbling around, holding his head. I spin back to the hedge of fire. Do I bust through or jump over? My knee makes the latter impossible.

"Lyssa," Aidan moans like wounded animal.

Go!

I protect my face with both hands and lunge forward, trying to dive over the flames. My body lands with a thud. I lift myself up on my elbows to catch my breath. My jeans are scorched and smoking, the hairs on my arms are brittle and singed, but I'm in one piece. The fire is all around me, licking the walls, curling onto the ceiling. Sparks rain down on my clothes. I slap at them before they catch.

It's at that moment the lights flicker and go out, making the glow of the flames seem brighter, but making the house seem darker. The smoke is so thick, I have to stay low to the floor just to breathe. I check behind me again for Aidan. It's a wall of black — I can't tell.

I'm hoping that I wrecked his face enough so that he can't see, so that he won't be able to find me, or better yet, that the fire hedge has him trapped.

Dragging my busted leg, I slowly inch along the hall, feeling my way. The sound of the fire is deafening — a million popcorn machines working overtime. The floor is littered with unidentifiable debris, and I wince when my hand comes down on broken glass.

I keep going. I brush up against something lumpy and bulky, and my heart instantly tightens in my chest. *A body.* Holding my breath, I tentatively pat the shape. Uncontrollable sobs burst from me when I realize it's just the duffle bag that I dropped in another life.

Using the bottom of my T-shirt, I wipe my eyes, wipe the sooty snot from my nose, and prepare to move on. If I squint, I can make out the outline of the front door. The smoke is thinner there — all the fire seems to be behind me.

I'm filled with hope, total elation.

I start crawling, wishing I could use my other leg to speed things up. I don't remember the hallway being so long. The front door is getting clearer. I'm almost there, when like something out of a horror movie, I feel the clamp of a hand on my foot.

"No!" I scream, turning onto my side. I know before I even look. There's Aidan on his stomach, his face puffy and mangled, unrecognizable, his hand wrapped around my ankle.

"Let go!" I twist my foot back and forth, bang it on the floor, anything to make him open his hand.

He squeezes harder.

This can't be happening. I reach out for something to hold on to. I manage to get my fingers around the door tread of the vestibule and pull, hoping I'll slide forward. But I'm not strong enough. He holds me back like an anchor.

"All I ever did was love you." His voice is broken, his breathing ragged.

"Aidan!"

"This isn't how it's supposed to end, not for us."

"Oh yeah?" I squirm some more, point my toe — better chance of my foot slipping out of my boot, and then his hand. It doesn't work. "How the hell is it supposed to end?"

"You're supposed to remember that you love me," he sobs.

"Jesus Christ, Aidan!" Then there's a sound. My eyes widen. *Sirens.* "Hear it? They're coming. It's over."

"It'll never be over."

In terror, I watch as tiny flames ignite on the back of his sweater and travel up his sleeve. His face is contorted in pain, but he still holds on. Then I smell a horrible smell. It's the skin on his hand as it turns black, shrivels and slides away, exposing red, jellied blood beneath.

"Aidan! Let go!" But as I shake and wiggle my foot, the flames follow a natural path and jump from his hand to my leg. White-hot, searing pain zaps through me like a current as my jeans start to burn. I'm sure I'm going to pass out. Frantically, I rock my leg in an attempt to smother the flames. "Aidan!" I shriek. "Please!"

I look ahead at the front door — so close I can almost touch it. I look back at Aidan. His hair is smoking. "Please," I beg.

For a split second, our eyes lock.

"Sometimes things just need to be done," he croaks. And I feel him let go.

I'm momentarily stunned by his release. But I snap out of it. I whip my legs up under me, get on my knees, and, with every last bit of life in me, I throw myself at the front door. My hands manage to grab on to the knob before I collapse. The door swings open, and I tumble onto the porch.

Freezing air fills my lungs.

I gulp and gulp.

It will never be enough.

Dragging my body down the steps, I land in a pile of snow. I cry out loud when the icy crystals touch my burning skin.

The sirens sound closer, mixing in with the roar of the trucks.

As I lie there, Aidan's last words to me echo in my head. A memory surfaces from some faraway place, and I'm transported back to that night so long ago. That night he beat those two guys almost to death. For me. After it was over, he said, "I only did what needed to be done." I remember how I felt. And now I remember what I said to him as I cleaned the bloodstains from his hands. *"In this whole world, Aidan, you're the only one I love."*

Aidan. I lift my head, look back at the front door. *Can I make it?* There's a rumble and a crack as the beams holding up the porch roof collapse, bringing it crashing down, blocking the door.

I lay my head down, close my eyes, and feel the tears trickle over the side of my face into my hair.

Everything gets quiet. Even all the pain goes away.

My life never does flash before my eyes. Only Aidan's face.

epilogue

Three Weeks Later

"It's pretty busy. We should buy all four tickets now in case it fills up."

"Good idea," I say, untangling my fingers from his to dig out my debit card.

He gives me a disgusted look. "Would you put that away?"

"Fine," I sigh and limp over to lean on the windowsill. My leg still aches when I put weight on it for too long. I slide my crutches along the wall behind my feet so I don't trip anyone coming and going from the theatre.

I watch him punch all the information into the ticket machine. He keeps glancing over at me like he's making sure I'm still here. Since the fire, he's been overprotective, but I don't mind. I sort of like it.

He checks his watch. "Erin's always late. Why don't you go find us some seats? Theatre 10. It'll be more comfortable than sitting on that."

I smile. Liam, my protector. "Okay, see you in there."

When I get to theatre 10, the usher won't let me in yet because they're cleaning up after the last showing. She takes in my crutches and points to an upholstered bench a little way down the hall.

I sit and read the posters advertising upcoming movies. People file past me, back and forth. I like to people-watch. But something draws my attention to two girls in particular. It takes a second for it to click, for the words to form. "Marla? Jodi?"

They stop and turn in my direction. We make eye contact. They both say, "Lyssa?" in unison.

A moment passes, like no one is sure what to do next.

Finally I stand and say awkwardly, "H-hi."

When they come over they see my crutches propped up against the wall. "Sit, sit," Marla says.

I do.

"This is so bizarre," Jodi says. "We were just talking about you, wondering about you. Marla saw someone who reminded her of Aidan. Freaked her out a bit."

"Of course I knew it wasn't," Marla explains. "It's just, well, it got me thinking, you know?"

"Sure." I nod. Another moment passes. "So ... how are you guys?"

"Never mind us," Jodi says. "How are *you*?"

"Yeah." Marla looks down at my leg stretched out straight in front of me. "Are you okay?"

I try to smile. "A little beat off, that's all."

"We heard about the fire. That you almost died."

"Yup." *That pretty much covers it.*

Jodi motions toward my crutches. "So what's the damage?"

I raise my eyebrows. "You mean to me?"

She gives me a sheepish look. "Yeah. For a start, anyway."

"Burns mostly. Some bad ones on my foot and leg, some not so bad ones on my stomach, arms, and hands. Oh, and I smashed my knee." I twist up my mouth. "Kid stuff, really."

"But you're going to be okay," Jodi says.

I nod, and Jodi shoots Marla a look. "I think I'll use the washroom before the movie starts," she says. "Give you two a chance to ... catch up."

We sit there, trying to figure out what to say to each other.

"You look good, Marla. How are you? Like really."

She smiles. "I'm good. Like really."

"You seem ... different. Happier."

"I am. I go to these group therapy sessions. It's done wonders for me. I'm back to work at the bookstore, I've registered for some courses at NSCAD — I'm actually excited about what's next."

"The College of Art and Design? That sounds amazing. I'm so happy for you. You deserve it after ... well, you know, after everything."

"It's not like you're not due for some happiness."

I don't say anything.

She frowns. "You must feel lucky, at least ... considering the alternative."

"Yeah," I say. "That's me. Lucky." I realize my tone sounds kind of sarcastic. "And they say I can have plastic surgery. It will help hide the scarring."

"Well, that's a good thing, isn't it?"

"I guess." I shrug. Maybe I'm supposed to keep the scars. As a reminder. "It's something I'll think about later, maybe."

She gets a thoughtful look on her face. "I'm sorry about Aidan," she says.

"Why?"

"I loved him. You did too."

When I don't respond, she asks, "So, any word? Have they found him?"

It's only been the last day or so that I've stopped jumping every time the phone rings. "No," I say.

"I can't believe he made it out," she says.

I think about the last time I saw Aidan, his face bashed in by my foot, his clothes catching fire ... it makes me cringe inside. "I can't believe it either."

"Are they really sure?"

"As sure as they can be. They didn't find a body in there."

"Couldn't he have just ... burned up?"

My throat clenches. "I don't know," I whisper.

"Sorry. You probably don't want to talk about it."

"I can't believe that you do."

"No, I talk about it a lot. It actually helps, it really does."

I give her a doubtful look and shift the way I'm sitting. A twinge of pain darts up my leg. "Can I ask you something?"

"Sure."

"What did Aidan say to you on the phone? What made you refuse to see me that day I came to your place?"

She looks all around the hall, everywhere but at me. I can tell she doesn't want to tell me. "He told me you guys were in love, always had been, and that you were moving back home together."

I'm not that surprised by her words. "Thanks," I say. "I just wondered, that's all ..."

We don't say anything for a bit after that. Marla breaks the silence first. "I read in the paper they discovered his car abandoned at Point Pleasant Park."

"Yeah, over by the beach."

"I don't get it. Like, didn't anyone see him drive off? Leave the scene?"

"The car was never at the house that night," I say. "They told me it was parked one street over. He must have gone through the backyard."

"He would have had to have planned that."

I nod. *He planned a lot of things.* "And then he just left it there, at the park.... His keys, phone, wallet, and watch were all in the trunk."

Her face goes a little pale. "Do you think he ... but the harbour's frozen, right?"

"Only along the shore, I think."

"I'm going to be dreading the spring thaw. I pray they don't find anything."

I turn my head for a second and swallow down something hard.

She smooths out some non-existent wrinkles on her pants. "I never thought he was in that bad of a way, you know?" she says softly. "You've got to wonder what made him just snap like that."

"Yeah." I don't bother to correct her, to tell her that Aidan didn't just snap. That this wasn't the first time. But I'm the only one who knows about what he did to his mom, what I think he *may* have done to Vince. I haven't told anyone, not even Liam. I don't know why. Or if I ever will. To change the subject, I say, "I still have Bingley."

"Oh God. Poor Bingley."

"Do you want him back?"

"Could you maybe keep him for now? Jodi and I are talking about getting a new place — one where the heat works when it's supposed to. I'll track you down if we do."

I remember the sauna-like apartment. "Sure, no problem. He and Liam have bonded anyway."

"Liam?"

"He's the guy I'm staying with. For now."

"Your boyfriend?"

"It's complicated." I use that word a lot now.

Suddenly she grabs my hand and squeezes. Still tender from the burns, I wince. "What?"

She releases her grip. "Sorry. It's just I see that guy again, the one who reminded me of Aidan." She shakes her head. "I guess I'm still a little on edge."

"No worries." I scan the sea of faces, hoping to see what, or who, she sees. But then I'm distracted as I spot Liam, Erin, and Josh coming toward us. I wave my hand so they can find me. Liam waves back. They're almost to us when something makes me turn to Marla. Her eyes are wide and flitting between me and Liam. In that moment I figure it out. Liam's the guy.

"That's Liam," I whisper. "He reminds you of Aidan?"

She coughs, seems momentarily flustered. "It was only for a second. I mean, obviously ... up close he doesn't."

"Yeah, because —" Too late, the gang arrives. "Um, h-hey guys," I say. "This is Marla. She's ... uh ..."

"Aidan's old girlfriend," Marla says without missing a beat, head held high like she's not ashamed of it. I'm in awe of her poise and confidence.

Sensing the weirdness of the situation, Liam holds out his hand. "I'm Liam." He points behind him. "This is Erin and Josh."

Marla shakes his hand, and everyone exchanges polite hellos.

"Well, I should go find Jodi," Marla says.

"Sure," I say. "It was really great to see you. Maybe I'll see you around?"

"Yeah. For sure."

We'll probably never see each other again.

after the movie Liam and I huddle in the lobby with Erin and Josh, discussing what to do next. We all agree we're hungry, so we decide to meet up at Pizzadelic for a slice. Erin and Josh leave right away to snag us a table — I don't move so fast anymore. As I button up my coat I glance around the crowd for Marla and Jodi. There's no sign of them. Then I notice Liam take out his phone, scroll down the screen, and frown. I know what he's doing.

"Don't worry," I say. "She'll agree to the paternity test eventually. She kind of doesn't have much choice, you know?"

He nods tightly and slides his phone back into his pocket.

Once outside, the wind hits me in the face, cooling my skin. I like being cold now. I like the way the freezing air makes my nose tingle inside.

A light dusting of fresh snow covers everything. Liam holds one of my crutches so I can hold on to him as he helps me across the slippery parking lot.

I study him out of the corner of my eye. *So they're both tall and thin with brown hair. Big whoop. So are a million other people.*

"I know I haven't felt like doing much lately," I say. "But I'm having fun. Thanks for making me get out."

"How grateful are you? Does it mean I don't have to sleep on the couch anymore?"

I jab him in the ribs with the handle of my crutch.

Smiling, he pulls me in closer, snug to his side.

When we get to the car he starts patting his coat pockets. "Shit. I think I left my gloves in the theatre. I'm gonna run back," he says as he digs out his keys, "but here, get in and I'll turn the heat on."

"I don't want to get in. I'll clean off the car while you go find your gloves."

"No way. You're supposed to be taking it easy."

"Well, I don't really consider flicking a few snowflakes off the windows hard labour."

He shakes his head. Gives me that look, like *what am I going to do with you?*

I roll my eyes. "I'm not an invalid, you know. Give me the sweeper thingy."

"Fine," he sighs, and pops open the trunk of the car. "But I expect a first-class job, missy. No slacking off just because of those crutches."

"Yeah, yeah," I say as he passes me the snow brush. "Just go, would ya?"

I lean my crutches against the side of the car, and starting at the back, I sweep off the snow and work my way to the front. I'm about to clear the windshield when I stop. The brush tumbles from my fingers, clattering against the side mirror on its way to the ground.

There's a loud pulsing sound in my head, like that's where all my blood is now.

Quickly I check over one shoulder, then the other. My eyes drop to the pavement. There's a smattering of footprints around the car — mine, Liam's, random others from people who parked beside us. Then I spy one lone set that breaks away from the pack. It leaves a diagonal trail leading down to the bottom of the parking lot, which edges along a four-lane highway. I stare at the cars whizzing by for a long time.

The electronic *beep-beep* of someone unlocking their car brings me back. I bend down and scoop up the brush. A sense of calm settles over me as I slowly make a sweep across the windshield, erasing the giant happy face drawn in the snow.

A tiny smile tugs at my lips.

acknowledgements

To my family, Ross, Lexi, William, and our new addition, Hermione. Thanks for your continued patience and support. Especially Lexi and William, for freely offering your advice and never, ever being sarcastic about it.

To my editor, Barry Jowett and the gang at Dancing Cat Books. Thanks for making me feel like part of the fam. It was great getting the band back together.

And of course, to my writing group, the Scribs: Jo Ann Yhard, Daphne Greer, Joanna Butler, Jennifer Thorne, and Graham Bullock. Thanks for leaving your fingerprints all over this book.